Courtesy Call

A hunter's wind blew down off the Mooncatcher Mountains and across the Rungn Valley. Night filled with the sounds of it, rustling forest, remote animal cries, and with odors of soil, growth, beast. The wish that it roused, to be yonder, to stalk and pounce and slay and devour, grew in Weoch-Captain until he trembled. The fur stood up on him. Claws slid out of their sheaths; fingers bent into the same saber curves. He had long been deprived.

Eastward stretched rangeland, wan beneath the stars. Westward, ahead, the woods loomed darkling, the game preserve part of Ress-Chiuu's vast domain. Far and high beyond glimmered snowpeaks. The chill that the wind also bore chastened bit by bit the lust in Weoch-Captain. Reason fought its way back. He reached the Admiral's lair with the turmoil no more than a drumbeat in his blood.

After an electronic gate identified and admitted him, the portal through which he passed was a tunnel wherein he moved blind. Primitive instincts whispered, "Beware!" He ignored them. Guided by echoes and subtle tactile sensations, his pace never slackened. Ress-Chiuu always ~~received visitors one way~~ or another. . . .

POUL ANDERSON

IRON

1

The kzin screamed and leaped.

In any true gravity field, Robert Saxtorph would have been dead half a minute later. The body has its wisdom, and his had been schooled through hard years. Before he really knew that a thunderbolt was coming at him, he had sprung aside—against the asteroid spin. As his weight dropped, he thrust a foot once more to drive himself off the deck, strike a wallfront, recover control over his mass, and bounce to a crouch.

The kzin was clearly not trained for such tricks. He had pounced straight out of a crosslane, parallel to Tiamat's rotation axis. Coriolis force was too slight to matter. But instead of his prey, he hit the opposite side of Ranzau Passage. Pastel plastic cracked under the impact; the metal behind it boomed. He recovered with the swiftness of his kind, whirled about, and snarled.

For an instant, neither being moved. Ten meters from him, the kzin stood knife-sharp in Saxtorph's

3

awareness. It was as if he could count every red-orange hair of the pelt. Round yellow eyes glared at him out of the catlike face, above the mouthful of fangs. Bat-wing ears were folded out of sight into the fur, for combat. The naked tail was angled past a columnar thigh, stiffly held. The claws were out, jet-black, on all four digits of either hand. Except for a phone on his left wrist, the kzin was unclad. That seemed to make even greater his 250 centimeters of height, his barrel thickness.

Before and behind the two, Ranzau Passage curved away. Windows in the wallfronts were empty, doors closed, signs turned off; workers had gone home for the nightwatch. They were always few, anyway. This industrial district had been devoted largely to the production of spaceship equipment which the hyperdrive was making as obsolete as fission power.

There was no time to be afraid. "Hey, wait a minute, friend," Saxtorph heard himself exclaim automatically, "I never saw you before, never did you any harm, didn't even jostle you—"

Of course that was useless, whether or not the kzin knew English. Saxtorph hadn't adopted the stance which indicated peacefulness. It would have put him off balance. The kzin bounded at him.

Saxtorph released the tension in his right knee and swayed aside. Coming upspin, his speed suddenly lessening his weight, the kzin—definitely not a veteran of space—went by too fast to change direction at once. As he passed, almost brushing the man, the gingery smell of his excitement filling the air, Saxtorph thrust fingers at an eye. That was just about the only vulnerable point when a human was unarmed. The kzin yowled; echoes rang.

Saxtorph was shouting, too. "Help, murder, help!" Somebody should be in earshot of that. The kzin skidded to a halt and whipped about. It would have been astounding how quick and agile his bulk was, if

Saxtorph hadn't seen action on the ground during the war.

Again saving his breath, the man backed downspin, but slantwise, so that he added little to his weight. Charging full-out, the kzin handicapped himself much more. The extra drag on his mass meant nothing to his muscles, but confused his reflexes. Dodging about, Saxtorph concentrated first on avoiding the sweeps of those claws, second on keeping the velocity parameters unpredictably variable. From time to time he yelled.

One slash connected. It ripped his tunic from collar to belt, and the undershirt beneath. Blood welled along shallow gashes. As he jumped clear, Saxtorph cracked the blade of his hand onto the flat nose before him. It did no real harm, but hurt. The kzin's eyes widened. The pupil of the undamaged one grew narrower yet. He had seen the scars across his opponent's chest. This human had encountered at least one kzin before, face to face.

But Saxtorph was fifteen years younger then, and equipped with a Gurkha knife. Now the wind was gusting out of him. His gullet was afire. Sluggishness crept into his motions. "Ya-a-ah, police, help! Ki-yai!"

A whistle skirled. The kzin halted. He stared past Saxtorph. The man dared not turn his head, but he heard cries and footfalls. The kzin turned and sped in the opposite direction, upspin. He whirled into the first crosslane he came to and disappeared.

And *that* wasn't like his breed, either. Saxtorph sagged back against a wallfront and sobbed breath into his lungs. Sweat was cold and acrid on him. He felt the beginnings of the shakes and started calling calm down on himself, as the Zen master who helped train him for war had taught.

One cop waved off a score or so of people whom the commotion had drawn after him and his companion. The other approached Saxtorph. He was stocky, clean-shaven, unremarkable except for the way he cocked his ears forward—neither aristocrat nor Belter, just a commoner from Wunderland. "*Was ist hier los?*" he demanded somewhat wildly.

Saxtorph could have recalled the Danish of his childhood, before the family moved to America, and brushed the rust off what German he'd once studied, and made a stab at this language. The hell with it. "Y-y-you speak English?" he panted.

"*Ja*, some," the policeman answered. "Vat is t'is? Don't you know not to push a kzin around?"

"I sure do know, and did nothing of the sort." Steadiness was returning. "He bushwhacked me, completely unprovoked. And, yes, this sort of thing isn't supposed to happen with kzinti, and I can't make any more sense of it than you. Aren't you going to chase him?"

"He's gone," said the policeman glumly. "He vill be back in Tigertown and t'e trail lost before ve can bring a sniffer to follow him. How you going tell vun of t'ose *Teufeler* from anot'er? You come along to t'e station, sir. Ve vill give you first aid and take your statement."

Saxtorph drew a long breath, grinned lopsidedly, and replied, "Okay. I'll want to make a couple of phone calls. My wife, and—it'd be smart to ask Commissioner Markham if I can put off my appointment with him."

2

Tiamat is much less known outside its system than it deserves to be. Once hyperdrive transport has become readily available and cheap, it may well be receiving tourists from all of human space: for it is a curious object, with considerable historical significance as well.

Circling Alpha Centauri A near the middle of those asteroids called the Serpent Swarm, it was originally a chondritic body with a sideritic component giving it more structural strength than is usual for that kind. A rough cylinder, about 50 kilometers in length and 20 in diameter, it rotated on its long axis in a bit over ten hours; and at the epoch when humans arrived, that axis happened to be almost normal to the orbital plane. Those who settled on Wunderland paid it no attention; they had a habitable planet. The Belters who came later, from the asteroids of the Solar System, realized what a treasure was theirs. Little work was needed to make the cylinder smooth, control precession, and give it a centrifugal acceleration of one g at the circumference. With its axial orientation, the velocity changes for spacecraft to dock were minimal, and magnetic anchors easily held them fast until they were ready to depart. The excavation of rooms and passages in the yielding material went rapidly. Thereafter, spaces just under the surface provided Earth-weight for such activities as required it, including the bringing of babies to term; farther inward were the levels of successively lower weight, where Belters felt comfortable and where other undertakings were possible.

Everywhere around orbited members of the Swarm, their mineral wealth held in negligible gravity wells. Tiamat boomed. It became an industrial center, devoted especially to the production of things associated with spacefaring.

When the kzinti invaded, they were quick to realize its importance. Their introduction of the gravity polarizer changed many of the manufacturing programs, but scarcely affected Tiamat itself; one seldom had any reason to adjust the field in a given section, since one could have whatever weight was desired simply by going to the appropriate level.

Out of the years that followed have come countless stories of heroism, cowardice, resistance, collaboration, sabotage, salvage, ingenuity, intrigue, atrocity, mercy. Some are true. Certainly, when the human hyperdrive armada entered the Centaurian System, Tiamat might well have been destroyed, had not the Belter freedom fighters taken it over from within.

So ended its heroic age. The rest is anticlimax. More and more, new technologies and new horizons are making it a relic.

However, it is still populous and interesting. Not least of its attractions, though a mixed blessing, are the kzinti. Of those who stayed behind at this sun, or actually sought there, after the war—disgraced combatants, individuals who had formed ties too strong to break, Kdaptist refugees, eccentrics, and others less understandable—a goodly proportion have their colony within Tiamat. Tigertown is well worth visiting, in a properly briefed tour group with an experienced guide.

Tiamat also contains the headquarters of the Interworld Space Commission, which likewise is not as much in the awareness of the general public as it ought to be. Now that the hyperdrive has abruptly opened a way to far more undertakings than there are ships and personnel to carry out, rivalry for those resources often gets bitter. It can become political, planet versus planet at a time when faster-than-light travel has made peace between them as necessary as peace between nations on Earth had become when humankind was starting its outward venture. Until we have created enough capability to satisfy everyone, we must allocate. Alpha Centauri—Wunderland, parts of the Serpent Swarm—alone among human dwelling places, suffered kzin occupation, almost half a century of it. Alpha Centaurian men and women endured, or waged guerrilla warfare from remote and desolate bases, until the liberation. Who would question *their* dedication to our species as a whole?

At least, it was an obvious symbolism to make them the host folk of the Commission; and Tiamat, not yet into its postwar decline, was a natural choice for the seat.

3

"Good evening," replied Dorcas Glengarry Saxtorph. The headwaiter had immediately identified her as being from the Solar System and greeted her in English. "I was to meet Professor Tregennis. The reservation may be in the name of Laurinda Brozik." You didn't just walk into the Star Well; it was small and expensive.

Very briefly, his smoothness failed him and he let his gaze linger. Ten years after the end of the war, when outworlders had become a substantial fraction of the patronage, she was nonetheless a striking sight. A Belter, 185 centimeters in height, slender to the point of leanness, she was not in that respect different from those who had inhabited the Swarm for generations. However, you seldom met features so severely classic, fair-skinned, with large green eyes under arching brows. The molding of her head was emphasized by the Sol-Belter style, scalp depilated except for a crest of mahogany hair that in her case swept halfway down her back. A shimmery gray gown folded and refolded itself around carriage and gestures which, even for a person of spacer ancestry, were extraordinarily precise.

The headwaiter regained professionalism. "Ah, yes, of course, madame." Dorcas didn't show her forty Earthyears much, but nobody would take her for a girl. "This way, please."

The tables were arranged around a sunken transparency, ten meters across, which gave on the surface of Tiamat and thus the sky beyond. Nonreflecting, in the dim interior light it seemed indeed a well of night which the stars crowded, slowly streaming. The table Dorcas reached was on the bottom tier, with a view directly down into infinity. A glowlamp on it cast softness over cloth, silver, ceramic, and the two people already seated.

Arthur Tregennis rose, courtly as ever. A Plateaunian of Crew descent, the astrophysicist stood as tall as she did and still more slim, practically skeletal. He had the flared hook nose and high cheekbones of his kindred; the long nail on his left little finger proclaimed him an aristocrat of his planet, never subject to manual labor. Dorcas sometimes wondered why he kept that affectation, when he admitted to having sympathized with the democrats and their revolution, 33 years ago. Habit, perhaps. Otherwise he was an unassuming old fellow.

"Welcome, my lady," he said. His English was rather flat. Since the advent of hyperdrive and hyperwave, he'd been to so many scientific conferences, or in voice-to-voice contact with colleagues, that native accent seemed to have worn off—except, maybe, when he was with his own folk on top of Mount Lookitthat. "Ah, is Robert detained?"

"I'm afraid so." Dorcas let the waiter seat her. She'd reacquired a little sophistication since the war. "He had a nasty encounter, and the aftermath is still retro on him. He told me to come alone, give you his regrets, and bring back whatever word you have for us."

"Oh, dear," Laurinda Brozik whispered. "He's all right, isn't he?"

The English of Tregennis' graduate student was harder for Dorcas to follow than his. It was from We Made It.

The young woman was not a typical Crashlander—is there any such thing as a typical anything?—but she could not have been mistaken for a person from anywhere else. Likewise tall and finely sculptured, she seemed attenuated, arachnodactylic, somehow both awkward and eerily graceful, as if about to go into a contortion such as her race was capable of. She belonged to the large albino minority on the planet, with snowy skin, big red eyes, white hair combed straight down to the shoulders. In contrast to Tregennis' quiet tunic and trousers, she wore a gown of golden-hued fabric—an expert would have identified it as Terrestrial silk—and an arrowhead pendant of topaz; but somehow she wore them shyly.

"Well, he survived, not too upset." Glancing at the waiter, Dorcas ordered a dry martini, "—and I mean *dry*." She turned to the others. "He was on his way to talk with Markham," she explained. "Late hour, but the commissioner said he was too busy to receive him earlier. In fact, the meeting was to be at an auxiliary office. The equipment at the regular place is all tied up with—I'm not sure what. Well, Bob was passing through a deserted section when a kzin came out of nowhere and attacked him. He kept himself alive, without any serious damage, till the noise drew the police. The kzin fled."

"Oh, dear!" Laurinda repeated. She looked appalled.

Tregennis had a way of attacking problems from unexpected angles. "Why was Robert on foot?" he asked.

"What?" said Dorcas, surprised. She considered.

"The tubeway wasn't convenient for his destination, and it's not much of a walk. What of it?"

"There have been ample incidents, I hear. Kzinti with their hair-trigger tempers; and many humans bear an unreasoning hatred of them. I should think Robert would take care." Tregennis chuckled. "He's too seasoned a warrior to want any trouble."

"He had no reason to expect any, I tell you." Dorcas curbed her irritation. "Never mind. It was doubtless just one of those things. He has a ruined tunic and four superficial cuts, but he gave as good as he got. The point is, the police are in an uproar. They were nervous enough, now they're afraid of more fights. They've kept him at the station, questioning him over and over, showing him stereograms of this or that kzin—you can imagine. When last he called, he didn't expect to be free for another couple of hours, and then, on top of having nearly gotten killed, he'll be wrung out. So he told me to meet you on behalf of us both."

"Horrible," Laurinda said. "But at least he is safe."

"We regret his absence, naturally," Tregennis added, "and twice so when we had invited you two to dinner here in celebration of good news."

Dorcas smiled. "Well, I'll be your courier. What is the message?"

"It is for you to tell, Laurinda," the astrophysicist said gently.

The girl swallowed, leaned forward, and blurted, "This mornwatch I got the word I'd hoped for. On the hyperwave. My father, he, he'd been away, and afterward I suppose he needed to think about it, because that is a lot of money, but—but if necessary, he'll give us a grant. We won't have to depend on the Commission. We can take off on our own!"

"Wow-oo," Dorcas breathed.

Though it made no sense, for a tumbling few seconds her mind was on Stefan Brozik, whom she had never met. He had been among those on We Made

It quickest to seize the chance when the Outsiders came by with their offer to sell the hyperdrive technology. For a while he was an officer in one of the fleets that drove the kzin sublight ships back and back into defeat. Returning, he made his fortune in the production of hyperdrives for both government and private use; and Laurinda was his adored only daughter—

"It will take a time," came Tregennis' parched voice. "First the draft must clear the banks, then we must order what we need and wait for delivery. The demand exceeds the supply, after all. However, in due course we will be able to go."

His white head lifted. Dorcas remembered what he had said to Markham, when the commissioner declared: "Professor, this star of yours does appear to be an interesting object. I do not doubt an expedition to it would have scientific value. But space is full of urgent work to do, human work to do. Your project can wait another ten or fifteen years."

Iron had been in Tregennis' answer: "I cannot."

"Wonderful!" exclaimed Dorcas. Her jubilation was moderate merely because she had expected this outcome. The only question had been how long it would take. Stefan Brozik wouldn't likely deny his little girl a chance to go visit the foreign sun which she, peering from orbit around Plateau, had discovered, and which could make her reputation in her chosen field.

Nonetheless, Dorcas' gaze left the table and went off down the well of stars. Alpha Centauri B, dazzling bright, had drifted from it. She had a clear view toward the Lesser Magellanic Cloud. In yonder direction lay Beta Hydri, and around it swung Silvereyes, the most remote colony that humankind had yet planted. Beyond Silvereyes—But glory filled vision. Laurinda's sun was a dim red dwarf, invisible to her. Strange thought, that such a thing might be a key to mysteries.

Anger awoke. "Maybe we won't need your father's

money," Dorcas said. "Maybe the prospect will make that slime-bugger see reason."

"I beg your pardon?" asked Tregennis, shocked.

"Markham." Dorcas grinned. "Sorry. You haven't been toe-to-toe with him, over and over, the way Bob and I have. Never mind. Don't let him or a quantum-headed kzin spoil our evening. Let's enjoy. We're going!"

4

The office of Ulf Reichstein Markham was as austere as the man himself. Apart from a couple of chairs, a reference shelf, and a desk with little upon it except the usual electronics, its largeness held mostly empty space. Personal items amounted to a pair of framed documents and a pair of pictures. On the left hung his certificate of appointment to the Interworld Space Commission and a photograph of his wife with their eight-year-old son. On the right were his citation for extraordinary heroism during the war and a portrait painting of his mother. Both women showed the pure bloodlines of Wunderland aristocracy, the older one also in her expression; the younger looked subdued.

Markham strove to maintain the same physical appearance. His father had been a Belter of means, whom his mother married after the family got in trouble with the kzinti during the occupation and fled to the Swarm. At age 50 he stood a slender, swordblade-straight 195 centimeters. Stiff gray-blond hair grew over a narrow skull, above pale eyes, long nose, outthrust chin that sported the asymmetric beard, a point on the right side. Gray and close-fitting, his garb suggested a military uniform.

"I trust you have recovered from your experience, Captain Saxtorph," he said in his clipped manner.

"Yah, I'm okay, aside from puzzlement." The space-man settled back in his chair, crossed shank over thigh. "Mind if I smoke?" He didn't wait for an answer before reaching after pipe and tobacco pouch.

Markham's lips twitched the least bit in disdain of the uncouthness, but he replied merely, "We will doubtless never know what caused the incident. You should not allow it to prey on your mind. The resident kzinti are under enormous psychological stress, still more so than humans would be in comparable circumstances. Besides uprootedness and culture shock, they must daily live with the fact of defeat. Acceptance runs counter to an instinct as powerful in them as sexuality is in humans. This individual, who-ever he is, must have lashed out blindly. Let us hope he doesn't repeat. Perhaps his friends can prevail on him."

Saxtorph scowled. "I thought that way, too, at first. Afterward I got to wondering. I hadn't been near any kzinti my whole time here, this trip. They don't mingle with humans unless business requires, and then they handle it by phone if at all possible. This fellow was way off the reservation. He lurked till I arrived, in that empty place. He was wearing a phone. Somebody else, shadowing me, could have called to tell him I was coming and the coast was clear."

"Frankly, you are being paranoid. Why in creation should he, or anyone, wish you harm? You specifi-cally, I mean. Furthermore, conspiracy like that is not kzin behavior. It would violate the sense of honor that the meanest among them cherishes. No, this poor creature went wandering about, trying to walk off his anger and despair. When you chanced by, like a game animal on the ancestral planet passing a hunter's blind, it triggered a reflex that he lost control of."

"How can you be sure? How much do we really know about that breed?"

"I know more than most humans."

"Yah," drawled Saxtorph, "I reckon you do."

Markham stiffened. His glance across the desk was like a levelled gun. For a moment there was silence.

Saxtorph got his pipe lit, blew a cloud of smoke, and through it peered back in more relaxed wise. He could afford to; somatic presence does make a difference. Barely shorter than the Wunderlander, he was hugely broader of shoulders and thicker of chest. His face was wide, craggy-nosed, shaggy-browed, with downward-slanted blue eyes and reddish hair that, at age 45, was getting thin. Whatever clothes he put on, they soon looked rumpled, but this gave the impression less of carelessness than of activity.

"What are you implying, Captain?" Markham asked low.

Saxtorph shrugged. "Nothing in particular, Commissioner. It's common knowledge that you have quite a lot to do with 'em."

"Yes. Certain among the rabble have called me 'kzin-lover.' I did not believe you shared their sewer mentality."

"Whoa, there." Saxtorph lifted a palm. "Easy, please. Of course you'd take a special interest. After all, the kzin empire, if that's what we should call it, it's still out yonder, and we still know precious little about it. Besides handling matters related to kzin comings and goings, you have to think about the future in space. Getting a better handle on their psychology is a real service."

Markham eased a bit. "Learning some compassion does no harm either," he said unexpectedly.

"Hm? Pardon me, but I should think that'd be extra hard for you."

Markham's history flitted through Saxtorph's mind. His mother had apparently married his commoner father out of necessity. Her husband died early, and she raised their son in the strictest aristocratic and martial tradition possible. By age 18 Markham was in the resistance forces. As captain of a commando ship, he led any number of raids and gained a reputation for kzin-like ruthlessness. He was 30 when the hyperdrive armada from Sol liberated Alpha Centauri. Thereafter he was active in restoring order and building up a Wunderland navy. Finally leaving the service, he settled on the planet, on a restored Reichstein estate granted him, and attempted a political career; but he lacked the needful affability and willingness to compromise. It was rumored that his appointment to the Space Commission had been a way of buying him off—he had been an often annoying gadfly—but he was in fact well qualified and worked conscientiously.

The trouble was, he had his own views on policy. With his prestige and connections, he had managed in case after case to win agreement from a voting majority of his colleagues.

Saxtorph smiled and added, "Well, Christian charity is all the more valuable for being so rare."

Markham pricked up his ears. The pale countenance flushed. "Christian!" he snapped. "A religion for slaves. No, I learned to respect the kzinti while I fought them. They were valiant, loyal, disciplined—and in spite of the propaganda and horror stories, their rule was by no means the worst thing that ever happened to Wunderland."

He calmed, even returned the smile. "But we have drifted rather far off course, haven't we? I invited you here for still another talk about your plans. Have I no hope of persuading you the mission is wasteful folly?"

"You've said the same about damn near every proposal to do any real exploring," Saxtorph growled.

"You exaggerate, Captain. Must we go over the old, trampled ground again? I am simply a realist. Ships, equipment, trained crews are in the shortest supply. We need them closer to home, to build up interstellar commerce and industry. Once we have that base, that productivity, yes, then of course we go forward. But we will go cautiously, if I have anything to say about it. Was not the kzin invasion a deadly enough surprise? Who knows what dangers, mortal dangers, a reckless would-be galaxytrotter may stir up?"

Saxtorph sighed. "You're right, this has gotten to be boringly familiar territory. I'll spare you my argument about how dangerous ignorance can be. The point is, I never put in for anything much. For a voyage as long as we intend, we need adequate supplies, and our insurance carrier insists we carry double spares of vital gear. The money Professor Tregennis wangled out of his university for the charter won't stretch to it. So we all rendezvoused here to apply for a government donation of stuff sitting in the warehouses.

"It just might buy you a scientific revolution."

He had rehashed this with malice, to repay Markham for the latter's own repetition. It failed to get the man's goat. Instead, the answer was, mildly, "I saw it as my duty to persuade the Commission to deny your request. Please believe there was no personal motive. I wish you well."

Saxtorph grinned, blew a smoke ring, and said, "Thanks. Want to come wave goodbye? Because we are going."

Markham took him off guard with a nod. "I know. Stefan Brozik has offered you a grant."

"Huh?" Saxtorph grabbed his pipe just before it landed in his lap. He recovered his wits. "Did you have the hyperwave monitored for messages to members of our party?" His voice roughened. "Sir, I resent that."

"It was not illegal. I was . . . more concerned than you think." Markham leaned forward. "Listen. A man does not necessarily like doing what duty commands. Did you imagine I don't regret choking off great adventures, that I do not myself long for the age of discovery that must come? In my heart I feel a certain gratitude toward Brozik. He has released me.

"Now, since you are inevitably going, it would be pointless to continue refusing you what you want. That can only delay, not stop you. Better to cooperate, win back your goodwill, and in return have some influence on your actions. I will contact my colleagues. There should be no difficulty in getting a reversal of our decision."

Saxtorph sagged back in his chair. "Judas . . . priest."

"There are conditions," Markham told him. "If you are to be spared a long time idle here, prudent men must be spared nightmares about what grief you might bring on us all by some blunder. Excuse my blunt language. You are amateurs."

"Every explorer is an amateur. By definition."

"You are undermanned."

"I wouldn't say so. Captain; computerman; two pilots, who're also experienced rockjacks and planetsiders; quartermaster. Everybody competent in a slew of other specialties. And, this trip, two scientists, the prof and his student. What would anybody else *do?*"

"For one thing," Markham said crisply, "he would counsel proper caution and point out where this was not being exercised. He would keep official policy in your minds. The condition of your obtaining what you need immediately is this. You shall take along a man who will have officer status—"

"Hey, wait a minute. I'm the skipper, my wife's the mate as well as the computerman, and the rest have shaken down into a damn good team. I don't aim to shake it back up again."

"You needn't," Markham assured him. "This man will be basically an observer and advisor. He should prove useful in several additional capacities. In the event of . . . disaster to the regular officers, he can take command, bring the ship back, and be an impartial witness at the inquiry."

"M-m-m." Saxtorph frowned, rubbed his chin, pondered. "Maybe. It'll be a long voyage, you know, about ninety days cooped up together, with God knows what at the end. Not that we expect anything more than interesting astronomical objects. Still, you're right, it is unpredictable. We're a close-knit crew, and the scientists seem to fit in well, but what about this stranger?"

"I refer you to my record," Markham replied. When Saxtorph drew a sharp breath, the Wunderlander added, "Yes, I am doubtless being selfish. However, my abilities in space are proven, and—in spite of everything, I share the dream."

5

In her youth, before she became a tramp, *Rover* was a naval transport, UNS *Ghost Dance*. She took men and matériel from their sources to bases around the Solar System, and brought some back for furlough or repair. A few times she went into combat mode. They were only a few. The kzinti hurled a sublight fleet out of Alpha Centauri at variable intervals, but years apart, since one way or another they always lost heavily in the sanguinary campaigns that followed. *Ghost Dance* would release her twin fighters to escort her on her rounds. Once they came under attack, and were the survivors.

Rover might now be less respectable, maybe even a bit shabby, but was by no means a slattern. The Saxtorphs had obtained her in a postwar sale of surplus and outfitted her as well as their finances permitted. On the outside she remained a hundred-meter spheroid, its smoothness broken by airlocks, hatches, boat bays, instrument housings, communications boom, grapples, and micrometeoroid pocks that had

given the metal a matte finish. Inboard, much more
had changed. Automated as she was, she never needed
more than a handful to man her; on a routine interplanetary flight she was quite capable of being her
own crew. Most personnel space had therefore been
converted for cargo stowage. Those people who did
travel in her had more room and comfort than for-
merly. Instead of warcraft she carried two Prospector
class boats, primarily meant for asteroids and the like
but well able to maneuver in atmosphere and set
down on a fair-sized planet. Other machinery was
equally for peaceful, if occasionally rough use.

"But how did the Saxtorphs ever acquire a hyperdrive?" asked Laurinda Brozik. "I thought licensing
was strict in the Solar System, too, and they don't
seem to be terribly influential."

"They didn't tell you?" replied Kamehameha Ryan.
"Bob loves to guffaw over that caper."

Her lashes fluttered downward. A tinge of pink
crossed the alabaster skin. "I, I don't like to . . .
pry—ask personal questions."

He patted her hand. "You're too sweet and consider-
ate, Laurinda. Uh, okay to call you that? We are in
for a long haul. I'm Kam."

The quartermaster was showing her around while
Rover moved up the Alpha Centaurian gravity well
until it would be safe to slip free of Einsteinian
space. Her holds being vacant, the acceleration was
several g, but the interior polarizer maintained weight
at the half Earth normal to which healthy humans
from every world can soon adapt. "You want the
grand tour, not a hasty look-around like you got
before, and who'd be a better guide than me?" Ryan
had said. "I'm the guy who takes care of inboard
operations, everything from dusting and polishing,
through mass trim and equipment service, on to
cooking, which is the real art." He was a stocky man
of medium height, starting to go plump, round-faced,
dark-complexioned, his blue-black hair streaked with

the earliest frost. A gaudy sleeveless shirt bulged above canary-yellow slacks and thong sandals.

"Well, I—well, thank you, Kam," Laurinda whispered.

"Thank you, my dear. Now this door I'd better not open for you. Behind it we keep chemical explosives for mining-type jobs. But you were asking about our hyperdrive, weren't you?

"Well, after the war Bob and Dorcas—they met and got married during it, when he was in the navy and she was helping beef up the defenses at Ixa, with a sideline in translation—they worked for Solar Minerals, scouting the asteroids, and did well enough, commissions and bonuses and such, that at last they could make the down payment on this ship. She was going pretty cheap because nobody else wanted her. Who'd be so crazy as to compete with the big Belter companies? But you see, meanwhile they'd found the real treasure, a derelict hyperdrive craft. She wasn't UN property or anything, she was an experimental job a manufacturer had been testing. Unmanned; a monopole meteoroid passed close by and fouled up the electronics; she looped off on an eccentric orbit and was lost; the company went out of business. She'd become a legend of sorts, every search had failed, on which basis Dorcas figured out where she most likely was, and she and Bob went looking on their own time. As soon as they were ready they announced their discovery, claimed salvage rights, and installed the drive in this hull. Nobody had foreseen anything like that, and besides, they'd hired a smart lawyer. The rules have since been changed, of course, but we come under a grandfather clause. So here we've got the only completely independent starship in known space."

"It is very venturesome of you."

"Yeah, things often get precarious. Interstellar commerce hasn't yet developed regular trade routes, except what government-owned lines monopolize.

We have to take what we can get, and not all of it has been simple hauling of stuff from here to there. The last job turned out to be a lemon, and frankly, this charter is a godsend. Uh, don't quote me. I talk too much. Bob bears with me, but a tongue-lashing from Dorcas can take the skin off your soul."

"You and he are old friends, aren't you?"

"Since our teens. He came knocking his way around Earth to Hawaii, proved to be a good guy for a *haole*, I sort of introduced him to people and things, we had some grand times. Then he enlisted, had a real yeager of a war career, but you must know something about that. He looked me up afterward, when he and Dorcas were taking a second honeymoon, and later they offered me this berth."

"You had experience?"

"Yes, I'd gone spaceward, too. Civilian. Interesting work, great pay, glamor to draw the girls, because not many flatlanders wanted to leave Earth when the next kzin attack might happen anytime."

"It seems so romantic," Laurinda murmured. "Superficially, at least, and to me."

"What do you mean, please?" Ryan asked, in the interest of drawing her out. Human females like men who will listen to them.

"Oh, that is—What have I done except study? And, well, research. I was born the year the Outsiders arrived at We Made It, but of course they were gone again long before I could meet them. In fact, I never saw a nonhuman in the flesh till I came to Centauri and visited Tigertown. You and your friends have been out, active, in the universe."

"I don't want to sound self-pitying," Ryan said, unable to quite avoid sounding smug, "but it's been mostly sitting inboard, then working our fingers off, frantic scrambles, shortages of everything, and moments of stark terror. A wise man once called adventure 'somebody else having a hell of a tough time ten light-years away.'"

She looked at him from her slightly greater elevation and touched his arm. "Lonely, too. You must miss your family."

"I'm a bachelor type," Ryan answered, forbearing to mention the ex-wives. "Not that I don't appreciate you ladies, understand—"

At that instant, luck brought them upon Carita Fenger. She emerged from a cold locker with a hundred-liter keg of beer, intended for the saloon, on her back, held by a strap that her left hand gripped. High-tech tasks were apportioned among all five of *Rover's* people, housekeeping chores among the three crewmen. This boat pilot was a Jinxian. Her width came close to matching her short height, with limbs in proportion and bosom more so. Ancestry under Sirius had made her skin almost ebony, though the bobbed hair was no longer sun-bleached white but straw color. Broad nose, close-set brown eyes, big mouth somehow added up to an attractive face, perhaps because it generally looked cheerful. "Well, hi," she hailed. "What's going on here?"

Ryan and Laurinda halted. "I am showing our passenger around the ship," he said stiffly.

Carita cocked her head. "Are you, now? That isn't all you'd like to show her, I can see. Better get back to the galley, lad. You did promise us a first-meal feast." To the Crashlander: "He's a master chef when he puts his mind to it. Good in bed, too."

Laurinda dropped her gaze and colored. Ryan flushed likewise. "I'm sorry," he gobbled. "Pilot Fenger's okay, but she does sometimes forget her manners."

Carita's laugh rang. "I've not forgotten this nightwatch is your turn, Kam. I'll be waiting. Or shall I seduce Commissioner Markham—or Professor Tregennis?" To Laurinda: "Sorry, dear, I shouldn't have said that. Being coarse goes with the kind of life I've led. I'll try to do better. Don't be afraid of Kam. He's harmless as long as you don't encourage him."

She trudged off with her burden. To somebody born to Jinx gravity, the weight was trifling. Ryan struggled to find words. All at once Laurinda trilled laughter of her own, then said fast, "I apologize. Your arrangements are your own business. Shall we continue for as long as you can spare the time?"

6

The database in *Rover* contained books as well as musical and video performances. Both the Saxtorphs spent a considerable amount of their leisure reading, she more than he. Their tastes differed enough that they had separate terminals in their cabin. He wanted his literature, like his food, plain and hearty; Dorcas ranged wider. Ever since hyperwave made transmission easy, she had been putting hundreds of writings by extrasolar dwellers into the discs, with the quixotic idea of eventually getting to know most of them.

The ship was a few days into hyperspace when she entered the saloon and found Tregennis. A couple of hours' workout in the gym, followed by a shower and change of coverall, left her aglow. The Plateaunian sat talking with Markham. That was unusual; the commissioner had kept rather to himself.

"Indeed the spectroscope, interferometer, the entire panoply of instruments reveals much," Tregennis was saying. "How else did Miss Brozik discover her star and learn of its uniqueness? But there is no substitute for a close look, and who would put a hyperdrive in an unmanned probe?"

"I know," Markham replied. "I was simply inquiring what data you already possess. That was never made clear to me. For example, does the star have planets?"

"It's too small and faint for us to establish that, at the distance from which we observed. Ah, I am surprised, sir. Were you so little interested that you didn't ask questions?"

"Why should he, when he was vetoing our mission?" Dorcas interjected. It brought her to their notice. Tregennis started to rise. "No, please stay seated." He looked so fragile. "No offense intended, Landholder Markham. I'm afraid I expressed myself tactlessly, but it seemed obvious. After all, you were— are a busy man with countless claims on your attention."

"I understand, Mme. Saxtorph," the Wunderlander said stiffly. "You are correct. Feeling as I did, I took care to suppress my curiosity."

Tregennis shook his head in a bemused fashion. He doubtless wasn't very familiar with the twists and turns the human mind can take. Dorcas recalled that he had never been married, except to his science— though he did seem to regard Laurinda as a surrogate daughter.

The computerman sat down. "In fact," she said conciliatingly, "I still wonder why you felt you could be spared from your post for as long as we may be gone. You could have sent somebody else."

"Trustworthy persons are hard to find," Markham stated, "especially in the younger generation."

"I've gathered you don't approve of postwar developments on your planet." Dorcas glanced at Tregennis. "That's apropos the reason I hoped you would be here, Professor. I'm reading *The House on Crowsnest*—"

"What do you mean?" Markham interrupted. "Crowsnest is an area on top of Mount Lookitthat."

Dorcas curbed exasperation. Maybe he couldn't help being arrogant. "I understand it's considered the greatest novel ever written on Plateau," she said.

Tregennis nodded. "Many think so. I confess the language in it gets too strong for my taste."

"Well, the author is a Colonist, telling how things were before and during the revolution," Dorcas said in Markham's direction. "Oppression does not make people nice. The wonder is that Crew rule was overthrown almost bloodlessly."

"If you please," Tregennis responded, "we of the Crew families were not monsters. Many of us realized reform was overdue and worked for it. I sympathized myself, you know, although I did not take an active role. I do believe Nairn exaggerates the degree and extent of brutality under the old order."

"That's one thing I wanted to ask you about. His book's full of people, places, events, practices that must be familiar to you but that nobody on any other planet ever heard of. Laurinda herself couldn't tell me what some passages refer to."

Tregennis smiled. "She has only been on Plateau as a student, and was born into a democracy. Why should she concern herself about old, unhappy, far-off things? Not that she is narrow, she comes from a cultured home, but she is young and has a whole universe opening before her."

Dorcas nodded. "A lucky generation, hers."

"Yes, indeed. Landholder Markham, I must disagree with views you have expressed. Taken as a whole, on every world the young are rising marvelously well to their opportunities—better, I fear, than their elders would have done."

"It makes a huge difference, being free," Dorcas said.

Markham sat bolt upright. "Free to do what?" he

snapped. "To be vulgar, slovenly, ignorant, self-centered, materialistic, *common*? I have seen the degradation go on, year by year. You have stayed safe in your ivory tower, Professsor. You, Mme. Saxtorph, operate in situations where a measure of discipline, sometimes old-fashioned self-sacrifice, is a condition of survival. But I have gotten out into the muck and tried to stem the tide of it."

"I heard you'd run for your new parliament, and I know you don't care for the popular modern styles," Dorcas answered dryly. She shrugged. "I often don't myself. But why should people not have what they want, if they can come by it honestly? Nobody forces you to join them. It seems you'd force them to do what pleases you. Well, that might not be what pleases me!"

Markham swallowed. His ears lay back. "I suspect our likes are not extremely dissimilar. You are a person of quality, a natural leader." Abruptly his voice quivered. He must be waging battle to keep his feelings under control. "In a healthy society, the superior person is recognized for what he or she is, and lesser ones are happy to be guided, because they realize that not only they but generations to come will benefit. The leader is not interested in power or glory for their own sake. At most, they are means to an end, the end to which he gives his life, the organic evolution of the society toward its destiny, the full flowering of its soul. But we are replacing living *Gemeinschaft* with mechanical *Gesellschaft*. The cyborg civilization! It goes as crazy as a cyborg individual. The leading classes also lose their sense of responsibility. Those members who do not become openly corrupt turn into reckless megalomaniacs."

Dorcas paled, which was her body's way of showing anger. "I've seen that kind of thinking described in history books," she said. "I thought better of you, sir. For your information, my grandfather was a cyborg after an accident. Belters always believed it was as criminal to send convicts into the organ banks as any crime of theirs could be. He was the sanest man I've known. Nor have I noticed leaders of free folk doing much that is half as stupid or evil as what the master classes used to order. I'll make my own mistakes, thank you."

"You certainly will. You already have. I must speak plainly. Your husband's insistence on this expedition, against every dictate of sound judgment, merely because it suits him to go, is a perfect example of a leader who has ceased to be a shepherd. Or perhaps you yourself are, since you have aided and abetted him. *You* could have remembered how full of terrible unknowns space is. Belters are born to that understanding. He is a flatlander."

Dorcas whitened entirely. Her crest bristled. She stood up, fists on hips, to loom over Markham and say word by word: "That will do. We have endured your presence, that you pushed on us, in hopes you would prove to be housebroken. We have now listened to your ridiculous rantings because we believe in free speech where you do not, and in hopes you would soon finish. Instead, you have delivered an intolerable racist insult. You will go to your cabin and remain there for twenty-four hours. Bread and water will be brought to you."

Markham gaped. "What? Are you mad?"

"Furious, yes. As for sanity, I refrain from expressing an opinion about who may lack it." Dorcas consulted her watch. "You can walk to your cabin in about five minutes. Therefore, do not be seen outside it, except for visits to the head, until 1737 hours tomorrow. Go."

He half rose himself, sank back down, and exclaimed, "This is impossible! Professor Tregennis, I call you to witness."

"Yes," Dorcas said. "Please witness that he has received a direct order from me, who am second in command of the ship. Shall we call Captain Saxtorph to confirm it? You can be led off in irons, Markham. Better you obey. Go."

The commissioner clambered to his feet. He breathed hard. The others could smell his sweat. "Very well," he said tonelessly. "Of course I will file a complaint when we return. Meanwhile we shall minimize further conversation. Good day." He jerked a bow and marched off.

After a time in which only the multitudinous low murmurings of the vessel had utterance, Tregennis breathed, "Dear me. Was that not a . . . slightly excessive reaction?"

Dorcas sat down again. Her iciness was dissolving in calm. "Maybe. Bob would think so, though naturally he'd have backed me up. He's more good-natured than I am. I do not tolerate such language about him. This hasn't been the only incident."

"There is a certain prejudice against the Earth-born among the space-born. I understand it is quite widespread."

"It is, and it's not altogether without foundation—in a number of cases." Dorcas laughed. "I shared it, at the time Bob and I met. It caused some monumental quarrels the first couple of years, years when we could already have been married. I finally got rid of it and took to judging individuals on their merits."

"Forgive me, but are you not a little intolerant of those who have not had your enlightening experience?"

"Doubtless. However, between you and me, I welcomed the chance to show Markham who's boss here. I worried that if we have an emergency he could get insubordinate. That would be an invitation to disaster."

"He is a strange man," Tregennis mused. "His behavior, his talk, his past career, everything seems such a welter of contradictions. Or am I being naive?"

"Not really, unless I am, too. Oh, people aren't self-consistent like the laws of mechanics—even quantum mechanics. But I do think we lack some key fact about Landholder Markham, and will never understand him till we have it." Dorcas made a gesture of dismissal. "Enough. Now may I do what I originally intended and quiz you about Plateau?"

7

While *Rover* was in hyperspace, all five of her gang stood mass detector watch, six hours a day for four days, fifth day off. It was unpopular duty, but they would have enjoyed still less letting the ship fly blind, risking an entry into a gravity well deep enough to throw her to whatever fate awaited vessels which did not steer clear. The daydream was becoming commonplace among their kind, that someday somebody would gain sufficient understanding of the psionics involved that the whole operation could be automated.

It wasn't torture, of course, once you had schooled yourself never to look into the Less Than Void which filled the single port necessarily left unshuttered. You learned how to keep an eye on the indicator globe while you exercised, read, watched a show, practiced a handicraft. On the infrequent occasions when it registered something, matters did get interesting.

"And I've decided I don't mind it in the least,"

said Juan Yoshii after Kamehameha Ryan had relieved him.

"Really?" asked Laurinda Brozik. She had met him below the flight deck by agreement.

He offered her his arm, a studied, awkward gesture not used in his native society. She smiled and took it. He was a young Sol-Belter. Unlike Dorcas Saxtorph, or most folk of his nation, he eschewed spectacular garb. Small, slim, with olive-skinned, almost girlish features, he did wear his hair in the crest, but it was cut short.

"I have just heard complaints about the monotony," Laurinda said.

"Monotony, or peacefulness?" he countered in his diffident fashion. "I chafed, too. Then gradually I realized what an opportunity this is to be alone and think. Or compose."

"You don't sound like a rockjack," she said needlessly. It was what had originally attracted her to him.

He chuckled. "How are rockjacks supposed to sound? We have the rough, tough image, yes. Pilot the boat, find the ore, wrench it out, bring it home, and damn the meteoroids. Or the sun-flare or the fusion generator failure or anything else. But we are simply persons making a living. Quite a few of us look forward to a day when we can use different talents."

"What else would you like to do?"

His smile was stiff. He stared before him. "Prepare yourself to laugh."

"Oh, no." Her tone made naught of the eight centimeters by which she topped him. "How could I laugh at a man who handles the forces that I only measure?"

He flushed and had no answer. They walked on. The ship hummed around them. Bulkheads were brightly painted, pictures were hung on them and often changed, here and there were pots whose flowers Carita Fenger maintained, but nonetheless this was a barren environment. The two had a date in his cabin, where he would provide tea while they screened d'Auvergne's Fifth Chromophony. An appreciation of her work was one thing among others that they discovered they had in common.

"What is your hope?" Laurinda asked at last, low.

He gulped. "To be a poet."

"Why, how . . . how remarkable."

"Not that there's a living in it," he said hastily. "I'll need a groundside position. But I will anyway when I get too old for this berth—and am still fairly young by most standards." He drew breath. "In the centuries of spaceflight, how much true poetry has been written? Plenty of verse, but how much that makes your hair rise and you think yes, this is the real truth? It's as if we've been too busy to find the words for what we've been busy with. I want to try. I am trying, but know quite well I won't have a chance of succeeding with a single line till I've worked at it for another ten years or more."

"You're too modest, Juan. Genius flowers early oftener than not. I would like to see what you have done."

"No, I, I don't think it's that good. Maybe my efforts never will be. Not even equal to—well, actually minor stuff, but it does have the spirit—"

"Such as what?"

"Oh, ancient pieces, mostly, pre-space.

" *'To follow knowledge like a sinking star,*

"Beyond the utmost bound of human thought.' "

Yoshii cackled a laugh. "I'm really getting bookish, am I not? An easy trap to fall into. Spacemen have a lot of free time in between crises."

"You've put yours to good use," she said earnestly. "Is that poem you quoted from in the ship's database? I'd like to read it."

"I don't know, but I can recite it verbatim."

"That would be much better. Romantic—" Laurinda broke off. She turned her glance away.

He sensed her confusion and blurted in his own, "Please don't misunderstand me. I know—your customs, your mores—I mean to respect them. Completely."

She achieved a smile, though she could not yet look back his way. "Why, I'm not afraid of you." Unspoken: You're not unbearably frustrated. It's obvious that Carita is your mistress as well as Kam's. "You are a gentleman." And what we have coming to life between us is still small and frail, but already very sweet.

8

Rover re-entered normal space ten astronomical units from the destination star. That was unnecessarily distant for a mass less than a fourth of Sol's, but the Saxtorphs were more cautious than Markham admitted. Besides, the scientists wanted to begin with a long sweep as baseline for their preliminary observations, and it was their party now.

As soon as precise velocity figures were available, Dorcas computed the vectors. The star was hurtling at well over a thousand kilometers per second with respect to galactic center. That meant the ship needed considerable delta v to get down to interplanetary speeds and into the equatorial plane where any attendant bodies were likeliest to be. That boost phase must also serve those initial requirements of the astronomers. Course and thrust could be adjusted as data came in and plans for the future were developed.

The star's motion meant, too, that it was escaping the galaxy, bound for the gulfs beyond. Presumably an encounter with one or more larger bodies had cast it from the region where it formed. A question the expedition hoped to get answered, however incompletely, was where that might have happened—and when.

Except for Dorcas, who worked with Tregennis to process the data that Laurinda mostly gathered, the crew had little to do but housekeeping. Occasionally someone was asked to lend a hand with some task of the research.

Going off watch, Carita Fenger stopped by the saloon. A large viewscreen there kept the image of the sun at the cross-haired center. Else nobody could have identified it. It was waxing as the ship drove inward but thus far remained a dim dull-red point, outshone by stars light-years away. The undertone of power through the ship was like a whisper of that which surged within, around, among them, nuclear fires, rage of radiation, millennial turmoil of matter, births and funeral pyres and ashes and rebirths, the universe forever in travail. Like most spacefarers, Carita could lose herself, hour upon hour, in the contemplation of it.

She halted. Markham sat alone, looking. His face was haggard.

"Well, hi," she said tentatively.

Markham gave her a glance. "How do you do, Pilot Fenger." The words came flat.

She plumped herself down in the chair beside him. "Quite a sight, eh?"

He nodded, his gaze back on the screen.

"A trite thing to say," she persisted. "But I suspect Juan's wrong. He hopes to find words grand enough. I suspect it can't be done."

"I was not aware Pilot Yoshii had such interests," said Markham without unbending.

"Nah, you wouldn't be. You've been about as outgoing as a black hole. What's between you and Dorcas? You seem to be off speaking terms with her."

"If you please, I am not in the mood for gossip." Markham started to rise, to leave.

Carita took hold of his arm. It was a gentle grip but he could easier have broken free of a salvage grapple. "Wait a minute," she said. "I've been halfway on the alert for a chance to talk with you. Who does any more, except 'Pass the salt' at mess, that sort of thing? How lonesome you must be."

He refrained from ineffectual resistance, continued to stare before him, and clipped, "Thank you for your concern, but I manage. Kindly let go."

"Look," she said, "we're supposed to be shipmates. It's a hell of an exciting adventure—Christ, we're the first, the very first, in all this weird wonder— but it's cold out, too, and doesn't care an atom's worth about human beings. I keep thinking how awful it must be, cut off from any friendship the way you are. Not that you've exactly encouraged us, but we could try harder."

Now he did regard her. "Are you inviting me to your bed?" he asked in the same tone as before.

Slightly taken aback, she recovered, smiled, and replied, "No, I wasn't, but if it'll make you feel better we can have a go at it."

"Or make you feel better? I am not too isolated to have noticed that lately Pilot Yoshii has ceased visiting your cabin. Is Quartermaster Ryan insufficient?"

Carita's face went sulfur black. She dragged her fingers from him. "My mistake," she said. "The rest were right about you. Okay, you can take off."

"With pleasure." He stalked out.

She mumbled an oath, drew forth a cigar, lit and blew fumes that ran the ventilators and air renewers up to capacity. Calm returned after a while. She laughed ruefully. Ryan had told her more than once that she was too soft-hearted; and he was a man prone to fits of improvident generosity.

She was about to go when Saxtorph's voice boomed

from the intercom: "Attention, please. Got an announcement here that I'm sure will interest everybody.

"We'll hold a conference in a few days, when more information is in. Then you can ask whatever questions you want. Meanwhile, I repeat my order, do not pester the science team. They're working around the clock and don't need distractions.

"However, Arthur Tregennis has given me a quick rundown on what's been learned so far, to pass on to you. Here it is, in my layman's language. Don't blame him for any garbling.

"They have a full analysis of the sun's composition, along with other characteristics. That wasn't too easy. For one thing, it's so cool that its peak emission frequency is in the radio band. Because the absorption and re-emission of the interstellar medium in between isn't properly known, we *had* to come here to get decent readings.

"They bear out what the prof and Laurinda thought. This sun isn't just metal-poor, it's metal-impoverished. No trace of any element heavier than iron, and little of that. Yes, you've all heard as how it must be very old, and has only stayed on the main sequence this long because it's such a feeble dwarf. But now they have a better idea of just how long 'this' has been.

"Estimated age, fifteen billion years. Our star is damn near as old as the universe.

"It probably got slung out of its parent galaxy early on. In that many years you can cover a lot of kilometers. We're lucky that we—meaning the human species—are alive while it's in our neighborhood.

"And . . . in the teeth of expectations, it's got planets. Already the instruments are finding signs of oddities in them, no two alike, nothing we could have foreseen. Well, we'll be taking a close look. Stand by. Over."

Carita sprang to her feet and cheered.

9

Once when they were young bucks, chance-met, beachcombing together in the Islands, Kam Ryan and Bob Saxtorph acquired a beat-up rowboat, cat-rigged it after a fashion, stowed some food and plenty of beer aboard, and set forth on a shakedown cruise across Kaulakahi Channel. Short runs off Waimea had gone reasonably well, but they wanted to be sure of the seaworthiness before making it a lure for girls. They figured they could reach Niihau in 12 or 15 hours, land if possible, rest up in any case, and come back. They didn't have the price of an outboard, but in a pinch they could row.

To avoid coping with well-intentioned busybodies, they started after dark. By that time sufficient beer had gone down that they forgot about tuning in a weather report before leaving their tent—at the verge of kona season.

It was a beautiful night, half a moon aloft and so many stars they could imagine they were in space. Wind lulled, seas whooshed, rigging creaked, the boat rocked forward and presently a couple of dolphins appeared, playing alongside for hours, a marvel that made even Kam sit silent in wonder. Then toward dawn, the goal a vague darkness ahead, clouds boiled out of the west, wind sharpened and shrilled, suddenly rain slanted like a flight of spears and through murk the mariners heard waves rumble against rocks.

It wasn't much of a storm, really, but ample to deal with *Wahine*. Seams opened, letting in water to join that which dashed over the gunwales. Sail first reefed, soon struck, stays nonetheless gave way and the mast went. It would have capsized the hull had Bob not managed to heave it free. Thereafter he had the oars, keeping bow on to the waves, while Kam bailed. A couple of years older, and no weakling, the Hawaiian couldn't have rowed that long at a stretch. Eventually he did his share and a bit at the rudder, when somehow he worked the craft through a gap between two reefs which roared murder at them. They hit coral a while later, but close enough to shore that they could swim, never sure who saved the life of who in the surf. Collapsing behind a bush, they slept the weather out.

Afterward they limped off till they found a road and hitched a ride. They'd been blown back to Kauai. Side by side, they stood on the carpet before a Coast Guard officer and endured what they must.

Next day in their tent, Kam said, unwontedly solemn—the vast solemnity of youth—"Bob, listen. You've been my *hoa* since we met, you became my *hoaloha*, but what we've been through, what you did, makes you a *hoapili*."

"Aw, wasn't more'n I had to, and you did just as much," mumbled the other, embarrassed. "If you mean what I suppose you do, okay, I'll call you *kammerat*, and let's get on with whatever we're going to do."

"How about this? I've got folks on the Big Island. A tiny little settlement tucked away where nobody ever comes. Beautiful country, mountains and woods. People still live in the old kanaka style. How'd you like that?"

"Um-m, how old a style?"

Kam was relieved at being enabled to laugh. "You won't eat long pig! Everybody knows English, though they use Hawaiian for choice, and never fear, you can watch the Chimp Show. But it's a great, relaxed, cheerful life—you've got to experience the girls to believe—the families don't talk about it much when they go outside, or invite *haolena* in, because tourists would ruin it—but you'll be welcome, I guarantee you. How about it?"

The month that followed lived up to his promises, and then some.

Recollections of it flew unbidden across the years as Ryan worked in the galley. Everybody else was in the gym, where chairs and projection equipment had been brought, for the briefing the astronomers would give. *Rover* boosted on automatic; her instruments showed nothing ahead that she couldn't handle by herself for the next million kilometers. The quartermaster could have joined the group, but he wanted to make a victory feast ready. Before long, they'd be too busy to appreciate his art.

He did have a screen above the counter, monitoring the assembly.

Tregennis and Laurinda stood facing their audience. The Plateaunian said, with joy alive beneath the dry words:

"It is a matter of semantics whether we call this a first- or a second-generation system. Hydrogen and helium are overwhelmingly abundant, in proportions consistent with condensation shortly after the Big Bang—about which, not so incidentally, we may learn something more than hitherto. However, oxygen, nitrogen, carbon, silicon, and neon are present in significant quantities; magnesium and iron are not insignificant; other elements early in the periodic table are detectable. There has naturally been a concentration of heavier atoms in the planets, especially the inner ones, as gases selectively escaped. They are not mere balls of water ice.

"It seems clear, therefore, that this system formed out of a cloud which had been enriched by mass loss from older stars in their red giant phase. A few supernovae may have contributed, too, but any elements heavier than iron which they may have supplied are so scant that we will only find them by mass spectrography of samples from the solid bodies. They may well be nonexistent. Those older stars must have come into being as soon after the Beginning as was physically possible, in a proto-galaxy not too far then from the matter which was to become ours, but now surely quite distant from us."

"As we dared hope," said the Crashlander. Tears glimmered in her eyes like dew on rose petals.

"Oh, good for you!" called Yoshii.

"A relic—hell, finding God's fingerprints," Carita said, and clapped a hand to her mouth. Ryan grinned. Nobody else noticed.

"How many planets?" asked Saxtorph.

"Five," Tregennis replied.

"Hm. Isn't that kind of few, even for a dwarf? Are you sure?"

"Yes. We would have found anything of a size much less than what you would call a planet's."

"Especially since the Bode function is small, as you'd expect," Dorcas added. Having worked with the astronomers, she scarcely needed this session. "The planets huddle close in. We haven't found an Oort cloud either. No comets at all, we think."

"Outer bodies may well have been lost in the collision that sent this star into exile," Laurinda said. "And in fifteen billion years, any comets that were left got . . . used up."

"There probably was a sixth planet until some unknown date in the past," Tregennis stated. "We have indications of asteroids extremely close to the sun. Gravitational radiation—no, it must chiefly have been friction with the interstellar medium that caused a parent body to spiral in until it passed the Roche limit and was disrupted."

"Hey, wait," Saxtorph said. "Dorcas talks of a Bode function. That implies the surviving planets are about where theory says they ought to be. How'd they avoid orbital decay?"

Tregennis smiled. "That's a good question."

Saxtorph laughed. "Shucks, you sound like I was back in the Academy."

"Well, at this stage any answers are hypothetical, but consider. In the course of its long journey, quite probably through more galaxies than ours, the system must sometimes have crossed nebular regions where matter was comparatively dense. Gravitation would draw the gas and dust in, make it thickest close to the sun, until the sun swallowed it altogether. As a matter of fact, the planetary orbits have very small eccentricities—friction has a circularizing effect—and their distances from the primary conform only roughly to the theoretical distribution." Tregennis paused. "A further anomaly we cannot explain, though it may be related. We have found—marginally; we think we have found—molecules of water and OH radicals among the asteroids, almost like a ring around the sun." He spread his hands. "Well, I won't live to see every riddle we may come upon solved."

He had fought to get here, Ryan remembered.

"Let's hear about those planets," Carita said impatiently. Her job would include any landings. "Uh, have you got names for them? One, Two, Three might cause mixups when we're in a hurry."

"I've suggested using Latin ordinals," Laurinda answered. She sounded almost apologetic.

"Prima, Secunda, Tertia, Quarta, Quinta," Dorcas supplied. "Top-flight idea. I hope it becomes the standard for explorers." Laurinda flushed.

"I have agreed," Tregennis said. "The philologists can bestow official names later, or whoever is to be in charge of such things. Let us give you a précis of what we have learned to date."

He consulted a notator in his hand. "Prima," he recited. "Mean orbital radius, approximately 0.4 A. U. Diameter, approximately 16,000 kilometers. Since it has no satellite, the mass is still uncertain, but irradiation is such that it cannot be icy. We presume the material is largely silicate, which—allowing for self-compression—gives a mass on the order of Earth's. No signs of air.

"Secunda, orbiting at 0.7 A.U., resembles Prima, but is slightly larger and does have a thin atmosphere, comparable to Mars'. It has a moon as well. Remarkably, the moon has a higher albedo than expected, a yellowish hue. The period tells us the mass, of course, which reinforces our guess about Prima.

"Tertia is almost exactly one A.U. out. It is a superterrestrial, mass of five Earths, as confirmed by four moons, also yellowish. A somewhat denser atmosphere than Secunda's; we have confirmed the presence of nitrogen and traces of oxygen."

"What?" broke from Saxtorph. "You mean it might have life?"

Laurinda shivered a bit. "The water is forever frozen," she told him. "Carbon dioxide must often freeze. We don't know how there can be any measurable amount of free oxygen. But there is."

Tregennis cleared his throat. "Quarta," he said. "A gas giant at 1.5 A.U., mass 230 Earths, as established by ten moons detected thus far. Surprisingly, no rings. Hydrogen and helium, presumably surrounding a vast ice shell which covers a silicate core with some iron. It seems to radiate weakly in the radio frequencies, indicating a magnetic field, though the radio background of the sun is such that at this distance we can't be sure. We plan a flyby on our way in. Quarta will be basic to understanding the dynamics of the system. It is its equivalent of Jupiter."

"Otherwise we have only detected radio from Secunda," Laurinda related, "but it is unmistakable, cannot be of stellar origin. It is really curious—intermittent, seemingly modulated, unless that is an artifact of our skimpy data." She smiled. "How lovely if intelligent beings are transmitting."

Markham stirred. He had put his chair behind the row of the rest. "Are you serious?" he nearly shouted.

Surprised looks went his way. "Oh, no," Laurinda said. "Just a daydream. We'll find out what is actually causing it when we get there."

"Well, Quinta remains," Tregennis continued, "in several respects, the most amazing object of all. Mass 103 Earths—seven moons found—at 2.8 A.U. It does have a well-developed ring system. Hydrogen-helium atmosphere, but with clear spectra of methane, ammonia, and . . . water vapor. Water in huge quantities. Turbulence, and a measured temperature far above expectations. Something peculiar has happened.

"Are there any immediate questions? If not, Laurinda and Dorcas have prepared graphics—charts, diagrams, tables, pictures—which we would like to show. Please feel free to inquire, or to propose ideas. Don't be bashful. You are all intelligent people with a good understanding of basic science. Any of you may get an insight which we specialists have missed."

Markham rose. "Excuse me," he said.

"Huh?" asked Saxtorph, amiably enough. "You want to go now when this is really getting interesting?"

"I do not expect I can make a contribution." Markham hesitated. "I am a little indisposed. Best I lie down for a while. Do not worry. I will soon be well. Carry on." He sketched a bow and departed.

"What do you know, he is human," Carita said.

"We ought to be kinder to him than we have been, poor man," Laurinda murmured.

"He hasn't given us much of a chance, has he?" replied Yoshii.

"Stow that," Saxtorph ordered. "No backbiting."

"Yes," added Dorcas, "let's proceed with the libretto."

Eagerness made Tregennis tremble as he obliged.

In his galley, Ryan frowned. Something didn't feel quite right. While he followed the session he continued slicing the mahimahi he had brought frozen from Earth, but his mind was no longer entirely on either.

Time passed. It became clear that the Quarta approach was going to be an intellectual orgy, the more so because Quinta happened to be near inferior conjunction and thus a lot of information about that planet would be arriving, too. Ryan wiped hands on apron, left his preparations, and stumped up toward the flight deck.

He met Markham coming back. They halted and regarded each other. The companionway thrummed around them. "Hello, there," the quartermaster said slowly. "I thought you were in your cabin."

Markham stiffened. "I am on my way, if it is any of your business."

"Long way 'round."

"It . . . occurred to me to check certain stations. This is an old ship, refitted. Frankly, Captain Saxtorph relies too much on his machinery."

"What sort of thing did you want to check on?"

"Who are you to ask?" Markham flung. "You are the quartermaster."

"And you are the passenger." Ryan's bulk blocked the stairs. "I wouldn't be in this crew if I didn't have a pretty fair idea of how all the equipment works. I'm responsible for maintaining a lot of it."

"I have commanded spacecraft."

"Then you know each system keeps its own record." Ryan's smile approximated a leer, or a snarl. "Save the skipper a bunch of data retrievals. Where were you and what were you doing?"

Markham stood silent while the ship drove onward. At length: "I should, I shall report directly to the captain. But to avoid rumors, I tell you first. Listen well and do not distort what I say if you are able not to. I beamed a radio signal on a standard band at Secunda. It is against the possibility—the very remote possibility, Mlle. Brozik assured us— that sentient beings are present. Natives, Outsiders, who knows? In the interest of peaceful contact, we must provide evidence that we did not try to sneak in on them. Not that it is likely they exist, but—this is the sort of contigency I am here for. Saxtorph and I can dispute it later if he wishes. I have presented him with a *fait accompli*. Now let me by."

Ryan stood aside. Markham passed downward. Ryan stared after him till he was gone from sight, then went back to his galley.

10

Quarta fell astern as *Rover* moved on sunward. In the boat called *Fido*, Juan Yoshii swung around the giant planet and accelerated to overtake his ship. Vectors programmed, he could relax, look out the ports, seek to sort the jumbled marvels in his mind. Most had gone directly from instruments to the astronomers; he was carrying back certain observations taken farside. A couple of times there had been opportunity for Laurinda Brozik to tell him briefly about the latest interpretation, but he had been too busy on his flit to think much beyond the piloting.

Stars thronged, the Milky Way torrented, a sky little different from the skies he remembered. Less than 30 light-years' travel—a mite's leap in the galaxy. Clearly alien was the sun ahead. Tiny but perceptible, its ember of a disc was slow to dazzle his eyes, yet already cast sufficient light for him to see things by.

An outer moon drifted across vision. This was his last close passage, and instruments worked greedily.

Clicks and whirrs awoke beneath the susurrus of air through the hull. Yoshii pointed his personal camera; photography was an enthusiasm of his. The globe glimmered wan red under its sun. It was mainly ice, and smooth; any cracks and craters had slumped in the course of gigayears. The surface was lighter than it might have been and mottled with yellow spots. Ore deposits? The same material that tinted most airless bodies here? Tregennis was puzzled. You got dark spots in Solar-type systems. They were due to photolysis of frozen methane. Of course, this sun was so feeble. . . .

It nonetheless illuminated the planet aft. Quarta's hue was pale rose, overlaid with silvery streaks that were ice clouds: crystals of carbon dioxide, ammonia, in the upper levels methane. No twists, no vortices, no sign of any Jovian storminess marred the serenity. Though the disc was visibly flattened, it rotated slowly, taking more than 40 hours. Tidal forces through eons had worn down even the spin of this huge mass. They had likewise dispersed whatever rings it once had, and surely drawn away moons. The core possessed a magnetic field, slight, noticeable only because it extended so far into space that it snatched radio waves out of incoming cosmic radiation—remanent magnetism, locked into iron as that core froze. For gravitational energy release had long since reached its end point; and long, long before then, K-40 and whatever other few radionuclei were once on hand had guttered away beyond measurement. The ice sheath went upward in tranquil allotropic layers to a virtually featureless surface and an enormous, quietly circulating atmosphere of starlike composition. Quarta had reached Nirvana.

It fell ever farther behind. *Fido* closed in on *Rover*. The ship swelled until she might have been a planet herself. Instructions swept back and forth, electronic, occasionally verbal. A boat bay opened its canopy. Yoshii maneuvered through and docked. The canopy

closed, shutting off heaven. Air hissed back in from
the recovery tanks. A bulb flashed green. Yoshii
unharnessed, operated the lock, crawled forth, and
walked under the steady weight granted him by the
ship's polarizer, into her starboard reception room.

Laurinda waited.

Yoshii stopped. She was alone. White hair tumbled past delicate features to brush the dress, new to
him, that hugged her slenderness. She reached out.
Her eyes glowed. "W-welcome back, Juan," she
whispered.

"Why, uh, thanks, thank you. You're the . . .
committee?"

She smiled, dropped her glance, became briefly
the color of the world he had rounded. "Kam
met Carita. As for you, Dorcas—Mate Saxtorph suggested—"

He took her hands. They felt reed-thin and silk-
soft. "How nice of her. And the rest. I've data discs
for you."

"They'll keep. We have more work than we can
handle. Observations of Quinta were, have been incredibly fruitful." Ardor pulsed in her voice. The
outermost planet was a safe subject. "We think we
can guess its nature, but of course there's no end of
details we don't understand, and we could be entirely wrong—"

"Good for you," he said, delighted by her delight.
"I missed out on that, of course." Transmissions to
him, including hers, had dealt with the Quartan
system exclusively; any bit of information about it
might perhaps save his life. "Tell me."

"Oh, it's violent, multi-colored, with spots like
Jupiter's—one bigger than the Red—and—the surface is liquid water. It's Arctic-like; we imagine
continent-sized ice floes clashing together."

"But warmer than Quarta! Why?"

"We suppose a large satellite crashed, a fraction of
a million years ago. Debris formed the rings. The

main mass released enough heat to melt the upper part of the planetary shell, and, and we'll need years, science will, to learn what else has happened."

He stood for an instant in awe, less of the event than of the time-scale. That moon must have been close to start with, but still it had taken the casual orbital erosion of . . . almost a universe's lifespan so far—how many passages through nebulae, galaxies, the near-ultimate vacuum of intergalactic space?—to bring it down. *What is man, that thou art mindful of him—?*

What is man, that he should waste the little span which is his?

"That's wonderful," he said, "but—we—"

Impulsively, he embraced her. Astoundingly, she responded.

Between laughter and tears she said in his ear, "Come, let's go, Kam's spread a feast for the two of us in my cabin."

Set beside that, the cosmos was trivial.

Saxtorph's voice crackled from the intercom: "Now hear this. Now hear this. We've just received a message from what claims to be a kzin warship. They're demanding we make rendezvous with them. Keep calm but think hard. We'll meet in the gym in an hour, 1530, and consider this together."

Standing with back to bulkhead, the captain let silence stretch, beneath the pulsebeat and whispers of the ship, while he scanned the faces of those seated before him. Dorcas, her Athene countenance frozen into expressionlessness; Kam Ryan's full lips quirked a bit upward, defiantly cheerful; Carita Fenger a-scowl; Juan Yoshii and Laurinda Brozik unable to keep from glancing at each other, hand gripping hand; Arthur Tregennis, who seemed almost as concerned about the girl; Ulf Markham, well apart from the rest, masked in haughtiness—Ulf *Reichstein* Markham, if you please. . . . The air renewal cycle was at its daily point of ozone injection. That tang smelled like fear.

Which must not be let out of its cage. Saxtorph cleared his throat.

"Okay, let's get straight to business," he said. "You must've noticed a quiver in the interior *g*-field and change in engine sound. You're right, we altered acceleration. *Rover* will meet the foreign vessel, with velocities matched, in about 35 hours. It could be sooner, but Dorcas told them we weren't sure our hull could take that much stress. What we wanted, naturally, was as much time beforehand as possible."

"Why don't we cut and run?" Carita asked.

Saxtorph shrugged. "Whether or not we can out-run them, we for sure can't escape the stuff they can throw, now that they've locked onto us. If they really are kzinti navy, they'll never let us get out where we can go hyperspatial. They may be lying, but Dorcas and I don't propose to take the chance."

"I presume evasion tactics are unfeasible," said Tregennis in his most academic voice.

"Correct. We could stop the engine, switch off the generator, and orbit free, with batteries supplying the life support systems, but they'd have no trouble computing our path. As soon as they came halfway close, they'd catch us with a radar sweep.

"From what data we have on them, I believe they were searching for some time before they acquired us, probably with amplified optics. That's assuming they were in orbit around Secunda when they first learned of our arrival. The assumption is consistent with what would be a reasonable search curve for them and with the fact that there are modulated radio bursts out of that planet—transmissions to and from their base."

Nobody before had seen Yoshii snarl. "And how did they learn about us?" he demanded.

Looks went to Markham. He gave them back. "Yes, undoubtedly through me," he said. Strength rang in the words. "You all know I took it upon myself to beam a signal at Secunda—in my capacity as this expedition's officer of the government. The result has surprised me, too, but I acknowledge no need to apologize. If we, approaching a kzin base unbeknownst, had suddenly become manifest to their detectors, they would most likely have blown us out of existence."

Ryan nodded. "Without stopping to ask questions," he supplied. "Yeah, that'd be kzin style. If they are. How're you so sure?"

"I think we can take it for granted," Dorcas said. "Who else would have reason to call themselves kzinti?"

"Who else would want to?" Carita growled.

"Save the cuss words for later," Saxtorph counselled. "We're in too much of a pickle for luxuries. I might add that although the vocal transmission was through a translator, the phrasing, the responses to us, everything was pure kzin. They are here—on the far side of human space from their own. You realize what this means, don't you, folks? The kzinti have gotten the hyperdrive."

That conclusion had indeed become clear to everyone, but Laurinda asked, "How could they?" as if in pain.

Yoshii grimaced. "Once you know something can be done, you're halfway to doing it yourself," he told her.

"I know," she answered. "But I had the, the impression they aren't quite as clever at engineering as humans, even if they did invent the gravity polarizer. And, and wouldn't we have known?"

"Collecting intelligence in kzin space isn't exactly easy," Saxtorph explained. "Anyhow, they may have done the R and D on some planet we aren't aware of. I'll grant you, I'm surprised myself that they've been this quick. Well, they were." His grin was lopsided. "Once I heard about an epitaph on an old New England tombstone. 'I expected this, but not so soon.'"

"Why have they established themselves here?" Tregennis wondered. "As you observed, it is a long journey for them, especially if they went around human space in order to avoid any chance that their possession of the hyperdrive would be discovered. True, this system is uniquely interesting, but I didn't think kzin civilization gave scientific research as high a value as ours does."

"That's a good question," Saxtorph said.

His gallows humor drew a chuckle from none but Ryan. Dorcas uttered the thought in every mind: "They won't let us go home to tell about them if they can help it."

"Which is why we are being nice and meeting them as they request," Saxtorph added. "It gives them an alternative to putting a nuke on our track."

Markham folded his arms and stated, "I hope you people have the wit to be glad, at last, that I came along. They will understand that I am authorized to negotiate with them. They will likewise understand that my disappearance would in due course cause a second expedition to come, with armed escort, as the loss of an entirely private group might not."

"Could be," Saxtorph said. "However, I can think of several ways to fake a natural disaster for us."

"Such as?"

"Well, for instance, giving us a lethal dose of radiation, then sending the corpses back with the ship gimmicked to seem this was an accident. The kzin pilot could return on an accompanying vessel after ours left hyperspace."

"What would the log show?"

"What the 'last survivor' was tortured into entering."

"Nonsense. You have been watching too many spy dramas."

"I disagree. Besides, that was just one of the notions that occurred to Dorcas and me. The kzinti might be more inventive yet."

"We have decided not to rely exclusively on their sweet nature," the mate declared. "Listen carefully.

"We can launch the boats without them detecting it, if we act soon. They'll float free while *Rover* proceeds to rendezvous. When she's a suitable distance off, nobody looking for any action in this volume of space, they'll scramble."

Carita smacked fist in palm. "Hey, terrific!" she cried.

Markham sounded appalled: "Have you gone crazy? How will you survive, let alone return, in two little interplanetary flitters?"

"They're more than that," Saxtorph reminded. "They're rugged and maneuverable and full to the scuppers with delta v. In either of 'em I'd undertake to outrace or dodge a tracking missile, and make it tough or impossible to hold a laser beam on her long enough to do much damage. Air and water recycler are in full working order and rations for one man-year are stowed aboard."

"I, I ate some," Yoshii stammered. "Carita must have, too."

"I've already replaced it," Ryan informed them.

"Good thinking!" Saxtorph exclaimed. "Did you expect this tactic?"

"Oh, general principles. Take care of your belly and your belly will take care of you."

"Stop that schoolboy chatter," Markham snapped. "What in the cosmos can you hope to do but antagonize the kzinti?"

"How do you tell an antagonized kzin from an unantagonized one?" Saxtorph retorted. "I am dead serious. Nobody has to follow me who doesn't want to."

"I certainly do not. Someone has to stay and . . . try to repair the harm your lunacy will have done."

"I figured you would. But I supposed you, of all people, would have a better hold on kzin psychology than you're showing. You ought to know they don't resent an opponent giving them a proper fight. Fighting's their nature. Whoever surrenders becomes no more than a captured animal in their eyes. Dorcas and I aim to put some high cards in your hand before you sit down at their poker table. A spacecraft on the loose is a weapon. The drive, or the sheer kinetic energy, can wreck things quite as thoroughly as the average nuke. Come worst to worst, we might smash a boat into their base at several thousand k.p.h. The other boat might take out their ship and leave them stranded; I've a hunch they've kept just a single hyperdrive vessel, as scarce as those must still be among them. Yah, going out like that would be a sight better than going into the stewpot. Kzinti like long pig."

Yoshii brightened. He and Laurinda exchanged a wonder-smitten look. Carita whooped. Tregennis smiled faintly. Ryan went oddly, abruptly thoughtful.

Markham gnawed his lip a moment, then straightened in his chair and rapped, "Very well. I do not approve, and I ask the crew to refrain from this foolishness of yours, but I cannot stop you. Therefore I must factor your action into my calculations. What terms shall I try to get for us?"

"Freedom to leave, of course," Dorcas responded. "Let *Rover* retreat to hyperspacing distance and wait, while the kzinti withdraw too far to intercept our boats. We can verify that on instruments before we come near. We'll convey any message they want, or even a delegate."

"There could be a delegation on board, waiting," Ryan warned.

Tregennis stirred. "I will remain behind," he said.

Tears sprang into Laurinda's eyes. "Oh, no!" she pleaded.

He smiled again, at her. "I am too old to go blatting around space like that. I would merely be a burden, and quite likely die on your hands. Not only will I be more comfortable here, I will be an extra witness to the bona fides of the kzinti. Landholder Markham alone could not keep track of everything they might stealthily do."

"It will show them there are two reasonable human beings in this outfit," the Wunderlander said. "That might be marginally helpful to me. Anyone else?"

"Speaking," Ryan answered.

"Huh?" broke from Saxtorph. "Hey, Kam, no. Whatever for?"

"For this," the quartermaster said calmly. "Haven't you thought of it yourself? The boats will be on the move, or holed up someplace unknown to the kzinti. They can only be reached by broadcast. Planar broadcast, maybe, but still the signal's bound to be down in the milliwatts or microwatts when it reaches your receivers—with the sun's radio background to buck. Nothing but voice transmission will carry worth diddly. Given a little time to record how the humans talk who were left behind, the kzinti can write a computer program to fake it. 'Sure, come on back, fellows, all is forgiven and they've left a case of champagne for us to celebrate with.' How're you going to know that's for real?"

Dorcas frowned. "We did consider it," she told him. "We'll use a secret password."

"Which a telepath of theirs can fish right out of a human skull, maybe given a spot of torture to unsettle the brain first. Nope, I know a trick worth two of that. How well do you remember your Hawaiian, Bob? You picked up a fair amount while we were in the village." Ryan laughed. "That worked on the girls like butter on a toboggan slope."

Saxtorph was a long while silent before he answered: "I think, if I practiced for a few days, I think . . . enough of it . . . would come back to me."

Ryan nodded. "The kzinti have programs for the important human languages in their translators, but I doubt Hawaiian is included. *Or* Danish."

Yoshii swallowed. "You'd certify everything is kosher?" he mumbled. "But what if—well—"

"If the kzinti aren't stupid, they won't try threatening or torturing me into feeding you a lie," Ryan responded. "How'd they savvy what I was saying? I assure you, it wouldn't be complimentary to them."

"A telepath would know."

Ryan shrugged. "He'd know I was not going to be their Judas goat, no matter what they did. Therefore they won't do it."

Saxtorph's right hand half reached out. "Kam, old son—" he croaked. The hand dropped.

Dorcas rose and confronted the rest, side by side with her husband. "I'm sorry, but time is rationed for us and you must decide at once," she said. "If you think you'd better stay, then do. We won't consider you a coward or anything. You may be right. We can't be sure at this stage. All we are certain of is that we don't have time for debate. Who's going?"

Hands went up, Carita's, Yoshii's, and after an instant Laurinda's.

"Okay," Dorcas continued. "Now we're not about to put our bets on a single number. The boats will go separate ways. Which ways, we'll decide by tight beam once we're alone in space. You understand, Kam, Arthur, Landholder Markham. What you don't know, a telepath or a torturer can't get out of you. Bob and I have already considered the distribution. Carita and Juan will take *Fido*. We thought Kam would ride with them, but evidently not. Laurinda, you'll be with Bob and me in *Shep*."

"Wait a minute!" Yoshii protested. The girl brought fingertips to open mouth.

"Sorry, my dears," Dorcas said. "It's a matter of practicality, as nearly as we could estimate on short notice. Not that we imagine you two would play Romeo and Juliet to the neglect of your duties. However, Juan and Carita are our professional pilots, rockjacks, planetside prospectors. Together they make our strongest possible team. They can pull stunts Bob and I never could. We need that potential, don't we? Bob and I are no slouches, but we do our best work in tandem. To supply some of what we lack as compared to Juan and Carita, Laurinda has knowledge, including knowledge of how to use instruments we plan to pack along. Don't forget, more is involved than us. The whole human race needs to know what the kzinti are up to. We must maximize our chances of getting the news home. Agreed?"

Yoshii clenched his free hand into a fist, stared at it, raised his head, and answered, "Aye. And you can take better care of her."

The Crashlander flushed. "I'm no piece of porcelain!" Immediately contrite, she stroked the Belter's cheek while she asked unevenly, "How soon do we leave?"

Dorcas smiled and made a gesture of blessing. "Let's say an hour. We'll need that much to stow gear. You two can have most of it to yourselves."

12

The kzin warship was comparatively small, Prowling Hunter class, but not the less terrifying a sight. Weapon pods, boat bays, sensor booms, control domes studded a spheroid whose red hue, in the light of this sun, became like that of clotted blood. Out of it and across the kilometers between darted small fierce gleams that swelled into space-combat armor enclosing creatures larger than men. They numbered a dozen, and each bore at least two firearms.

Obedient to orders, Ryan operated the main personnel airlock and cycled four of them through. The first grabbed him and slammed him against the bulkhead so hard that it rang. Stunned, he would have slumped to the deck were it not for the bruising grip on his shoulders. The next two crouched with weapons ready. The last one took over the controls and admitted the remaining eight.

At once, ten went off in pairs to ransack the ship. It was incredible how fast they carried the mass of metal upon them. Their footfalls cast booming echoes down the passageways.

Markham and Tregennis, waiting in the saloon, were frisked and put under guard. Presently Ryan was brought to them. "My maiden aunt has better manners than they do," he muttered, and lurched toward the bar. The kzin used his rifle butt to push him into a chair and gestured for silence. Time passed.

Within an hour, which felt longer to the humans, the boarding party was satisfied that there were no traps. Somebody radioed a report from the airlock; the rest shed their armor and stood at ease outside the saloon. Its air grew full of their wild odor.

A new huge and ruddy-gold form entered. The guard saluted, sweeping claws before his face. Markham jumped up. "For God's sake, stand," he whispered. "That's the captain."

Tregennis and, painfully, Ryan rose. The kzin's gaze flickered over them and came back to dwell on Markham, recognizing leadership. The Wunderlander opened his mouth. Noises as of a tiger fight poured forth.

Did the captain register surprise that a man knew his language? He heard it out and spat a reply. Markham tried to continue. The captain interrupted, and Markham went mute. The captain told him something.

Markham turned to his companions. "He forbids me to mangle the Hero's Tongue any more," he related wryly. "He grants my request for a private talk—in the communications shack, where our translator is, since I explained that we do have one and it includes the right program. Meanwhile you may talk with each other and move freely about this cabin. If you must relieve yourselves, you may use the sink behind the bar."

"How gracious of him," Ryan snorted.

Markham raised brows. "Consider yourselves fortunate. He is being indulgent. Don't risk provoking him. High-ranking kzinti are even more sensitive about their honor than the average, and he has earned a partial name, Hraou-Captain."

"We will be careful," Tregennis promised. "I am sure you will do your best for us."

The commander went majestically out. Markham trailed. Ryan gusted a sigh, sought the bar, tapped a liter of beer, and drained it in a few gulps. The guard watched enviously but then also left. Discipline had prevented him from shoving the human aside and helping himself. He and a couple of his fellows remained in the passage. They conversed a bit, rumbling and hissing.

"We'll be here a while," Ryan sighed. "Care for a round of gin?"

"It would be unwise of us to drink," Tregennis cautioned. "Best you be content with that mugful you had."

"I mean gin rummy."

"What is that, if not a, ah, cocktail?"

"A card game. They don't play it on Plateau? I can teach you."

"No, thank you. Perhaps I am too narrow in my interests, but cards bore me." Tregennis brightened. "However, do you play chess?"

Ryan threw up his hands. "You expect me to concentrate on woodpushing *now?* Hell, let's screen a show. Something light and trashy, with plenty of girls in it. Or would you rather seize the chance to at last read *War and Peace?*"

Tregennis smiled. "Believe it or not, Kamehameha, I have my memories. By all means, girls."

The comedy was not quite finished when a kzin appeared and jerked an unmistakable gesture. The men followed him. He didn't bother with a companion or with ever glancing rearward. At the flight deck he proceeded to Saxtorph's operations cabin, waved them through, and closed the door on them.

Markham sat behind the desk. He was very pale

and reeked of the sweat that stained his tunic, but his visage was set in hard lines. Hraou-Captain loomed beside him, too big to use a human's chair, doubtless tired of being cramped in the comshack and maybe choosing to increase his dominance by sheer height. Another kzin squatted in a far corner of the room, a wretched-looking specimen, fur dull and unkempt, shoulders slumped, eyes turned downward.

"Attention," rasped Markham. "I wish I did not have to tell you this—I hoped to avoid it—but the commander says I must. He . . . feels deception is pointless and . . . besmirches his honor. His superior on Secunda agrees; we have been in radio contact."

The newcomers braced themselves.

Nonetheless it was staggering to hear: "For the past five years I have been an agent of the kzinti. Later I will justify myself to you, if your minds are not totally closed. It is not hatred for my species that drove me to this, but love and concern for it, hatred for the decadence that is destroying us. Later, I say. We dare not waste Hraou-Captain's time with arguments."

Regarding the faces before him, Markham made his tone dry. "The kzinti never trusted me with specific information, but after I began sending them information about hyperdrive technology, they gave me a general directive. I was to use my position as commissioner to forestall, whenever possible, any exploration beyond the space containing the human-occupied worlds. That naturally gave me an inkling of the reason—to prevent disclosure of their activities—and it became clear to me that some of the most important must be in regions distant from kzin space. When hope was lost of keeping you from this expedition, I decided my duty was to join it and stand by in case of need. Not that I anticipated the need, understand. The star looked so useless. But when you did get those radio indications, I knew better than you what they could mean, and was glad I had provided against the contingency, and beamed a notice of our arrival."

"Your parents were brothers," Ryan said.

Markham laid back his ears. "Spare the abuse. Remember, by forewarning the kzinti I saved your lives. If you had simply blundered into detector range—"

"They may be impulsive," Tregennis said, "but they are not idiotic. I do not accept your assertion that they would reflexively have annihilated us."

Markham trembled. "Silence. Bear in mind that I am all that stands between you and—It has been a long time since the kzinti in this project tasted fresh meat."

"What are they doing?" Ryan asked.

"Constructing a naval base. They chose the system precisely because it seemed insignificant—the dimmest star in the whole region, devoid of heavy elements and impoverished in the light—though it does happen to have a ready source of iron and certain other crucial materials, together with a strategic location. They never expected humans to seek it out. They underestimated the curiosity of our species. They are . . . cats, not monkeys."

"Uh-huh. Not noisy, sloppy, free-swinging monkeys like you despise. Kzinti respect rank. Once they've overrun us, they'll put the niggers back in their proper place. From here they can grab off Beta Hydri, drive a salient way into our space—How many more prongs will there be to the attack? When is the next war scheduled for?"

"Silence!" Markham shouted. "Hold your mouth! One word from me, and—"

"And what? You need us, Art and me, you need us, else we wouldn't be having this interview. Kill us, and your boss just gets a few meals."

"Killing can be in due course. I imagine he would enjoy your testicles for tomorrow's breakfast."

Ryan rocked on his feet. Tregennis' lips squeezed together till they were white.

Markham's voice softened. "I am warning, not threatening," he said in a rush. "I'll save you if I can, unharmed, but if you don't help me I can promise nothing."

He leaned forward. "Listen, will you? Obviously you can't be released to spread the news—not yet—but some years of detention are better than death." He could not quite hold back the sneer. "In *your* minds, I suppose. You're lucky, lucky that I was aboard. Once my status has been verified, the high commandant can let me bring home a convincing tale of disaster. Else he would probably have had to kill us and make our bodies stage props, as Saxtorph suggested. I think he will spare you if I ask; it will cost him little, and kzinti reward faithful service. They also keep their promises. But you must earn your lives."

"The boats," Tregennis whispered.

Ryan nodded. "You've got a telepath on hand, I see," he said flat-voiced. "He could make sure that my call in Hawaiian tells how everything is hearts and flowers. Except if he reads my mind, he'll see that I ain't gonna do it, no matter what. Or, okay, maybe they can break me, but Bob will hear that in his old pal's voice."

"I've explained this to Hraou-Captain," Markham said, cooler now. "It is necessary to neutralize those boats, but they don't pose any urgent threat, so we will start with methods less time-consuming than . . . interrogation and persuasion. Later, though, when we are on Secunda—that's where we are going—later your cooperation in working up a plausible disaster for me to return with, that is what will buy you your lives. If you refuse, you'll die for nothing, because we can always devise some deception which will keep humans away from here. You'll die for nothing."

"What the hell can we do about the boats? We don't know where they've gone."

Markham's manner became entirely impersonal. "I have explained this to Hraou-Captain. I went on to explain that their actions will not be random. What Captain Saxtorph decides—has decided to do is a multi-variable function of the logic of the situation and of his personality. You and he are good friends, Ryan. You can make shrewd guesses as to his behavior. They won't be certain, of course, but they will eliminate some possibilities and assign rough probabilities to others. Your input may have some value, too, Professor. And even mine—in the course of establishing that I have been telling the truth.

"Sit down on the deck. This will not be pleasant, you know."

Hraou-Captain, who had stood like a pillar, turned his enormous body and growled a command. The telepath raised his head. Eyes glazed by the drug that called forth his total abilities came to a focus.

In their different ways, the three humans readied for what was about to happen. They'd have sundering headaches for hours afterward, too.

13

Small though it was, at its distance from Prima the sun showed more than half again the disc which Sol presents to Earth. Blotches of darkness pocked its sullen red. Corona shimmered around the limb, not quite drowned out of naked-eye vision.

Yoshii ignored it. His attention was on the planet which *Fido* circled in high orbit. Radar, spectroscope, optical amplifier, and a compact array of other instruments fed data to a computer which spun forth interpretations on screen and printout. Click and whirr passed low through the rustling ventilation, the sometimes uneven human breath within the control cabin. Body warmth and a hint of sweat tinged the air.

Yoshii's gaze kept drifting from the equipment, out a port of the globe itself. "Unbelievable," he murmured.

Airless, it stood sharp-edged athwart the stars, but the illuminated side was nearly a blank, even at first and last quarter when shadows were long. Then a few traces of hill and dale might appear, like time-worn Chinese brush strokes. Otherwise there was yellowish-white smoothness, with ill-defined areas of faint gray, brown, or blue. The whole world could almost have been a latex ball, crudely made for a child of the giants.

"What now?" Carita asked. She floated, harnessed in her seat, her back to him. They had turned off the gravity polarizer and were weightless, to eliminate that source of detectability. Her attention was clamped to the long-range radar with which she swept the sky, to and fro as the boat swung around.

"Oh, everything," said the Belter.

"Any ideas? You've had more chance to think, these past hours, than I have."

"Well, a few things *look* obvious, but I wouldn't make book on their being what they seem."

"Why don't you give me a rundown?" proposed the Jinxian. "Never mind if you repeat what I've already heard. We should try putting things in context."

Yoshii plunged into talk. It was an escape of sorts from their troubles, from not knowing what the fate of *Shep* and those aboard her might be.

"The planet's about the mass of Earth but only about half as dense. Must be largely silicate, some aluminum, not enough iron to form a core. Whatever atmosphere and hydrosphere it once outgassed, it lost—weak gravity, and temperatures around 400 K at the hottest part of the day. That day equals 131 of Earth's; two-thirds rotational lock, like Mercury. No more gas comes out, because vulcanism, tectonics, all geology ended long ago. Unless you want to count meteoroid erosion wearing down the surface; and I'd guess hardly any objects are left that might fall on these planets.

"Then what is that stuff mantling the surface? The computer can't figure it out. Shadows of what relief there is indicate it's thin, a few centimeters deep, with local variations. Reflection spectra suggest carbon compounds but that's not certain. It just lies there, you see, doesn't do anything. Try analyzing a lump of some solid plastic across a distance. Is that what we have here, a natural polymer? I wish I knew more organic chemistry."

"Can't help you, Juan," Carita said. "All I remember from my class in it, aside from the stinks in the lab, is that the human sex hormones are much the same, except that the female is ketonic and the male is alcoholic."

"We'll have time to look and think further, of course." Yoshii sighed. "Time and time and time. I never stopped to imagine how what fugitives mostly do is sit. Hiding, huddling, while—" He broke off and struggled for self-command.

"And we don't dare let down our guard long enough to take a little recreation," Carita grumbled.

Yoshii reddened. "Uh, if we could, I—well—"

She chuckled and said ruefully, "I know. The fair Laurinda. Don't worry, your virtue will be safe with me till you realize it can't make any possible diff— Hold!" she roared.

He tensed where he floated. "What?"

"Quiet. No, secure things and get harnessed."

For humming minutes she studied the screen and meters before her. Yoshii readied himself. Seated at her side he could see the grimness grow. Pale hair waved around sable skin when at last she nodded. "Yes," she said, "somebody's bound this way. From the direction of the sun. About ten million klicks off. He barely registered at first, but it's getting stronger by the minute. He's boosting *fast*. We'd tear our hull apart if we tried to match him, supposing we had that kind of power. Definitely making for Prima."

"What . . . is it?"

"What but a kzin ship with a monster engine? I'm afraid they've caught on to our strategy." Carita's tone grew wintry. "I'd rather not hear just how they did."

"G-guesswork?" Yoshii faltered.

"Maybe. I don't know kzin psych. How close to us can they make themselves think?" She turned her head to clamp her vision on him. "Well, maybe the skipper's plan failed and it's actually drawn the bandits to us. Or maybe it's the one thing that can save us."

(Saxtorph's words drawled through memory: "We don't know how much search capability the kzin have, but a naval vessel means auxiliaries, plus whatever civilian craft they can press into service. A boat out in the middle of the far yonder, drifting free, would be near-as-damn impossible to find. But as soon as she accelerates back toward where her crew might do something real, she screams the announcement to any alert, properly organized watchers—optical track, neutrino emission, the whole works till she's in effective radar range. After that she's sold to the licorice man, as they say in Denmark. On the other hand, if she can get down onto a planetary surface, she can probably make herself almost as invisible as out in the deep. A worldful of topography, which the kzinti cannot have had time or personnel to map in anything but the sketchiest way. So how about one of ours goes to Prima, the other to Tertia, and lies low in orbit? Immediately when we get wind of trouble, we drop down into the best hidey-hole the planet has got, and wait things out.")

(It had been the most reasonable idea that was broached.)

"You've been doing our latest studies," Carita went on. "Found any prospective burrows? The kzinti may or may not have acquired us by now. Maybe not. That vessel may not be as well equipped to scan as this prospector, and she's probably a good deal bigger. But they're closing in fast, I tell you."

Yoshii made a shushing gesture, swiveled his seat,

and evoked pictures, profiles, data tabulations. Shortly he nodded. "I think we have a pretty respectable chance." Pointing: "See here. Prima isn't all an unbroken plain. This range, it's small valleys—and on the night side, too."

Carita whistled. "Hey, boy, we live right!"

"I'll set up for a detailed scan and drop into low orbit to make it. We should find some cleft we can back straight down into. The kzinti would have to arc immediately above and be on the lookout for that exact spot to see us." Yoshii said nothing about what a feat of piloting he had in mind. He was a Belter. She had almost comparable experience, together with Jinxian reflexes.

14

"Yah, I do think our best bet is to land and snuggle in." Saxtorph's look ranged through the port and across the planet, following an onward sweep of daylight as *Shep* orbited around to the side of the sun.

That disc was less than half the size of Sol's at Earth, its coal-glow light little more than one one-hundredth. Nevertheless Tertia shone so brightly as to dazzle surrounding stars out of sight. Edges softened by atmosphere, it was bestrewn with glaciers, long streaks and broad plains and frozen seas bluishly aglimmer from pole to pole. Bared rock reached darkling on mountainsides or reared in tablelands. Five Terrestrial masses had been convulsed enough as they settled toward equilibrium that the last of the heights they thrust upward had not worn away entirely during the post-tectonic eons.

The glaciers were water, with some frozen carbon dioxide overlying them in the antarctic zone where winter now reigned. The air, about twice as dense as Earth's, was almost entirely nitrogen, the oxygen in it insufficient to sustain fire or life. It was utterly clear save where slow winds raised swirls of glitter, dust storms whose dust was fine ice.

A small moon, inmost of four, hove in view. It sheened reddish-yellow, like amber. The largest, Luna-size, was visible, too, patched with the same hue, ashen where highlands were uncovered. It had no craters; spalling and cosmic sand had long since done away with them.

"But, but on the surface we'll see only half the sky at best," Laurinda ventured. "And atmospherics will . . . hinder the seeing."

Saxtorph nodded. "True. Ordinarily I'd opt for staying in space in hopes of early warning. That does have its own drawbacks, though. A kzin search vessel could likelier than not detect us the moment we commenced boost. Since we might not be able to skedaddle flat-out from them, we'd probably drop planetside. That's the whole idea of being where we are, remember? If we did it right, the ratcats wouldn't know where we'd squatted, but they'd know we were someplace yonder for sure, and that would be a bigger help to them than they deserve."

"Treacherous terrain for landing," Dorcas warned.

Saxtorph nodded again. "Indeed. Which means we'll be smart to take our time while we've still got it, come down cautiously and settle in thoroughly. As for knowing when a spacecraft is in the neighborhood, at a minimum there's our neutrino detector. It's not what you'd call precise, but it will pick up an operating fusion generator within a couple million klicks, clear through the body of the planet."

He paused before adding, "I realize this isn't quite what we intended when we said goodbye. But we didn't know what Tertia is like. Doctrine exists to be modified as circumstances dictate. I'd guess the sensible thing for Juan and Carita to do is quite different."

Laurinda's fingers twisted together. She turned her face from the other two.

"I vote with you," Dorcas declared. They had been considering tactics for hours, while they gained knowledge of the world they had reached. "What are the specs of a landing site? Safe ground; concealment from anything except an unlikely observation from directly overhead, unless we can avoid that, too; but we don't want to be in a radio shadow, because we hope for—we expect—a broadcast message in the fairly near future."

"Don't forget defensibility," Saxtorph reminded.

"What?" asked Laurinda, startled. "How can we possibly—"

The man grinned. "I didn't tell you, honey, because it's not a thing to blab about, but Dorcas and I always travel with a few weapons. I took them along packed among my personal effects. Managed to slip Carita a rifle and some ammo when nobody else was looking. That leaves us with another rifle, a Pournelle rapid-fire automatic, choice of solid or explosive shells; a .38-caliber machine pistol with detachable stock; and a 9-mm. mulekiller."

"Plus a certain amount of blasting sticks," Dorcas informed him.

Saxtorph goggled. "Huh?" He guffawed. "That's my nice little wifey. The standard mining equipment aboard includes knives, geologists' hammers, crowbars, and such, useful for mayhem." He sobered. "Not that we want a fight. God, no! But if we're able to give a good account of ourselves—it might make a difference."

"A single small warhead will make a much bigger difference, unless we have dispersal and concealment capability," Dorcas observed. "All right, let's take a close look at what topographical data we've collected."

The choice was wide, but decision was quick. *Shep* dropped out of orbit and made for a point about 30 degrees north latitude. It was at midafternoon, which was a factor. Lengthening shadows would bring out details, while daylight would remain—in a rotation period of 40 hours, 37-plus minutes—for preliminary exploration of the vicinity.

A mesa loomed stark, thinly powdered with ice crystals, above a glacier that had flowed under its own weight, down from the heights, until a jumble of hills beneath had brought it to a halt. As it descended, the glacier had gouged a deep, almost sheer-walled coulee through slopes and steeps. The bottom was talus, under a dusting of sand, but solid; with gravity a third higher than on Earth, and epochs of time, shards and particles had settled into gridlock.

Or so the humans reasoned. The last few minutes of maneuver were very intent, very quiet except for an occasional low word of business. Saxtorph, manning the console, was prepared to cram on emergency boost at the first quiver of awryness. But Dorcas talked him down and *Shep* grounded firmly. For a while, nobody spoke or moved. Then husband and wife unharnessed and kissed. After a moment, Laurinda made it a threeway embrace.

Saxtorph peered out. The canyon walls laid gloom over stone. "You ladies unlimber this and stow that while I go take a gander," he said. "Yes, dear, I won't be gone long and I will be careful."

His added weight dragged at him, but not too badly. It wasn't more than physiology could take, even a Belter's or a Crashlander's, and distributed over the whole body. The women would get used to it, sort of, and in fact it ought to be valuable, continuous exercise in the cramped quarters of the boat. The spacesuit did feel pretty heavy.

He cycled through and stood for a few minutes learning to see the landscape. Every cue was alien, subtly or utterly, light, shadow, shapes. The cobbles underfoot were smooth as those on a beach. They and the rubble along the sides and the cliffs above were tawny-gray, sparked with bits of what might be mica but was likelier something strange—diamond dust? Several crags survived, eroded to laciness. The lower end of the gorge, not far off, was blocked by a wall of glacier. Above reached purple sky. An ice-devil whirled on the heights. Wind whittered.

Saxtorph decided his party had better plant an antenna and relay inconspicuously up there. Any messages ought to be on a number of simultaneous bands, at least one of which could blanket a Tertian hemisphere, but the signal would be tenuous and these depths might screen it out altogether. He walked carefully from the arrowhead of the boat to the right-hand side and started downslope, looking for safe routes to the top. Lateral ravines appeared to offer them.

Abruptly he halted. What the flapping hellfire?

He stooped and stared. Could it be—? No, some freak of nature. He wasn't qualified to identify a fossil.

He went on. By the time he had tentatively found the path he wanted, he was so near the glacier that he continued. It lifted high, not grimy like its counterparts on terrestroid planets but clear, polished glassy-smooth, a cold and mysterious blue. Whatever mineral grains once lay on it had sunken to the bottom, and—

And—

Saxtorph stood moveless. The time was long before he breathed, "Oh. My. God."

From within the ice, the top half of a skull stared at him. It could only be that, unhuman though it was. And other bones were scattered behind, and shaped stones, and pieces of what was most surely earthenware—

Chill possessed him from within. How old were those remnants?

Big Tertia must in its youth have had a still denser atmosphere than now, greenhouse effect, heat from a contracting interior, and . . . those molecules that are the kernel from which life grows, perhaps evolved not here but in interstellar space, organics which the wan sun did not destroy as they drifted inward. . . . Life arose. It liberated oxygen. It gave birth to beings that made tools and dreams. But meanwhile the planetary core congealed and chilled, the oceans began to freeze, plants died, nothing replaced the oxygen that surface rocks bound fast. . . . Without copper, tin, gold, iron, any metal they could know for what it was, the dwellers had never gone beyond their late stone age, never had a chance to develop the science that might have saved them or at least have let them understand what was happening. . . .

Saxtorph shuddered. He turned and hastened back to the boat.

15

Unsure what kind of surface awaited them, Carita and Yoshii descended on the polarizer and made a feather-soft landing. They were poised to spring instantly back upward. All they felt was a slight resilience, more on their instruments than in their bones. It damped out and *Fido* rested quiet.

"Elastic?" Yoshii wondered. "Or viscous, or what?"

"Never mind, we'll investigate later, right now we're down safe," Carita replied. She wiped her brow. "Hoo, but I need a stiff drink and a hot shower!"

Yoshii leered at her. "In the opposite order, please." She cuffed him lightly. The horseplay turned into mutual unharnessing and a hug.

"Hey-y," she purred, "you really do want to celebrate, don't you? Later, we'll share that shower."

His arms dropped. She released him in her turn and he made a stumbling backward step. "I, I'm sorry, I didn't intend—Well, we should take a good look outside, shouldn't we?"

The Jinxian was briefly silent before she smiled

wryly and shrugged. "Okay. I'll forgive you this time if you'll fix dinner. Your yakitori tacos are always consoling. You're right, anyway."

They turned off the fluoros and peered forth. As their eyes adapted, they saw well enough through airlessness, by the thronging stars and the cold rush of the Milky Way. Bowl-shaped, the dell in which they were parked curved some 50 meters wide to heights twice as far above the bottom. *Fido* sat close to one side; direct sunlight would only touch her for a small part of the day, weeks hence. Every edge and lump was rounded off by the covering of the planet. In this illumination it appeared pale gray.

"What *is* the stuff?" Carita muttered.

"I've hit on an idea," Yoshii said. "I do not warrant that it is right. It may not even make sense."

Her teeth flashed white in the darkness. "The universe is not under obligation to make sense. Speak your piece." She switched cabin illumination back on. Radiance made the ports blank.

"I think it must be organic—carbon-based," Yoshii said. "It doesn't remotely match any mineral I've ever seen or heard of or imagined, whereas it does resemble any number of plastics."

"Hm, yeah, I had the same thought, but discarded it. Where would the chemistry come from? Life can't have started in the short time Prima hung onto its atmosphere, can it? Whatever carbon, hydrogen, oxygen, nitrogen are left must be locked up in solid-state materials. At most we might find hydrates or something."

"This could have come from space."

"What?" She gaped at him. "If that's a joke, it's too deep for me."

"There is matter in space, in the nebulae and even in the emptiest stretches between. It includes organic compounds, some of them fairly complex."

"Not quite concentrated enough for soup."

"Sure, the densest nebula is still a pretty hard

vacuum by Terrestrial standards. However, this system has had time to pass through many. Between them, too—yes, between galaxies—gravity has found atoms and molecules to draw in. During any single year, hardly a measurable amount. But it's been fifteen *billion* years, Carita."

"Um'h," she uttered, almost as if punched in the stomach.

"The sun doesn't give off any ultraviolet to speak of," Yoshii pursued. "Its wind is puny. Carbon-based molecules land intact. The sun does maintain a daytime temperature at which they can react with each other. I daresay cosmic radiation energizes the chemistry, too. Fine grains of sand and dust—crumbled off rocks, together with meteoroid powder—provide colloidal surfaces where the stuff can cluster till there's a fairly high concentration and complicated exchanges become possible. Unsaturated bonds grab the free atoms of carbon, hydrogen, oxygen, anything included in the downdrift except noble gases, and incorporate them. Maybe, here and there, some such growing patch 'learns' how to take stuff from surface rocks. It's a slow, slow process—or set of processes—but it's had time. Eventually patches meet as they expand. What happens then depends on just what their compositions happen to be. I'd expect some weird interactions while they join. Those could be going on yet. That would explain why we saw differently colored areas. But it's only the terminal reactions."

Yoshii's words had come faster and faster. He was developing his idea as he described it. Excitement turned into awe and he whispered, "A polymer. A single multiplex molecule, the size of this planet."

Carita was mute for a whole minute before she murmured, "Whew! But why isn't the same stuff on every airless body? . . . No, wait. Stupid of me to ask. This is the only one where conditions have been right."

Yoshii nodded. "I suspect that what yellows the

rest is a carbon compound, too, but something formed in space. You get some fairly complicated ones there, you know. If that particular one can't react with the organics I was talking about—too cold—then they are a minor part of the downdrift compared to it. We haven't noticed the same thing in other planetary systems because they are all too young, and maybe because none of them have made repeated passages through nebulae."

"You missed your calling," Carita said tenderly. "Should've been a scientist. Is it too late? We can go out, take samples, put 'em through our analyzers. When we get home, you can write a paper that'll have scholarships piled around you up to your bellybutton. Though I hope you'll keep on with the poetry. I like what you—"

A quiver went through the boat. "What the Finagle!" she exclaimed.

"A quake?" Yoshii asked.

"The prof's told us these planets are as far beyond quakes as a mummy is beyond hopscotch," Carita snapped.

Another tremor made slight noises throughout the hull. Yoshii reached for the searchlight switch. Carita caught his arm. "Hold that," she said. "The kzinti— No, unless they beef up that already wild boost they are under, they won't arrive for a couple more hours." Nevertheless he refrained.

The pair studied their instrument panel. "We've been tilted a bit," Yoshii pointed out. "Should we reset the landing jacks?"

"Let's wait and see," Carita said. "I'd guess the rock beneath has settled under our weight, or one layer has slid over another, or something like that. If it's reached a new equilibrium, we don't want to upset it by shifting mass around. No sense in moving yet, when we can't tell what the ground is like anywhere else."

"Right. I'm afraid, though, we can't relax as we had hoped."

"How much relaxing could we do anyway, with kzinti sniffing after us?"

"And Laurinda—" Yoshii whispered. Harshly: "Do you want to take the controls, stand by to jump out of here, in case? I'll snug things down and, yes, throw a meal together."

Lightfoot under the low gravity, he descended aft to the engine compartment. Delicate work needed doing. The idling fusion generator must be shut down entirely, lest its neutrino smoke betray the boat—not that the kzinti could home in on it, but they would know with certainty the humans were on Prima, and in which quadrant. Batteries, isotopic and crystalline as well as chemical, held energy for weeks of life support and ordinary operations. Yet it had to be possible to restart the generator instantly, full power within a second, should there be a sudden need to scramble. That meant disconnecting the safety interlocks. Yoshii fetched tools and got busy. The task was demanding, but not too much for his spirit to wing elsewhere in space, elsewhen in time—the Belt, Plateau, We Made It, *Rover*'s folk on triumphal progress after their return. . . .

Carita's voice came over the intercom. "This is dull duty. I think I will turn on the searchlight while it's still safe to do so. Might get a clue to what caused those jolts."

"Good idea," he agreed absent-mindedly, and continued his task.

The metal around him throbbed. Small objects rattled on the deck.

"Juan!" Carita shouted. "The, the material—it's rippling, crawling—" The hull rocked. "I'm getting us out of here!"

"Yes, do," he called back, and grabbed for the nearest handhold.

Within its radiation shield, the generator hummed.

Needles sprang across dials, displays onto screens. Yoshii felt the upward thrust of the deck against his feet. It was slight. Carita was a careful pilot, applying barely sufficient boost to rise off the ground before she committed to a leap.

The boat screamed. Things tilted. Yoshii clung. Loose things hailed around him. A couple of them drew blood. The boat canted over, toppled, struck lengthwise, tolled so that he was half deafened

Stillness crashed down, except for a shrill whistle that he knew too well. Air was escaping from one or more rents nearby. He hauled himself erect and out of his daze. The emergency valve had already shut, sealing off this section. He had to get through the lock built into it before the pressure differential made operation fatally slow.

Somehow he passed forth, and on along the companionway that was now a corridor, toward the control cabin. Lights were still shining, ventilators still whirring, and few articles lay strewn around. This was a good, sturdy craft, kept shipshape. How had she failed?

Carita met him in the entrance. "Hey, you sure got battered, didn't you? I was secured. Here, let me help you." She practically carried him to his chair, which she had adjusted for the new orientation. Meanwhile she talked on: "The trouble's with the landing gear, I think. Is that damn stuff a glue? No, how could it be? Take over. I'm going to suit up and go out for a look."

"Don't," he protested. "You might get stuck there, too."

"I'll be careful. Keep watch. If I don't make it back—" She stooped, brushed lips across his, and hurried aft.

His ears rang and pained him, his head ached, he was becoming conscious of bruises, but his eyes worked. The searchlight made clear the motion in the mantle. It was slight in amplitude, as thin as the

layer was, and slow, but intricate, like wave patterns
spreading from countless centers to form an ever-
changing moiré. Those nodes were darker than the
ripple-shadows and seemed to pass the darknesses on
from one to the next, so that a shifting stipple went
outward from the boat, across the dell floor and, as
he watched, up the side. The hull rocked a little, off
and on, in irregular wise.

"Do you read me?" he heard after a while. "I'm in
the Number Two lock, outer valve open, looking
over the lip."

"I read you," he answered unevenly. At least the
radio system remained intact. "What do you see?"

"The same turbulence in the . . . stuff. Nothing
clear aft, where the main damage is. The searchbeam
doesn't diffuse, and—I'm off to inspect."

"Better not. If you lost your footing and fell down
into—"

She barked scorn. "If you think I could, then I'm
for sure the right person for this job." He clenched
his fists but must needs admit that induction boots
gave plenty of grip on the metal for a rockjack—a
rockjill, she often called herself. "I'm crawling out.
. . . Standing. . . . On my way." The hull pitched.
"Hey! That damn near threw me." Starkly: "I think
Fido just settled more at the after end."

"But into what?" he cried. "Solid rock?"

"No, I guess not. I do know what we *are* deep
down into. . . . Okay, proceeding. Landing gear in
sight now, spraddled against the sky. It's dark, I
can't see much except stars. Let me unlimber my
flashlight. . . . A-a-ah!" she nearly screamed.

He half rose in his seat. "What happened? Carita,
dear, are you there?"

"Yes. A nasty shock, that sight. Listen, the Number Three leg is off the ground. The bottom end
sticks up—ragged, holes in it—like a badly corroded
thing that got so weak it tore apart when it came

under stress. . . . But, Juan, this is melded steel and titanium alloy. What could've eaten it?"

"We can guess," Yoshii said between his teeth. "Come back."

"No, I need to see the rest. Don't worry, I'll creep down the curve like a cat burglar. . . . I'm at the socket of Number Two. I'm shining my light along it. Yes. Nothing left of the foot. Seems to be sort of—absorbed into the ground. Number One—more yet is missing, and, yes, that's the unit which pulled partly loose from its mounting and made the hole in the engine compartment. I can see the skin ripped and buckled—"

The boat swayed. Her nose twisted about and lifted a few degrees as her tail sank. Groans went through the hull.

"I'm okay, mate. Well anchored. But holy Finagle! The stuff is going wild underneath. Has it come to a boil?"

Yoshii could not see that where he was, but he did spy the quickening and thickening of the wave fronts farther off. Understanding blasted him. "Douse your flash!" he yelled. "Get back inside!" He grabbed for the searchlight switch as for the throat of a foeman.

"Hey, what is this?" Carita called.

"Douse your flash, I said. Can't you see, bright light is what causes the trouble? Find your way by the stars." He clutched his shoulders and shivered in the dark. The boat shivered with him, diminuendo.

"I read you," Carita said faintly.

Yoshii darkened the cabin as well. "Let's meet in my stateroom," he proposed. The sarcastically named cubbyhole did not give on the outside. He groped till he found it. When again he dared grant himself vision, he bent above the locker where a bottle was, shook his head, straightened, and stood looking at a photograph of Laurinda on the bulkhead.

Carita entered. Her coverall was wet and pungent.

Sweat glistened on the dark face. "Haven't you poured me a drink?" she asked hoarsely.

"I decided that would be unwise."

"Maybe for you, sonny boy. Not for me." The Jinxian helped herself, tossed off two mouthfuls, and sighed. That's better. Thank you very much."

Yoshii gestured at his bunk. It was roughly horizontal, that being how the polarizer field was ordinarily set in flight. They sat down on it, side by side. Her bravado dwindled. "So you know what's happened to us?" she murmured.

"I have a guess," Yoshii replied with care. "It depends on my idea of the supermolecule being correct."

"Say on."

"Well, you see, it grew. Or rather, I think, different ones grew till they met and linked up. There must have been all possible combinations, permutations of radicals and bases and—every kind of chemical unit. Cosmic radiation drives that kind of change. So does quantum mechanics, random effects; that was probably dominant in intergalactic space. So the chemistry . . . mutated. Whatever structure was better at assimilating fresh material would be favored. It would grow at the expense of the rest."

Carita whistled. "Natural selection, evolution? You mean the stuff's alive?"

"No, not like you and me or bacteria or even viruses. But it would develop components which could grab onto new atoms, and other components that are catalytic, and—and I think ways of passing an atom on from ring to ring until it's gone as far as there are receptors for it. That would leave room for taking up more at the near end. Because I think finally the molecule evolved beyond the point of depending on whatever fell its way from the skies. I think it began extracting matter from the planet, whenever it spread to where there was a suitable substance. Breaking down carbonates and silicates and—and incorporating metallic atoms, too. Clathrate formation would promote growth, as well as chemical combination. But of course metal is ultra-scarce here, so the molecule became highly efficient at stealing it."

"At eating things." Carita stared before her. "That's close enough to life for me."

"The normal environment is low-energy," Yoshii said. "Things must go faster during the day. Not that there is much action then, either; nothing much to act on, any more. But we set down on our metal landing gear, and pumped out light-frequency quanta."

"And it . . . woke."

Yoshii grimaced but stayed clear of semantic argument. "It must be strongly bound to the underlying rock. It was quick to knit the feet of our landing jacks into that structure."

"And gnaw its way upward, till I—"

He caught her hand. "You couldn't have known. I didn't."

The deck swayed underfoot. The liquor sloshed in Carita's glass. "But we're blacked out now," she protested, as if to the devourer.

"We're radiating infrared," Yoshii answered. "The boat's warmer on the outside than her surroundings. Energy supply. The chemistry goes on, though slower. We can't stop it, not unless we want to freeze to death."

"How long have we got?" she whispered.

He bit his lip. "I don't know. If we last till sunrise we'll dissolve entirely soon after, like spooks in an ancient folk tale."

"That's more than a month away."

"I'd estimate that well before then, the hull will be eaten open. No more air."

"Our suits recycle. We can jury-rig other things to keep us alive."

"But the hull will weaken and collapse. Do you want to be tossed down into . . . that?" Yoshii sat straight. Resolution stiffened his tone. "I'm afraid we have no choice except to throw ourselves on the mercy of the kzinti. They must have arrived."

Carita ripped forth a string of oaths and obscenities, knocked back her drink, and rose. "*Shep* is still on the loose," she said.

Yoshii winced. "Man the control cabin. I'm going to suit up and get back into the engine compartment."

"What for?"

"Isn't it obvious? The energy boxes are stored there."

"Oh. Yes. You're thinking we'll have to take orbit under our own power and let the kzinti pick us up? I'm not keen on that."

"Nor I. But I don't imagine they'll be keen on landing here."

He rejoined her an hour later. By starlight she saw how he trembled. "I was too late," dragged from him. "Maybe if I hadn't had to operate the airlock hydraulics manually—What I found was a seething mass of—of—The entire locker where the boxes were is gone."

"That fast?" she wondered, stunned, though they had been in communication until he passed through into the after section. And then, slowly: "Well, the capacitors in those boxes are—were fully charged. Energy concentrated like the stuff's never known before. Too bad so much didn't poison it. Instead, it got a kick in the chemistry making it able to eat everything in three gulps. We're lucky the life-support batteries weren't there, too."

"Let's hope the kzinti want us enough to come down for us."

Shielding a flashlight with a clipboard, they activated the radio, standard-band broadcast. Yoshii spoke. "SOS. SOS. Two humans aboard a boat, marooned," he said dully. "We are sinking into a—solvent—the macromolecule—You doubtless know about it. Rescue requested.

"We can't lift by ourselves. The drive units in our spacesuits have only partial charge, insufficient to reach orbital speed in this field. We can't recharge. That equipment is gone. So are all the reserve energy boxes. We can flit a goodly distance around the planet or rise to a goodly height, but we can't escape.

"Please take us off. Please inform. We will keep our receiver open on this band, and continue transmission so you can locate us."

Having recorded his words, he set them to repeat directly on the carrier wave and leaned back. "Not the most eloquent speech ever made," he admitted. "But they won't care."

She took his hand. Heaven stood gleamful above them. Time passed. Occasionally the vessel moved a bit.

A spaceship flew low, from horizon to horizon. They had only the barest glimpse. Perhaps cameras took note of theirs.

Carita choked. "Alien."

"Kzin," Yoshii said. "Got to be."

"But I never heard of anything like—"

"Nor I. What did you see?"

"Big. Sphere with fins or flanges or—whatever they are—all around. Mirror-bright. Doesn't look like she's intended for planetfall."

Yoshii nodded. "Me, too. I wanted to make sure of my impression, as fast as she went by. Just the same, I think we have a while to wait." He stood up. "Suppose I go fix us some sandwiches and also bring that bottle. We may as well take it easy. We've played our hand out."

"But won't they—Oh, yes, I see. That's no patrol craft. She was called off her regular service to come check Prima. We being found, she'll call Secunda for further orders, and relay our message to a translator there."

"About a five-minute transmission lag either way, at the present positions. A longer chain-of-command lag, I'll bet. Leave the intercom on for me, please, but just for the sake of my curiosity. You can talk to them as well as I can."

"There isn't a lot to say," Carita agreed.

Yoshii was in the galley when he heard the computer-generated voice: "Werlith-Commandant addressing you directly. Identify yourselves."

"Carita Fenger, Juan Yoshii, of the ship *Rover*, stuck on Prima—on Planet One. Your crew has seen us. I suppose they realize our plight. We're being . . . swallowed. Please take us off. If your vessel here can't do it, please dispatch one that can. Over."

Silence hummed and rustled. Yoshii kept busy.

He was returning when the voice struck again: "We lost two boats with a total of eight heroes aboard before we established the nature of the peril. I will not waste time explaining it to you. Most certainly I will not hazard another craft and more lives. On the basis of observations made by the crew of *Sun Defier*, if you keep energy output minimal you have approximately five hundred hours left to spend as you see fit."

A click signalled the cutoff.

Werlith-Commandant had been quite kindly by his lights, Yoshii acknowledged.

He entered the control cabin. "I'm sorry, Carita," he said.

She rose and went to meet him. Starlight guided her through shadows and glinted off her hair and a few tears. "I'm sorry, too, Juan," she gulped. "Now let's both of us stop apologizing. The thing has happened, that's all. Look, we can try a broadcast that maybe they'll pick up in *Shep*, so they'll know. They won't dare reply, I suppose, but it's nice to think they might know. First let's eat, though, and have a couple of drinks, and talk, and, and go to bed. The same bed."

He lowered his tray to the chart shelf. "I'm exhausted," he mumbled.

She threw her arms around him and drew his head down to her opulent bosom. "So'm I, chum. And if you want to spend the rest of what time we've got being faithful, okay. But let's stay together. It's cold out there. Even in a narrow bunk, let's be together while we can."

16

The sun in the screen showed about half the Sol-disc at Earth. Its light equaled more than 10,000 full Lunas, red rather than off-white but still ample to make Secunda shine. The planetary crescent was mostly yellowish-brown, little softened by a tenuous atmosphere of methane with traces of carbon dioxide and ammonia. A polar cap brightened its wintered northern hemisphere, a shrunken one the southern. The latter was all water ice, the former enlarged by carbon dioxide and ammonia that had frozen out. These two gases did it everywhere at night, most times, evaporating again by day in summer and the tropics, so that sunrises and sunsets were apt to be violent. Along the terminator glittered a storm of fine silicate dust mingled with ice crystals.

The surface bore scant relief, but the slow rotation, 57 hours, was bringing into view a gigantic crater and a number of lesser neighbors. Probably a moon had crashed within the past billion years; the scars remained, though any orbiting fragments had dissipated. A sister moon survived, three-fourths Lunar diameter, dark yellowish like so many bodies in this system.

Thus did Tregennis interpret what he and Ryan saw as they sat in *Rover*'s saloon watching the approach. Data taken from afar, before the capture, helped him fill in details. Talking about them was an anodyne for both men.

Markham entered. Silence rushed through like a wind.

"I have an announcement," he said after a moment.

Neither prisoner stirred.

"We are debarking in half an hour," he went on. "I have arranged for your clothing and hygienic equipment to be brought along. Including your medication, Professor."

"Thank you," Tregennis said flatly.

"Why shouldn't he?" Ryan sneered. "Keep the animals alive till the master race can think of a need for them. I wonder if he'll share in the feast."

Markham's stiffness became rigidity. "Have a care," he warned. "I have been very patient with you." During the 50-odd hours of 3-g flight—during which Hraou-Captain allowed the polarizer to lighten weight—he had received no word from either, nor eye contact. To be sure, he had been cultivating the acquaintance of such kzinti among the prize crew as deigned to talk with him. "Don't provoke me."

"All right," Ryan answered. Unable to resist: "Not but what I couldn't put up with a lot of provocation myself, if I were getting paid what they must be paying you."

Markham's cheekbones reddened. "For your information, I have never had one mark of recompense, nor ever been promised any. Not one."

Tregennis regarded him in mild amazement. "Then why have you turned traitor?" he asked.

"I have not. On the contrary—" Markham stood for several seconds before he plunged. "See here, if you will listen, if you will treat me like a human being, you can learn some things you will be well advised to know."

Ryan scowled at his beer glass, shrugged, nodded, and grumbled, "Might as well."

"Can you talk freely?" Tregennis inquired.

Markham sat down. "I have not been forbidden to. Of course, what I have been told so far is quite limited. However, certain kzinti, including Hraou-Captain, have been reasonably forthcoming. They have been bored by their uneventful duty, are intrigued by me, and see no immediate threat to security."

"I can understand that," said Tregennis dryly.

Markham leaned forward. His assurance had shrunk enough to notice. He tugged his half-beard. His tone became earnest:

"Remember, for a dozen Earth-years I fought the kzinti. I was raised to it. They had driven my mother into exile. The motto of the House of Reichstein was '*Ehre*—' well, in English, 'Honor Through Service.' She changed it to 'No Surrender.' Most people had long since given up, you know. They accepted the kzin order of things. Many had been born into it, or had only dim childhood memories of anything before. Revolt would have brought massacre. Aristocrats who stayed on Wunderland—the majority—saw no alternative to cooperating with the occupation forces, at least to the extent of preserving order among humans and keeping industries in operation. They were apt to look on us who fought as dangerous extremists. It was a seductive belief. As the years wore on, with no end in sight, more and more members of the resistance despaired. Through the aristocrats at home they negotiated terms permitting them to come back and pick up the pieces of their lives. My mother was among those who had the greatness of spirit to refuse the temptation. 'No Surrender.' "

Ryan still glowered, but Tregennis said with a

dawn of sympathy, "Then the hyperdrive armada arrived and she was vindicated. Were you not glad?"

"Of course," Markham said. "We jubilated, my comrades and I, after we were through weeping for the joy and glory of it. That was a short-lived happiness. We had work to do. At first it was clean. The fighting had caused destruction. The navy from Sol could spare few units; it must go on to subdue the kzinti elsewhere. On the men of the resistance fell the tasks of rescue and relief.

"Then as we returned to our homes on Wunderland —I and many others for the first time in our lives—we found that the world for whose liberation we had fought, the world of our vision and hope, was gone, long gone. Everywhere was turmoil. Mobs stormed manor after manor of the 'collaborationist' aristocrats, lynched, raped, looted, burned—as if those same proles had not groveled before the kzinti and kept war production going for them! Lunatic political factions rioted against each other or did actual armed combat. Chaos brought breakdown, want, misery, death.

"My mother took a lead in calling for a restoration of law. We did it, we soldiers from space. What we did was often harsh, but necessary. A caretaker government was established. We thought that we could finally get on with our private lives—though I, for one, busied myself in the effort to build up Centaurian defense forces, so that never again could my people be overrun.

"In the years that my back was turned, they, my people, were betrayed." Markham choked on his bitterness.

"Do you mean the new constitution, the democratic movement in general?" Tregennis prompted.

Markham recovered and nodded. "No one denied that reform, reorganization was desirable. I will concede, if only because our time to talk now is limited, most of the reformers meant well. They did not foresee the consequences of what they enacted. I admit I did not myself. But I was busy, often away for long periods of time. My mother, on our estates, saw what was happening, and piece by piece made it clear to me."

"Your estates. You kept them, then. I gather most noble families kept a substantial part of their former holdings; and Wunderland's House of Patricians is the upper chamber of its parliament. Surely you don't think you have come under a . . . mobocracy."

"But I do! At least, that is the way it is tending. That is the way it will go, to completion, to destruction, if it is not stopped. A political Gresham's Law prevails; the bad drives out the good. Look at me, for example. I have one vote, by hereditary right, in the Patricians, and it is limited to federal matters. To take a meaningful role in restoring a proper society— through enactment of proper laws—a role which it is my hereditary duty to take—I must begin by being elected a consul of my state, Braefell. That would give me a voice in choosing who goes to the House of Delegates— No matter details. I went into politics."

"Holding your well-bred nose," Ryan murmured.

Markham flushed again. "I am for the people. The honest, decent, hard-working, sensible common people, who know in their hearts that society is tradition and order and reverence, not a series of cheap bargains between selfish interests. One still finds them in the countryside. It is in the cities that the maggots are, the mobs, the criminals, the parasites, the . . . politicians."

For the first time, Ryan smiled a little. "Can't say I admire the political process either. But I will say the cure is not to domesticate the lower class. How about letting everybody see to his own business, with a few cops and courts to keep things from getting too hairy?"

"I heard that argument often enough. It is stupid. It assumes the obvious falsehood that an individual can function in isolation like an atom. Oh, I did my share of toadying, I shook the clammy hands and said the clammy words, but it was hypocritical ritual, a sugar coating over the cynicism and corruption—"

"In short, you lost."

"I learned better than to try."

Ryan started to respond but checked himself. Markham smiled like a death's head. "Thereupon I decided to call back the kzinti, is that what you wish to say?" he gibed. Seriously: "No, it was not that simple at all. I had had dealings with them throughout my war career, negotiations, exchanges, interrogation and care of prisoners, the sort of relationships one always has with an opponent. They came to fascinate me and I learned everything about them that I could. The more I knew, the more effective a freedom fighter I would be, not so?

"After the . . . liberation, my knowledge and my reputation caused me to have still more to do with them. There were mutual repatriations to arrange. There were kzinti who had good cause to stay behind. Some had been born in the Centaurian System; the second and later fleets carried females. Others came to join such kinfolk, or on their own, as fugitives, because their society too was in upheaval and many of them actually admired us, now that we had fought successfully. Remember, most of those newcomers arrived on human hyperdrive ships. This was official policy, in the hope of earning goodwill, of learning more about kzinti in general, and of—frankly—having possible hostages. Even so, they were often subject to cruel discrimination or outright persecution. What could I do but intervene in their behalf? They, or their brothers, had been brave and honorable enemies. It was time to become friends."

"That was certainly a worthy feeling," Tregennis admitted.

Markham made a chopping gesture. "Meanwhile I not only grew more and more aware of the rot in

Wunderland, I discovered how much I had been lied to. The kzinti were never monsters, as propaganda had claimed. They were relentless at first and strict afterward, yes. They imposed their will. But it was a dynamic will serving a splendid vision. They were not wantonly cruel, nor extortionate, nor even pettily thievish. Humans who obeyed kzin law enjoyed its protection, its order, and its justice. Their lives went on peacefully, industriously, with old folkways respected—by the commoners *and* the kzinti. Most hardly ever saw a kzin. The Great Houses of Wunderland were the intermediaries, and woe betide the human lord who abused the people in his care. Oh, no matter his rank, he must defer to the lowliest kzin. But he received due honor for what he was, and could look forward to his sons rising higher, his grandsons to actual partnership."

"In the conquest of the galaxy," Ryan said.

"Well, the kzinti have their faults, but they are not like the Slavers that archaeologists have found traces of, from a billion years ago or however long it was. Men who fought the kzinti and men who served them were more fully *men* than ever before or since. My mother first said this to me, years afterward, my mother whose word had been 'No Surrender.'"

Markham glanced at his watch. "We must leave soon," he reminded. "I didn't mean to go on at such length. I don't expect you to agree with me. I do urge you to think, think hard, and meanwhile cooperate."

Regardless, Tregennis asked in his disarming fashion, "Did you actually decide to work for a kzin restoration? Isn't that the sort of radicalism you oppose?"

"My decision did not come overnight either," Markham replied, "nor do I want kzin rule again over my people. It would be better than what they have now, but manliness of their own is better still. Earth is the real enemy, rich fat Earth, its bankers and hucksters and political panderers, its vulgarity and whorishness that poison our young everywhere—on your world too, Professor. A strong planet Kzin will challenge humans to strengthen themselves. Those who do not purge out the corruption will die. The rest, clean, will make a new peace, a brotherhood, and go on to take possession of the universe."

"Together with the kzinti," Ryan said.

Markham nodded. "And perhaps other worthy races. We shall see."

"I don't imagine anybody ever promised you this."

"Not in so many words. You are shrewd, Quartermaster. But shrewdness is not enough. There is such a thing as intuition, the sense of destiny."

Markham waved a hand. "Not that I had a religious experience. I began by entrusting harmless, perfectly sincere messages to kzinti going home, messages for their authorities. 'Please suggest how our two species can reach mutual understanding. What can I do to help bring a détente?' Things like that. A few kzinti do still travel in and out, you know, on human ships, by prearrangement. They generally come to consult or debate about what matters of mutual concern our species have these days, diplomatic, commercial, safety-related. Some do other things, clandestinely. We haven't cut off the traffic on that account. It is slight—and, after all, the exchange helps us plant our spies in their space.

"The responses I got were encouraging. They led to personal meetings, even occasionally to coded hyperwave communications; we have a few relays in kzin space, you know, by agreement. The first requests I got were legitimate by anyone's measure. The kzinti asked for specific information, no state secrets, merely data they could not readily obtain. I felt that by aiding them toward a better knowledge of us I was doing my race a valuable service. But of course I could not reveal it."

"No, you had your own little foreign policy," Ryan

scoffed. "And one thing led to another, also inside your head, till you were sending stuff on the theory and practice of hyperdrive which gave them a ten- or twenty-year leg up on their R and D."

Markham's tone was patient. "They would inevitably have gotten it. Only by taking part in events can we hope to exercise any influence."

Again he consulted his watch. "We had better go," he said. "They will bring us to their base. You will be meeting the commandant. Perhaps what I have told will be of help to you."

"How about *Rover*?" Ryan inquired. "I hope you've explained to them she isn't meant for planetfall."

"That was not necessary," Markham said, irritated. "They know space architecture as well as we do— possibly better than you do, Quartermaster. We will go down in a boat from the warship. They will put our ship on the moon."

"What? Why not just in parking orbit?"

"I'll explain later. We must report now for debarkation. Have no fears. The kzinti won't willingly damage *Rover*. If they can—if we think of some way to prevent future human expeditions here that does not involve returning her—we'll keep her. The hyperdrive makes her precious. Otherwise *Kzarr-Siu*—*Vengeful Slasher*, the warship—is the only vessel currently in this system which has been so outfitted. They'll put *Rover* on the moon for safety's sake. Secunda orbits have become too crowded. The moon's gravity is low enough that it won't harm a freightship like this. Now come."

Markham rose and strode forth. Ryan and Tregennis followed. The Hawaiian nudged the Plateaunian and made little circling motions with his forefinger near his temple. Unwontedly bleak of countenance, the astronomer nodded, then whispered, "Be careful. I have read history. All too often, his kind is successful."

17

Kzinti did not use their gravity polarizers to maintain a constant, comfortable weight within spacecraft—unless accelerations got too high even for them to tolerate. The boat left with a roar of power. Humans sagged in their seats. Tregennis whitened. The thin flesh seemed to pull back over the bones of his face, the beaky nose stood out like a crag and blood trickled from it. "Hey, easy, boy," Ryan gasped. "Do you want to lose this man . . . already?"

Markham spoke to Hraou-Captain, who made a contemptuous noise but then yowled at the pilot. Weightlessness came as an abrupt benediction. For a minute silence prevailed, except for the heavy breathing of the Wunderlander and the Hawaiian, the rattling in and out of the old Plateaunian's.

Harnessed beside Tregennis, Ryan examined him as well as he could before muttering, "I guess he'll be all right in a while, if that snotbrain will take a little care." Raising his eyes, he looked past the other, out the port. "What's that?"

Close by, a kilometer or two, a small spacecraft—
the size and lines indicated a ground-to-orbit shuttle—
was docked at a framework which had been assembled
around a curiously spheroidal dark mass, a couple of
hundred meters in diameter. The framework secured
and supported machinery which was carrying out
operations under the direction of suited kzinti who
flitted about with drive units on their backs. Stars
peered through the lattice. In the distance passed a
glimpse of *Rover*, moon-bound, and the warship.

The boat glided by. A new approach curve computed, the pilot applied thrust, this time about a
single g's worth. Hraou-Captain registered impatience
at the added waiting aboard. Markham did not venture to address him again. It must have taken courage to do so at all, when he wasn't supposed to defile
the language with his mouth.

Instead the Wunderlander said to Ryan, on a note
of awe, "That is doubtless one of their iron sources.
Recently arrived, I would guess, and cooled down
enough for work to commence on it. From what I
have heard, a body that size will quickly be reduced."

Ryan stared at him, forgetting hostility in surprise.
"Iron? I thought there was hardly any in this system.
What it has ought to be at the center of the planets.
Don't the kzinti import their metals for construction?"

Markham shook his head. "No, that would be quite
impractical. They have few hyperdrive ships as yet—I
told you *Vengeful Slasher* alone is so outfitted here,
at present. Once the transports had brought personnel and the basic equipment, they went back for
duty closer to home. Currently a warship calls about
twice a year to bring fresh workers and needful items.
It relieves the one on guard, which carries back
kzinti being rotated. A reason for choosing this sun
was precisely that humans won't suspect anything
important can ever be done at it." He hesitated.
"Except pure science. The kzinti did overlook that."

"Well, where do they get their metals? Oh, the

lightest ones, aluminum, uh, beryllium, magnesium, . . . manganese?—I suppose those exist in ordinary ores. But I don't imagine those ores are anything but scarce and low-grade. And iron—"

"The asteroid belt. The planet that came too close to the sun. Disruption exposed its core. The metal content is low compared to what it would be in a later-generation world, but when you have a whole planet, you get an abundance. They have had to bring in certain elements from outside, nickel, cobalt, copper, et cetera, but mostly to make alloys. Small quantities suffice."

Tregennis had evidently not fainted. His eyelids fluttered open. "Hold," he whispered. "Those asteroids . . . orbit within . . . less than half a million kilometers . . . of the sun surface." He panted feebly before adding, "It may be a . . . very late type M . . . but nevertheless, the effective temperature—" His voice trailed off.

The awe returned to Markham's. "They have built a special tug."

"What sort?" Ryan asked.

"In principle, like the kind we know. Having found a desirable body, it lays hold with a grapnel field. I think this vessel uses a gravity polarizer system rather than electromagnetics. The kzinti originated that technology, remember. The tug draws the object into the desired orbit and releases it to go to its destination. The tug is immensely powerful. It can handle not simply large rocks like what you saw, but whole asteroids of reasonable size. As they near Secunda—tangential paths, of course—it works them into planetary orbit. That's why local space is too crowded for the kzinti to leave *Rover* in it unmanned. Besides ferrous masses on hand, two or three new ones are usually en route, and not all the tailings of worked-out old ones get swept away."

"But the heat near the sun," Ryan objected. "The crew would roast alive. I don't see how they can trust robotics alone. If nothing else, let the circuits get too hot and—"

"The tug has a live crew," Markham said. "It's built double-hulled and mirror-bright, with plenty of radiating surfaces. But mainly it's ship size, not boat size, because it loads up with water ice before each mission. There is plenty of that around the big planets, you know, chilled well below minus a hundred degrees. Heated, melted, evaporated, vented, it maintains an endurable interior until it has been spent."

"I thought we . . . found traces of water and OH . . . in a ring around the sun," Tregennis breathed. "Could it actually be—?"

"I don't know how much ice the project has consumed to date," Markham said, "but you must agree it is grandly conceived. That is a crew of heroes. They suffer, they dare death each time, but their will prevails."

Ryan rubbed his chin. "I suppose otherwise the only spacecraft are shuttles. And the warcraft and her boats."

"They are building more." Markham sounded proud. "And weapons and support machinery. This will be an industrial as well as a naval base."

"For the next war—" Tregennis seemed close to tears. Ryan patted his hand. Silence took over.

The boat entered atmosphere, which whined as she decelerated around the globe. A dawn storm, grit and ice, obscured the base, but the humans made out that it was in the great crater, presumably because the moonfall had brought down valuable ores and caused more to spurt up from beneath. Interconnected buildings made a web across several kilometers, with a black central spider. Doubtless much lay underground. An enterprise like this was large-scale or it was worthless. True, it had to start small, precariously—the first camp, the assembling of life support systems and food production facilities and a hospital for victims of disasters such as were inevitable when you drove hard ahead with your work on a strange world—but demonic energy had joined the exponential-increase powers of automated machines to bring forth this city of warriors.

No, Ryan thought, a city of workers in the service of future warriors. Thus far few professional fighters would be present except the crew of *Vengeful Slasher*. They weren't needed . . . yet. The warship was on hand against unlikely contingencies. Well, in this case kzin paranoia had paid off.

The pilot made an instrument landing into a cradle. Ryan spied more such units, three of them holding shuttles. The field on which they stood, though paved, must often be treacherous because of drifted dust. Secunda had no unfrozen water to cleanse its air; and the air was a chill wisp. Most of the universe is barren. Hawaii seemed infinitely far away.

A gang tube snaked from a ziggurat-like terminal building. Airlocks linked. An armed kzin entered and saluted. Hraou-Captain gestured at the humans and snarled an imperative before he went out. Markham unharnessed. "I am to follow him," he said. "You go with this guard. Quarters are prepared. Behave yourselves and . . . I will do my best for you."

Ryan rose. Two-thirds Earth weight felt good. He collected his and Tregennis' bags in his right hand and gave the astronomer his left arm for support. Kzinti throughout a cavernous main room stared as the captives appeared. They didn't goggle like humans, they watched like cats. Several naked tails switched to and fro. An effort had been made to brighten the surroundings, a huge mural of some hero in hand-to-hand combat with a monster; the blood jetted glaring bright.

The guard led his charges down corridors which pulsed with the sounds of construction. At last he opened a door, waved them through, and closed it behind them. They heard a lock click shut.

The room held a bed and a disposal unit, meant for kzinti but usable by humans; the bed was ample for two, and by dint of balancing and clinging you could take care of sanitation. "I better help you till you feel better, Prof," Ryan offered. "Meanwhile, why don't you lie down? I'll unpack." The bags and floor must furnish storage space. Kzinti seldom went in for clothes or for carrying personal possessions around.

They did hate sensory deprivation, still more than humans do. There was no screen, but a port showed the spacefield. The terminator storm was dying out as the sun rose higher, and the view cleared fast. Under a pale red sky, the naval complex came to an end some distance off. Tawny sand reached onward, strewn with boulders. In places, wind had swept clear the fused crater floor. It wasn't like lava, more like dark glass. Huge though the bowl was, Secunda— much less dense than Earth, but significantly larger— had a wide enough horizon that the nearer wall jutted above it in the west, a murky palisade.

Tregennis took Ryan's advice and stretched himself out. The quartermaster smiled and came to remove his shoes for him. "Might as well be comfortable," Ryan said, "or as nearly as we can without beer."

"And without knowledge of our fates," the Plateaunian said low. "Worse, the fates of our friends."

"At least they are out of Markham's filthy hands."

"Kamehameha, please. Watch yourself. We shall have to deal with him. And he—I think he too is feeling shocked and lonely. He didn't expect this either. His orders were merely to hamper exploration beyond the limits of human space. He wants to spare us. Give him the chance."

"Ha! I'd rather give a shark that kind of chance. It's less murderous."

"Oh, now, really."

Ryan thumped fist on wall. "Who do you suppose put that kzin up to attacking Bob Saxtorph back in

Tiamat? It has to have been Markham, when his earlier efforts failed. Nothing else makes sense. And this, mind you, this was when he had no particular reason to believe our expedition mattered as far as the kzinti were concerned. They hadn't trusted him with any real information. But he went ahead anyway and tried to get a man killed to stop us. That shows you what value he puts on human life."

"Well, maybe . . . maybe he is deranged," Tregennis sighed. "Would you bring me a tablet, please? I see a water tap and bowl over there."

"Sure. Heart, huh? Take it easy. You shouldn't've come along, you know."

Tregennis smiled. "Medical science has kept me functional far longer than I deserve.

" *'But fill me with the old familiar Juice,*
" *'Methinks I might recover by-and-by!'* "

Ryan lifted the white head and brought the bowl, from which a kzin would have lapped, carefully close to the lips. "You've got more heart than a lot of young bucks I could name," he said.

Time crept past.

The door opened. "Hey, food?" Ryan asked.

Markham confronted them, an armed kzin at his back. He was again pallid and stiff of countenance. "Come," he said harshly.

Rested, Tregennis walked steady-footed beside Ryan. They went through a maze of featureless passages with shut doors, coldly lighted, throbbing or buzzing. When they encountered other kzinti they felt the carnivore stares follow them.

After a long while they stopped at a larger door. This part of the warren looked like officer country, though Ryan couldn't be sure when practically everything he saw was altogether foreign to him. The guard let them in and followed.

The chamber beyond was windowless, its sole ornamentation a screen on which a computer projected colored patterns. Kzin-type seats, desk, and electronics suggested an office, but big and mostly empty. In one corner a plastic tub had been placed, about three meters square. Within stood some apparatus, and a warrior beside, and the drug-dazed telepath huddled at his feet.

The prisoners' attention went to Hraou-Captain and another—lean and grizzled by comparison—seated at the desk. "Show respect," Markham directed. "You meet Werlith-Commandant."

Tregennis bowed, Ryan slopped a soft salute.

The head honcho spat and rumbled. Markham turned to the men. "Listen," he said. "I have been in . . . conference, and am instructed to tell you . . . *Fido* has been found."

Tregennis made a tiny noise of pain. Ryan hunched his shoulders and said, "That's what they told you."

"It is true," Markham insisted. "The boat went to Prima. The interrogation aboard *Rover* led to a suspicion that the escapers might try that maneuver. *Ya-Nar-Ksshinn*—call it *Sun Defier*, the asteroid tug, it was prospecting. The commandant ordered it to Prima, since it could get there very fast. By then *Fido* was trapped on the surface. Fenger and Yoshii broadcast a call for help, so *Sun Defier* located them. Just lately, *Fido* has made a new broadcast which the kzinti picked up. You will listen to the recording."

Werlith-Commandant condescended to touch a control. From the desk communicator, wavery through a seething of radio interference, Juan Yoshii's voice came forth.

"Hello, Bob, Dorcas, Lau-laurinda—Kam, Arthur, . . . Ulf, if you hear—hello from Carita and me. We'll set this to repeat on different bands, hoping you'll happen to tune it in somewhere along the line. It's likely goodbye."

"No," said Carita's voice, "it's 'good luck.' To you. Godspeed."

"Right," Yoshii agreed. "Before we let you know what the situation is, we want to beg you, don't ever blame yourselves. There was absolutely no way to foresee it. And the universe is full of much worse farms we could have bought.

"However—" Unemotionally, now and then aided by his companion, he described things as they were. "We'll hang on till the end, of course," he finished. "Soon we'll see what we can rig to keep us alive. After the hull collapses altogether, we'll flit off in search of bare rock to sit on, if any exists. Do not, repeat do not risk yourselves in some crazy rescue attempt. Maybe you could figure out a safe way to do it if you had the time and no kzinti on your necks. Or maybe you could talk them into doing it. But neither one is in the cards, eh? You concentrate on getting the word home."

"We mean that," Carita said.

"Laurinda, I love you," Yoshii said fast. "Farewell, fare always well, darling. What really hurts is knowing you may not make it back. But if you do, you have your life before you. Be happy."

"We aren't glum." Carita barked a laugh. "I might wish Juan weren't quite so noble, Laurinda, dear. But it's no big thing either way, is it? Not any more. Good luck to all of you."

The recording ended. Tregennis gazed beyond the room—at this new miracle of nature? Ryan stood swallowing tears, his fists knotted.

"You see what Saxtorph's recklessness has caused," Markham said.

"No!" Ryan shouted. "The kzinti could lift them off! But they—tell his excellency yonder they're afraid to!"

"I will not. You must be out of your mind. Besides, *Sun Defier* cannot land on a planet, and carries no auxiliary."

"A shuttle—No. But a boat from the warship."

"Why? What have Yoshii and Fenger done to merit saving, at hazard to the kzinti for whom they only want to make trouble? Let them be an object lesson, gentlemen. If you have any care whatsoever for the rest of your party, help us retrieve them before it is too late."

"I don't know where they are. Not on P-prima, for sure."

"They must be found."

"Well, send that damned tug."

Markham shook his head. "It has better uses. It was about ready to return anyway. It will take Secunda orbit and wait for an asteroid that is due in shortly." He spoke like a man using irrelevancies to stave off the moment when he must utter his real meaning.

"Okay, the warship."

"It too has other duties. I've told them about Saxtorph's babbling of kamikaze tactics. Hraou-Captain must keep his vessel prepared to blow that boat out of the sky if it comes near—until Saxtorph's gang is under arrest, or dead. He will detach his auxiliaries to search."

"Let him," Ryan jeered. "Bob's got this whole system to skulk around in."

"Tertia is the first place to try."

"Go ahead. That old fox is good at finding burrows."

Werlith-Commandant growled. Markham grew paler yet, bowed, turned on Ryan and said in a rush: "Don't waste more time. The master wants to resolve this business as soon as possible. He wants Saxtorph and company preferably alive, dead will do, but disposed of, so we can get on with the business of explaining away at Wunderland what happened to *Rover*. You will cooperate."

Sweat studded Ryan's face. "I will?"

"Yes. You shall accompany the search party. Broadcast your message in Hawaiian. Persuade them to give themselves up."

Ryan relieved himself of several obscenities.

"Be reasonable," Markham almost pleaded. "Think

what has happened with *Fido*. The rest can only die in worse ways, unless you bring them to their senses."

Ryan shifted his feet wide apart, thrust his head forward, and spat, "No surrender."

Markham took a backward step. "What?"

"Your mother's motto, ratcat-lover. Have you forgotten? How proud of you she's going to be when she hears."

Markham closed his eyes. His lips moved. He looked forth again and said in a string of whipcracks: "You will obey. Werlith-Commandant orders it. Look yonder. Do you see what is in the corner? He expected stubbornness."

Ryan and Tregennis peered. They recognized frame and straps, pincers and electrodes; certain items were less identifiable. The telepath slumped at the feet of the torturer.

"Hastily improvised," Markham said, "but the database has a full account of human physiology, and I made some suggestions as well. The subject will not die under interrogation as often happened in the past."

Ryan's chest heaved. "If that thing can read my mind, he knows—"

Markham sighed. "We had better get to work." He glanced at the kzin officers. They both made a gesture. The guard sprang to seize Ryan from behind. The Hawaiian yelled and struggled, but that grip was unbreakable by a human.

The torturer advanced. He laid hands on Tregennis.

"Watch, Ryan," Markham said raggedly. "Let us know when you have had enough."

The torturer half dragged, half marched Tregennis across the room, held him against the wall, and, claws out on the free hand, ripped the clothes from his scrawniness.

"That's your idea, Markham!" Ryan bellowed. "You unspeakable—"

"Hold fast, Kamehameha," Tregennis called in his thin voice. "Don't yield."

"Art, oh, Art—"

The kzin secured the man to the frame. He picked up the electrodes and applied them. Tregennis screamed. Yet he modulated it: "Pain has a saturation point, Kamehameha. Hold fast!"

The business proceeded.

"You win, you Judas, okay, you win," Ryan wept.

Tregennis could no longer make words, merely noises.

Markham inquired of the officers before he told Ryan, "This will continue a few minutes more, to drive the lesson home. Given proper care and precautions, he should still be alive to accompany the search party." Markham breathed hard. "To make sure of your cooperation, do you hear? This is your fault!" he shrieked.

18

"No," Saxtorph had said, "I think we'd better stay put for the time being."

Dorcas had looked at him across the shoulder of Laurinda, whom she held close, Laurinda who had just heard her man say farewell. The cramped command section was full of the girl's struggles not to cry. "If they thought to check Prima immediately, they will be at Tertia before long," the captain's wife had stated.

Saxtorph had nodded. "Yah, sure. But they'll have a lot more trouble finding us where we are than if we were in space, even free-falling with a cold generator. We could only boost a short ways, you see, else they'd acquire our drive-spoor if they've gotten anywhere near. They'd have a fairly small volume for their radars to sweep."

"But to sit passive! What use?"

"I didn't mean that. Thought you knew me better. Got an idea I suspect you can improve on."

Laurinda had lifted her head and sobbed, "Couldn't

we . . . m-make terms? If we surrender to them . . . they rescue Juan and, and Carita?"

" 'Fraid not, honey," Saxtorph had rumbled. Anguish plowed furrows down his face. "Once we call 'em, they'll have a fix on us, and what's left to dicker with? Either we give in real nice or they lob a shell. They'd doubtless like to have us for purposes of faking a story, but we aren't essential—they hold three as is—and they've written *Fido's* people off. I'm sorry."

Laurinda had freed herself from the mate's embrace, stood straight, swallowed hard. "You must be right," she had said in a voice taking on an edge. "What can we do? Thank you, Dorcas, dear, but I, I'm ready now . . . for whatever you need."

"Good lass." The older woman had squeezed her hand before asking the captain: "If we don't want to be found, shouldn't we fetch back the relay from above?"

Saxtorph had considered. The same sensitivity which had received, reconstructed, and given to the boat a radio whisper from across more than two hundred million kilometers, could betray his folk. After a moment: "No, leave it. A small object, after all, which we've camouflaged pretty well, and its emission blends into the sun's radio background. If the kzinti get close enough to detect it, they'll be onto us anyway."

"You don't imagine we can hide here forever."

"Certainly not. They can locate us in two-three weeks at most if they work hard. However, meanwhile they won't know for sure we are on Tertia. They'll spread themselves thin looking elsewhere, too, or they'll worry. Never give the enemy a free ride."

"But you say you have something better in mind than simply distracting them for a while."

"Well, I have a sort of a notion. It's loony as it stands, but maybe you can help me refine it. At best, we'll probably get ourselves killed, but plain to see,

Markham's effort to cut a deal has not worked out, and—we can hope for some revenge."

Laurinda's albino eyes had flared.

—"*Aloha, hoapilina.*—"

Crouched over the communicator, Saxtorph heard the Hawaiian through. English followed, the dragging tone of a broken man:

"Well, that was to show you this is honest, Bob, if you're listening. The kzinti don't have a telepath along, because they know they don't need the poor creature. They do require me to go on in a language their translator can handle. Anyway, I don't suppose you remember much Polynesian.

"We're orbiting Tertia in a boat from the Prowling Hunter warship. 'We' are her crew, plus a couple of marines, plus Arthur Tregennis and myself. Markham stayed on Secunda. He's a kzin agent. Maybe you've gotten the message from *Fido*. I'm afraid the game's played out, Bob. I tried to resist, but they tortured—not me—poor Art. I soon couldn't take it. He's alive, sort of. They give you three hours to call them. That's in case you've scrammed to the far ends of the system and may not be tuned in right now. You'll've noticed this is a powerful planar 'cast. They think they're being generous. If they haven't heard in three hours, they'll torture Art some more. Please don't let that happen!" Ryan howled through the wail that Laurinda tried to stifle. "Please call back!"

Saxtorph waited a while, but there was nothing further, only the hiss of the red sun. He took his finger from the transmission key, which he had not pressed, and twisted about to look at his companions. Light streaming wanly through the westside port found Dorcas' features frozen. Laurinda's writhed; her mouth was stretched out of shape.

"So," he said. "Three hours. Dark by then, as it happens."

"They hurt him," Laurinda gasped. "That good old man, they took him and hurt him."

Dorcas peeled lips back from teeth. "Shrewd," she said. "Markham in kzin pay? I'm not totally surprised. I don't know how it was arranged, but I'm not too surprised. He suggested this, I think. The kzinti probably don't understand us that well."

"We can't let them go on . . . with the professor," Laurinda shrilled. "We can't, no matter what."

"He's been like a second father to you, hasn't he?" Dorcas asked almost absently. Unspoken: But your young man is down on Prima, and the enemy will let him die there.

"No argument," Saxtorph said. "We won't. We've got a few choices, though. Kzinti aren't sadistic. Merciless, but not sadistic the way too many humans are. They don't torture for fun, or even spite. They won't if we surrender. Or if we die. No point in it then."

Dorcas grinned in a rather horrible fashion. "The chances are we'll die if we do surrender," she responded. "Not immediately, I suppose. Not till they need our corpses, or till they see no reason to keep us alive. Again, quite impersonal."

"I don't feel impersonal," Saxtorph grunted.

Laurinda lifted her hands. The fingers were crooked like talons. "We made other preparations against them. Let's do what we planned."

Dorcas nodded. "Aye."

"That makes it unanimous," Saxtorph said. "Go for broke. Now, look at the sun. Within three hours, nightfall. The kzinti could land in the dark, but if I were their captain I'd wait for morning. He won't be in such a hurry he'll care to take the extra risk. Meanwhile we sit cooped for 20-odd hours losing our nerve. Let's not. Let's begin right away."

Willingness blazed from the women.

Saxtorph hauled his bulk from the chair. "Okay, first Dorcas and I suit up."

"Are you sure I can't join you?" Laurinda wellnigh beseeched.

Saxtorph shook his head. "Sorry. You aren't trained

for that kind of thing. And the gravity weighs you down still worse than it does Dorcas, even if she is a Belter. Besides, we want you to free us from having to think about communications. You stay inboard and handle the hardest part." He chucked her under the chin. "If we fail, which we well may, you'll get your chance to die like a soldier." He stooped, kissed her hand, and went out.

Returning equipped, he said into the transmitter: "*Shep* here. Spaceboat *Shep* calling kzin vessel. Hello, Kam. Don't blame yourself. They've got us. We'll leave this message replaying in case you're on the far side, and so you can zero in on us. Because you will have to. Listen, Kam. Tell that gonococcus of a captain that we can't lift. We came down on talus that slid beneath us and damaged a landing jack. We'd hit the side of the canyon where we are—it's narrow—if we tried to take off before the hydraulics have been repaired; and Dorcas and I can't finish that job for another several Earth-days, the two of us with what tools we've got aboard. The ground immediately downslope of us is safe. Or, if your captain is worried about his fat ass, he can wait till we're ready to come meet him. Please inform us. Give Art our love; and take it yourself, Kam."

The kzin skipper would want a direct machine translation of those words. They were calculated not to lash him into fury—he couldn't be such a fool— but to pique his honor. Moreover, the top brass back on Secunda must be almighty impatient. Kzinti weren't much good at biding their time.

Before they closed their faceplates at the airlock, Saxtorph kissed his wife on the lips.

—Shadows welled in the coulee and its ravines as the sun sank toward rimrock. Interplay of light and dark was shifty behind the boat, where rubble now decked the floor. The humans had arranged that by radio detonation of two of the blasting sticks Dorcas smuggled along. It looked like more debris than it was, made the story of the accident plausible, and guaranteed that the kzinti would land in the short stretch between *Shep* and glacier.

Man and woman regarded each other. Their spacesuits were behung with armament. She had the rifle and snub-nosed automatic, he the machine pistol; both carried potentially lethal prospector's gear. Wind skirled. The heights glowed under a sky deepening from royal purple to black, where early stars quivered forth.

"Well," he said inanely into his throat mike, "we know our stations. Good hunting, kid."

"And to you, hotpants," she answered. "See you on the far side of the monobloc."

"Love you."

"Love you right back." She whirled and hastened off. Under the conditions expected, drive units would have been a bad mistake, and she was hampered by a weight she was never bred to. Nonetheless she moved with a hint of her wonted gracefulness. Both their suits were first-chop, never mind what the cost had added to the mortgage under which Saxtorph Ventures labored. Full air and water recycle, telescopic option, power joints even in the gloves, selfseal throughout. . . . She rated no less, he believed, and she'd tossed the same remark at him. Thus they had a broad range of capabilities.

He climbed to his chosen niche, on the side of the canyon opposite hers, and settled in. It was up a boulderful gulch, plenty of cover, with a clear view downward. The ice cliff glimmered. He hoped that what was going to happen wouldn't cause damage yonder. That would be a scientific atrocity.

But those beings had had their day. This was humankind's, unless it turned out to be kzinkind's. Or somebody else's? Who knew how many creatures of what sorts were prowling around the galaxy? Saxtorph hunkered into a different position. He missed his pipe. His heart slugged harder than it ought and he could smell himself in spite of the purifier. Better do a bit of meditation. Nervousness would worsen his chances.

His watch told him an hour had passed when the kzin boat arrived. The boat! Good. They might have kept her safe aloft and dispatched a squad on drive. But that would have been slow and tricky; as they descended, the members could have been picked off, assuming the humans had firearms—which a kzin would assume; they'd have had no backup.

The sun had trudged farther down, but *Shep*'s nose still sheened above the blue dusk in the canyon, and the oncoming craft flared metallic red. He knew her type from his war years. Kam, stout kanaka, had passed on more information than the kzinti probably realized. A boat belonging to a Prowling Hunter normally carried six—captain, pilot, engineer, computerman, two fire-control officers; they shared various other duties, and could swap the main ones in an emergency. They weren't trained for groundside combat, but of course any kzin was pretty fair at that. Kam had mentioned two marines who did have the training. Then there were the humans. No wonder the complement did not include a telepath. He'd have been considered superfluous anyway, worth much more at the base. This mission was simply to collar three fugitives.

Sonic thunders rolled, gave way to whirring, and the lean shape neared. It put down with a care that Saxtorph admired, came to rest, instantly swiveled a gun at the human boat 50 meters up the canyon. Saxtorph's pulse leaped. The enemy had landed exactly where he hoped. Not that he'd counted on that, or on anything else.

His earphones received bland translator English; he could imagine the snarl behind. "Are you prepared to yield?"

How steady Laurinda's response was. "We yield on condition that our comrades are alive, safe. Bring

them to us." Quite a girl, Saxtorph thought. The
kzinti wouldn't wonder about her; their females not
being sapient, any active intelligence was, in their
minds, male.

"Do you dare this insolence? Your landing gear
does not seem damaged as you claimed. Lift, and we
fire."

"We have no intention of lifting, supposing we
could. Bring us our comrades, or come pry us out."

Saxtorph tautened. No telling how the kzin commander would react. Except that he'd not willingly
blast *Shep* on the ground. Concussion, in this thick
atmosphere, and radiation would endanger his own
craft. He might decide to produce Art and Kam—

Hope died. Battle plans never quite work. The
main airlock opened; a downramp extruded; two kzinti
in armor and three in regular spacesuits, equipped
with rifles and cutting torches, came forth. The smooth
computer voice said, "You will admit this party. If
you resist, you die."

Laurinda kept silence. The kzinti started toward
her.

Saxtorph thumbed his detonator.

In a well-chosen set of places under a bluff above a
slope on his side, the remaining sticks blew. Dust
and flinders heaved aloft. An instant later he heard
the grumble of explosion and breaking. Under one-
point-three-five Earth gravities, rocks hurtled, slid,
tumbled to the bottom and across it.

He couldn't foresee what would happen next, but
had been sure it would be fancy. The kzinti were
farther along than he preferred. They dodged leaping masses, escaped the landslide. But it crashed
around their boat. She swayed, toppled, fell onto the
pile of stone, which grew until it half buried her.
The gun pointed helplessly at heaven. Dust swirled
about before it settled.

Dorcas was already shooting. She was a crack marks-
man. A kzin threw up his arms and flopped, another,

another. The rest scattered. They hadn't thought to bring drive units. If they had, she could have bagged them all as they rose. Saxtorph bounded out and downslope, over the boulders. His machine pistol had less range than her rifle. It chattered in his hands. He zigzagged, bent low, squandering ammo, while she kept the opposition prone.

Out of nowhere, a marine grabbed him by the ankle. He fell, rolled over, had the kzin on top of him. Fingers clamped on the wrist of the arm holding his weapon. The kzin fumbled after a pistol of his own. Saxtorph's free hand pulled a crowbar from its sling. He got it behind the kzin's back, under the aircycler tank, and pried. Vapor gushed forth. His foe choked, went bug-eyed, scrabbled, and slumped. Saxtorph crawled from beneath.

Dorcas covered his back, disposed of the last bandit, as he pounded toward the boat. The outer valve of the airlock gaped wide. Piece of luck, that, though he and she could have gotten through both with a certain amount of effort. He wedged a rock in place to make sure the survivors wouldn't shut it.

She made her way to him. He helped her scramble across the slide and over the curve of hull above, to the chamber. She spent her explosive rifle shells breaking down the inner valve. As it sagged, she let him by.

He stormed in. They had agreed to that, as part of what they had hammered out during hour after hour after hour of waiting. He had the more mass and muscle; and spraying bullets around in a confined space would likely kill their friends.

An emergency airseal curtain brushed him and closed again. Breathable atmosphere leaked past it, a white smoke, but slowly. The last kzinti attacked. They didn't want ricochets either. Two had claws out—one set dripped red—and the third carried a power drill, whirling to pierce his suit and the flesh behind.

Saxtorph went for him first. His geologist's hammer knocked the drill aside. From the left, his knife stabbed into the throat, and slashed. Clad as he was, what followed became butchery. He split a skull and opened a belly. Blood, brains, guts were everywhere. Two kzinti struggled and ululated in agony. Dorcas came into the tumult. Safely point-blank, her pistol administered mercy shots.

Saxtorph leaned against a bulkhead. He began to shake.

Dimly, he was aware of Kam Ryan stumbling forth. He opened his faceplate—oxygen inboard would stay adequate for maybe half an hour, though God, the stink of death!—and heard:

"I don't believe, I can't believe, but you did it, you're here, you've won, only first a ratcat, must've lost his temper, he ripped Art, Art's dead, well, he was hurting so, a release, I scuttled aft, but Art's dead, don't let Laurinda see, clean up first, please, I'll do it, we can take time to bury him, can't we, this is where his dreams were—" The man knelt, embraced Dorcas' legs regardless of the chill on them, and wept.

19

They left Tregennis at the foot of the glacier, making a cairn for him where the ancients were entombed. "That seems very right," Laurinda whispered. "I hope the scientists who come in the future will—give him a proper grave   but leave him here."

Saxtorph made no remark about the odds against any such expedition. It would scarcely happen unless his people got home to tell the tale.

The funeral was hasty. When they hadn't heard from their boat for a while, which would be a rather short while, the kzinti would send another, if not two or three. Humans had better be well out of the neighborhood before then.

Saxtorph boosted *Shep* inward from Tertia. "We can get some screening in the vicinity of the sun, especially if we've got it between us and Secunda," he explained. "Radiation out of that clinker is no particular hazard, except heat; we'll steer safely wide and not linger too long." Shedding unwanted heat was always a problem in space. The best array of thermistors gave only limited help.

"Also—" he began to add. "No, never mind. A vague notion. Something you mentioned, Kam. But let it wait till we've quizzed you dry."

That in turn waited upon simple, dazed sitting, followed by sleep, followed by gradual regaining of strength and alertness. You don't bounce straight back from tension, terror, rage, and grief.

The sun swelled in view. Its flares were small and dim compared to Sol's, but their flame-flickers became visible to the naked eye, around the roiled ember disc. After he heard what Ryan knew about the asteroid tug, Saxtorph whistled. "Christ!" he murmured. "Imagine swinging that close. Damn near half the sky a boiling red glow, and you hear the steam roar in its conduits and you fly in a haze of it, and nevertheless I'll bet the cabin is a furnace you can barely endure, and if the least thing goes wrong— Yah, kzinti have courage, you must give them that. Markham's right—what you quoted, Kam—they'd make great partners for humans. Though he doesn't understand that we'll have to civilize them first."

Excitement grew in him as he learned more and his thoughts developed. But it was with a grim countenance that he presided over the meeting he called.

"Two men, two women, an unarmed interplanetary boat, and the nearest help light-years off," he said. "After what we've done, the enemy must be scouring the system for us. I daresay the warship's staying on guard at Secunda, but if I know kzin psychology, all her auxiliaries are now out on the hunt, and won't quit till we're either captured or dead."

Dorcas nodded. "We dealt them what was worse than a hurt, a humiliation," she confirmed. "Honor calls for vengeance."

Laurinda clenched her fists. "It *does*," she hissed.

Ryan glanced at her in surprise; he hadn't expected that from her.

"Well, they do have losses to mourn, like us," Dorcas said. "As fiery as they are by nature, they'll press the chase in hopes of dealing with us personally. However, they know our foodstocks are limited." Little had been taken from the naval lockers. It was unpalatable, and stowage space was almost filled already. "If we're still missing after some months, they can reckon us dead. Contrary to Bob, I suppose they'll return to base before then."

"Not necessarily," Ryan replied. "It gives them something to do. That's the question every military command has to answer, how to keep the troops busy between combat operations." For the first time since that hour on Secunda, he grinned. "The traditional human solutions have been either (a) a lot of drill or (b) a lot of paperwork; but you can't force much of either on kzinti."

"Back to business," Saxtorph snapped. "I've been trying to reason like, uh, Werlith-Commandant. What does he expect? I think he sees us choosing one of three courses. First, we might stay on the run, hoping against hope that there will be a human follow-up expedition and we can warn it in time. But he's got Markham to help him prevent that. Second, we might turn ourselves in, hoping against hope our lives will be spared. Third, we might attempt a suicide dash, hoping against hope we'll die doing him a little harm. The warship will be on the lookout for that, and in spite of certain brave words earlier, I honestly don't give us a tax collector's chance at Paradise of getting through the kind of barrage she can throw.

"Can anybody think of any more possibilities?"

"No," sighed Dorcas. "Of course, they aren't mutually exclusive. Forget surrender. But we can stay on the run till we're close to starvation and then try to strike a blow."

Laurinda's eyes closed. *Juan*, her lips formed.

"We can try a lot sooner," Saxtorph declared.

Breaths went sibilant in between teeth.

"What Kam's told us has given me an idea that I'll bet has not occurred to any kzin," the captain went on. "I'll grant you it's hairy-brained. It may very well get us killed. But it gives us the single possibility I see of getting killed while accomplishing something real. And we might, we just barely might do better than that. You see, it involves a way to sneak close to Secunda, undetected, unsuspected. After that, we'll decide what, if anything, we can do. I have a notion there as well, but first we need hard information. If things look impossible, we can probably flit off for outer space, the kzinti never the wiser." A certain vibrancy came into his voice. "But time crammed inside this hull is scarcely lifetime, is it? I'd rather go out fighting. A short life but a merry one."

His tone dropped. "Granted, the whole scheme depends on parameters being right. But if we're careful, we shouldn't lose much by investigating. At worst, we'll be disappointed."

"You do like to lay a long-winded foundation, Bob," Ryan said.

"And you like to mix metaphors, Kam," Dorcas responded.

Saxtorph laughed. Laurinda looked from face to face, bemused.

"Okay," Saxtorph said. "Our basic objective is to recapture *Rover*, agreed? Without her, we're nothing but a bunch of maroons, and the most we can do is take a few kzinti along when we die. With her—ah, no need to spell it out.

"She's on Secunda's moon, Kam heard. The kzinti know full well we'd like to get her back. I doubt they keep a live guard aboard against the remote contingency. They've trouble enough as is with personnel growing bored and quarrelsome. But they'll've planted detectors, which will sound a radio alarm if anybody comes near. Then the warship can land an armed party or, if necessary, throw a nuke. The warship also has the duty of protecting the planetside base. If I were in charge—and I'm pretty sure What's-his-screech-Captain thinks the same—I'd keep her in orbit about halfway between planet and moon. Wide field for radars, optics, every kind of gadget; quick access to either body. Kam heard as how that space is cluttered with industrial stuff and junk, but she'll follow a reasonably clear path and keep ready to dodge or deflect whatever may be on a collision course.

"Now. The kzinti mine the asteroid belt for metals, mainly iron. They do that by shifting the bodies into eccentric orbits osculating Secunda's, then wangling them into planetary orbit at the far end. Kam heard as how an asteroid is about due in, and the tug was taking station to meet it and nudge it into place. To my mind, 'asteroid' implies a fair-sized object, not just a rock.

"But the tug was prospecting, Kam heard, when she was ordered to Prima. Afterward she didn't go back to prospecting, because the time before she'd be needed at Secunda had gotten too short to make that worthwhile. However, since she was in fact called from the sun, my guess is that the asteroid's not in need of attention right away. In other words, the tug's waiting.

"Again, if I were in charge, I wouldn't keep a crew idle aboard. I'd just leave her in Secunda orbit till she's wanted. That needs to be a safe orbit, though, and inner space isn't for an empty vessel. So the tug's circling wide around the planet, or maybe the moon. Unless she sits on the moon, too."

"She isn't able to land anywhere," Ryan reminded. "Those cooling fins, if nothing else. I suppose the kzinti put *Rover* down, on the planet-facing side, the easier to keep an eye on her. She's a lure for us, after all."

Saxtorph nodded. "Thanks," he said. "Given that

the asteroid was diverted from close-in solar orbit, and is approaching Secunda, we can make a pretty good estimate of where it is and what the vectors are. How 'bout it, Laurinda?

"The kzinti are expecting the asteroid. Their instruments will register it. They'll say, 'Ah, yes,' and go on about their business, which includes hunting for us—and never suppose that we've glided to it and are trailing along behind."

Dorcas let out a war-whoop.

20

The thing was still molten. That much mass would remain so for a long while in space, unless the kzinti had ways to speed its cooling. Doubtless they did. Instead of venting enormous quantities of water to maintain herself near the sun, the tug could spray them forth. "What a show!" Saxtorph had said. "Pity we'll miss it."

The asteroid glowed ruddy, streaked with slag, like a lesser sun trundling between planets. Its diameter was ample to conceal *Shep*. Secunda gleamed ahead, a perceptible tawny disc. From time to time the humans had ventured to slip their boat past her shield for a quick instrumental peek. They knew approximately the rounds which *Vengeful Slasher* and *Sun Defier* paced. Soon the tug must come to make rendezvous and steer the iron into its destination path. Gigantic though her strength was, she could shift millions of tonnes, moving at kilometers per second, only slowly. Before this began, the raiders must raid.

Saxtorph made a final despairing effort: "Damn it to chaos, darling, I can't let you go. I can't."

"Hush," Dorcas said low, and laid her hand across his mouth. They floated weightless in semi-darkness, the bunk which they shared curtained off. Their shipmates had, unspokenly, gone forward from the cubbyhole where everyone slept by turns, to leave them alone.

"One of us has to go, one stay," she whispered redundantly, but into his ear. "Nobody else would have a prayer of conning the tug, and Kam and Laurinda could scarcely bring *Rover* home, which is the object of the game. So you and I have to divide the labor, and for this part I'm better qualified."

"Brains, not brawn, huh?" he growled half resentfully.

"Well, I did work on translation during the war. I can read kzin a little, which is what's going to count. Put down your machismo." She drew him close and fluttered eyelids against his. "As for brawn, fellow, you do have qualifications I lack, and this may be our last chance . . . for a spell."

"Oh, love—you, you—"

Thus their dispute was resolved. They had been through it more than once. Afterward there wasn't time to continue it. Dorcas had to prepare herself.

Spacesuited, loaded like a Christmas tree with equipment, she couldn't properly embrace her husband at the airlock. She settled for an awkward kiss and a wave at the others, then closed her faceplate and cycled through.

Outside, she streaked off, around the asteroid. Its warmth beat briefly at her. She left the lump behind and deployed her diriscope, got a fix on the planet ahead, compared the reading with the computed coordinates that gleamed on a databoard, worked the calculator strapped to her left wrist, made certain of what the displays on her drive unit meters said—

right forearm—and set the thrust controls for maximum. Acceleration tugged. She was on her way.

It would be a long haul. You couldn't eat distance in a spacesuit at anything like the rate you could in a boat. Its motor lacked the capacity—not to speak of the protections and cushionings possible within a hull. In fact, a large part of her load was energy boxes. To accomplish her mission in time, she must needs drain them beyond rechargeability, discard and replace them. That hurt; they could have been ferried down to Prima for the saving of Carita and Juan. Now too few would be left, back aboard *Shep*. But under present conditions rescue would be meaningless anyway.

She settled down for the hours. Her insignificant size and radiation meant she would scarcely show on kzin detectors. Occasionally she sipped from the water tube or pushed a foodbar through the chowlock. Her suit took care of additional needs. As for comfort, she had the stars, Milky Way, nebulae, sister galaxies, glory upon glory.

Often she rechecked her bearings and adjusted her vectors. Eventually, decelerating, she activated a miniature radar such as asteroid miners employ and got a lock on her objective. By then Secunda had swollen larger in her eyes than Luna over Earth. From her angle of view it was a scarred dun crescent against a circle of darkness faintly rimmed with light diffused through dusty air. The moon, where *Rover* lay, was not visible to her.

Saxtorph's guess had been right. Well, it was an informed guess. The warship orbited the planet at about 100,000 klicks. The supertug circled beyond the moon, twice as far out. She registered dark and cool on what instruments Dorcas carried; nobody aboard. Terminating deceleration, the woman approached.

What a sight! A vast, brilliant spheroid with flanges like convulsed meridians; drive units projecting within a shielding sheath; no ports, but receptors from which visuals were transmitted inboard; recesses for instruments; circular hatches which must cover steam vents; larger doors to receive crushed ice— How did you get in? Dorcas flitted in search. She could do it almost as smoothly as if she were flying a manwing through atmosphere.

There—an unmistakable airlock— She was prepared to cut her way in, but when she had identified the controls, the valves opened and shut for her. Who worries about burglars in space? To the kzinti, *Rover* was the bait that might draw humans.

The interior was dark. Diffusion of her flashbeam, as well as a gauge on her left knee, showed full pressure was maintained. Hers wasn't quite identical; she equalized before shoving back her faceplate. The air was cold and smelled musty. Pumps muttered.

Afloat in weightlessness, she began her exploration. She'd never been in a kzin ship before. But she had studied descriptions; and the laws of nature are the same everywhere, and man and kzin aren't terribly unlike—they can actually eat each other; and she could decipher most labels; so she could piecemeal trace things out, figure how they worked, even in a vessel as unusual as this.

She denied herself haste. If the crew arrived before she was done, she'd try ambushing them. There was no point in this job unless it was done right. As need arose she ate, rested, napped, adrift amidst machinery. Once she began to get a solid idea of the layout, she stripped it. Supplies, motors, black boxes, whatever she didn't think she would require, she unpacked, unbolted, torched loose, and carried outside. There the grapnel field, the same force that hauled on cosmic stones, low-power now, clasped them behind the hull.

Alone though she was, the ransacking didn't actually take long. She was efficient. A hundred hours sufficed for everything.

"Very well," she said at last; and she took a pill
and accepted ten hours of REM sleep, dreams which
had been deferred. Awake again, refreshed, she nour-
ished herself sparingly, exercised, scribbled a cross
in the air and murmured, "Into Your hands—" for
unlike her husband, she believed the universe was
more than an accident.

Next came the really tricky part. Of course Bob
had wanted to handle it himself. Poor dear, he must
be in absolute torment, knowing everything that could
go wrong. She was luckier, Dorcas thought: too busy
to be afraid.

Shep's flickering radar peeks had gotten fair-to-
middling readings on an object that must be the kzin
warship. Its orbit was only approximately known,
and subject both to perturbation and deliberate
change. Dorcas needed exact knowledge. She must
operate indicators and computers of nonhuman work-
manship so delicately that Hraou-Captain had no
idea he was under surveillance. Thereafter she must
guess what her best tactics might be, calculate the
maneuvers, and follow through.

When the results were in: "Here goes," she said
into the hollowness around. "For you, Arthur—" and
thought briefly that if the astronomer could have
roused in his grave on Tertia, he would have re-
proved her, in his gentle fashion, for being melodra-
matic.

Sun Defier plunged.

Unburdened by tonnes of water, she made nothing of ten g's, 20, 30, you name it. Her kzin crew
must often have used the polarizer to keep from
being crushed, as Dorcas did. "Hai-ai-ai!" she screamed,
and rode her comet past the moon, amidst the stars,
to battle.

She never knew whether the beings aboard the
warship saw her coming. Things happened so fast. If
the kzinti did become aware of what was bearing
down on them, they had scant time to react. Their

computers surely told them that *Sun Defier* was no
threat, would pass close by but not collide. Some
malfunction? The kzinti would not gladly annihilate
their iron gatherer.

When the precalculated instant flashed onto a screen
before her, Dorcas punched for a sidewise thrust as
great as the hull could survive. It shuddered and
groaned around her. An instant later, the program
that she had written cut off the grapnel field.

Those masses she had painstakingly lugged outside
—they now had interception vectors, and at a distance too small for evasion. *Sun Defier* passed within
50 kilometers while objects sleeted through *Vengeful
Slasher*.

The warship burst. Armor peeled back, white-hot,
from holes punched by monstrous velocity. Missiles
floated out of shattered bays. Briefly, a frost-cloud
betokened air rushing forth into vacuum. The wreck
tumbled among fragments of itself. Starlight glinted
off the ruins. Doubtless crew remained alive in this
or that sealed compartment; but *Vengeful Slasher*
wasn't going anywhere out of orbit, ever again.

Sun Defier swooped past Secunda. Dorcas commenced braking operations, for eventual rendezvous
with her fellow humans.

21

The moon was a waste of rock, low hills, boulderfields, empty plains, here and there a crater not quite eroded away. Darkling in this light, under Sol it would have been brighter than Luna, powdered with yellow which at the bottoms of slopes had collected to form streaks or blotches. The sun threw long shadows from the west.

Against them, *Rover* shone like a beacon. Saxtorph cheered. As expected, the kzinti had left her on the hemisphere that always faced Secunda. The location was, however, not central but close to the north pole and the western edge. He wondered why. He'd spotted many locations that looked as good or better, when you had to bring down undamaged a vessel not really meant to land on anything this size.

He couldn't afford the time to worry about it. By now the warboats had surely learned of the disaster to their mother ship and were headed back at top boost. Kzinti might or might not suspect what the cause had been of their supertug running amok, but

141

they would know when *Rover* took off—in fact, would probably know when he reached the ship. Their shuttles, designed for strictly orbital work, were no threat. Their gunboats were. If *Rover* didn't get to hyperspacing distance before those overtook her, she and her crew would be *ganz kaput*.

Saxtorph passed low overhead, ascended, and played back the pictures his scanners had taken in passing. As large as she was, the ship had no landing jacks. She lay sidelong on her lateral docking grapples. That stressed her, but not too badly in a gravity less than Luna's. To compound the trickiness of descent, she had been placed just under a particularly high and steep hill. He could only set down on the opposite side. Beyond the narrow strip of flat ground on which she lay, a blotch extended several meters across the valley floor. Otherwise that floor was strewn with rocks and somewhat downward sloping toward the hill. Maybe the kzinti had chosen this site precisely because it was a bitch for him to settle on.

"I can do it, though," Saxtorph decided. He pointed at the screen. "See, a reasonably clear area about 500 meters off."

Laurinda nodded. With the boat falling free again, the white hair rippled around her delicate features.

Saxtorph applied retrothrust. For thrumming minutes he backed toward his goal. Sweat studded his face and darkened his tunic under the arms. *Smell like a billy goat, I do,* he thought fleetingly. *When we come home, I'm going to spend a week in a Japanese hot bath. Dorcas can bring me sushi. She prefers showers, cold.* —He gave himself entirely back to his work.

Contact shivered. The deck tilted. Saxtorph adjusted the jacks to level *Shep*. When he cut the engine, silence fell like a thunderclap.

He drew a long breath, unharnessed, and rose. "I can suit up faster if you help me," he told the Crashlander.

"Of course," she replied. "Not that I have much experience."

Never mind modesty. It had been impossible to maintain without occasional failures, by four people crammed inside this little hull. Laurinda had blushed all over, charmingly, when she happened to emerge from the shower cubicle as Saxtorph and Ryan came by. The quartermaster had only a pair of shorts on, which didn't hide the gallant reflex. Yet nobody ever did or said anything improper, and the girl overcame her shyness. Now a part of Saxtorph enjoyed the touch of her spidery fingers, but most of him stayed focused on the business at hand.

"Forgive me for repeating what you've heard a dozen times," he said. "You are new to this kind of situation, and could forget the necessity of abiding by orders. Your job is to bring this boat back to Dorcas and Kam. That's *it*. Nothing else whatsoever. When I tell you to, you throw the main switch, and the program we've put in the autopilot will take over. I'd've automated that bit also, except rigging it would've taken time we can ill afford, and anyway, we do want some flexibility, some judgment in the control loop." Sternly: "If anything goes wrong for me, or you think anything has, whether or not I've called in, you go. The three of you must have *Shep*. The tug's fast but clumsy, impossible to make planetfall with, and only barely provisioned. Your duty is to *Shep*. Understood?"

"Yes," she said mutedly, her gaze on the task she was doing. "Besides, we have to have the boat to rescue Juan and Carita."

A sigh wrenched from Saxtorph. "I told you—" After Dorcas' flight, too few energy boxes remained to lift either of them into orbit. *Shep* could hover on her drive at low altitude while they flitted up, but she wasn't built for planetary rescue work, the thrusters weren't heavily enough shielded externally, at such a boost their radiation would be lethal.

Neither meek nor defiant, Laurinda replied, "I know. But after we've taken *Rover* to the right distance, why can't she wait, ready to flee, till the boat comes back from Prima?"

"Because the boat never would."

"The kzinti can land safely."

"More or less safely. They don't like to, remember. Sure, I can tell you how they do it. Obvious. They put detachable footpads on their jacks. The stickum may or may not be able to grab hold of, say, fluorosilicone, but if it does, it'll take a while to eat its way through. When the boat's ready to leave, she sheds those footpads."

"Of course. I've been racking my brain to comprehend why we can't do the same for *Shep*."

The pain in her voice and in himself brought anger into his. "God damn it, we're spacers, not sorcerers! Groundsiders think a spacecraft is a hunk of metal you can cobble anything onto, like a car. She isn't. She's about as complex and interconnected as your body is. A few milligrams of blood clot or of the wrong chemical will bring your body to a permanent halt. A spacecraft's equally vulnerable. I am *not* going to tinker with ours, light-years from any proper workshop. I am not. That's final!"

Her face bent downward from his. He heard her breath quiver.

"I'm sorry, dear," he added, softly once more. "I'm sorrier than you believe, maybe sorrier than you can imagine. Those are my crewfolk down and doomed. Oh, if we had time to plan and experiment and carefully test, sure, I'd try it. What should the footpads be made of? What size? How closely machined? How detached—explosive bolts, maybe? We'd have to wire those and—Laurinda, we won't have the time. If I lift *Rover* off within the next hour or two, we can pick up Dorcas and Kam, boost, and fly dark. If we're lucky, the kzin warboats won't detect us. But our margin is razor thin. We don't have the days or weeks your idea needs. *Fido*'s people don't either; their own time has gotten short. I'm sorry, dear."

She looked up. He saw tears in the ruby eyes, down the snowy cheeks. But she spoke still more quietly than he, with the briefest of little smiles. "No harm in asking, was there? I understand. You've told me what I was trying to deny I knew. You are a good man, Robert."

"Aw," he mumbled, and reached to rumple her hair.

The suiting completed, he took her hands between his gloves for a moment, secured a toolpack between his shoulders where the drive unit usually was, and cycled out.

The land gloomed silent around him. Nearing the horizon, the red sun looked bigger than it was. So did the planet, low to the southeast, waxing close to half phase. He could make out a dust storm as a deeper-brown blot on the fulvous crescent. Away from either luminous body, stars were visible—and yonder brilliancy must be Quarta. How joyously they had sailed past it.

Saxtorph started for his ship, in long low-gravity bounds. He didn't want to fly. The kzinti might have planted a boobytrap, such as an automatic gun that would lock on, track, and fire if you didn't radio the password. Afoot, he was less of a target.

The ground lightened as he advanced, for the yellow dust lay thicker. No, he saw, it was not actually dust in the sense of small solid particles, but more like spatters or films of liquid. Evidently it didn't cling to things, like that horrible stuff on Prima. A ghostly rain from space, it would slip from higher to lower places; in the course of gigayears, even cosmic rays would give some slight stirring to help it along downhill. It might be fairly deep near the ship, where its surface was like a blot. He'd better approach with care. Maybe it would prove necessary to fetch a drive unit and flit across.

Saxtorph's feet went out from under him. He fell slowly, landed on his butt. With an oath he started to get up. His soles wouldn't grip. His hands skidded on slickness. He sprawled over onto his back. And he was gliding down the slope of the valley floor, gliding down toward the amber-colored blot.

He flailed, kicked up dust, but couldn't stop. The damned ground had no friction, none. He passed a boulder and managed to throw an arm around. For an instant he was checked, then it rolled and began to descend with him.

"Laurinda, I have a problem," he managed to say into his radio. "Sit tight. Watch close. If this turns out to be serious, obey your orders."

He reached the blot. It gave way. He sank into its depths.

He had hoped it was a layer of just a few centimeters, but it closed over his head and still he sank. A pit where the stuff had collected from the heights— maybe the kzinti, taking due care, had dumped some extra in, gathered across a wide area—yes, this was very likely their boobytrap, and if they had ghosts, Hraou-Captain's must be yowling laughter. Odd how that name came back to him as he tumbled.

Bottom. He lay in blindness, fighting to curb his breath and heartbeat. How far down? Three meters, four? Enough to bury him for the next several billion years, unless— "Hello, *Shep*. Laurinda, do you read me? Do you read me?"

His earphones hummed. The wavelength he was using should have expanded its front from the top of the pit, but the material around him must be screening it. Silence outside his suit was as thick as the blackness.

Let's see if he could climb out. The side wasn't vertical. The stuff resisted his movements less than water would. He felt arms and legs scrabble to no avail. He could feel irregularities in the stone but he could not get a purchase on any. Well, could he swim? He tried. No. He couldn't rise off the bottom. Too high a mean density compared to the medium; and it didn't allow him even as much traction as water, it yielded to every motion, he might as well have tried to swim in air.

If he'd brought his drive unit, maybe it could have lifted him out. He wasn't sure. It was for use in space. This fluid might clog it or ooze into circuitry that there had never been any reason to seal tight. Irrelevant anyway, when he'd left it behind.

"My boy," he said, "it looks like you've had the course."

That was a mistake. The sound seemed to flap around in the cage of his helmet. If he was trapped, he shouldn't dwell on it. That way lay screaming panic.

He forced himself to lie quiet and think. How long till Laurinda took off? By rights, she should have already. If he did escape the pit, he'd be alone on the moon. Naturally, he'd try to get at *Rover* in some different fashion, such as coming around on the hillside. But meanwhile Dorcas would return in *Shep*, doubtless with the other two. She was incapable of cutting and running, off into futility. Chances were, though, that by the time she got here a kzin auxiliary or two would have arrived. The odds against her would be long indeed.

So if Saxtorph found a way to return topside and repossess *Rover*—soon—he wouldn't likely find his wife at the asteroid. And he couldn't very well turn back and try to make contact, because of those warboats and because of his overriding obligation to carry the warning home. He'd have to conn the ship all by himself, leaving Dorcas behind for the kzinti.

The thought was strangling. Tears stung. That was a relief, in the nullity everywhere around. Something he could feel, and taste the salt of on his lips.

Was the tomb blackness thickening? No, couldn't be. How long had he lain buried? He brought his time-piece to his faceplate, but the hell-stuff blocked off luminosity. The blood in his ears hammered against a wall of stillness. Had a whine begun to modulate the rasping of his breath? Was he going crazy? Sensory deprivation did bring on illusions, weirdnesses, but he wouldn't have expected it this soon.

He made himself remember—sunlight, stars, Dorcas, a sail above blue water, fellowship among men, Dorcas, the tang of a cold beer, Dorcas, their plans for children—they'd banked gametes against the day they'd be ready for domesticity but maybe a little too old and battered in the DNA for direct begetting to be advisable—

Contact ripped him out of his dreams. He reached wildly and felt his gloves close on a solid object. They slid along it, along humanlike lineaments, a spacesuit, no, couldn't be!

Laurinda slithered across him till she brought face-plate to faceplate. Through the black he recognized the voice that conduction carried: "Robert, thank God, I'd begun to be afraid I'd never find you, are you all right?"

"What the, the devil are you doing here?" he gasped.

Laughter crackled. "Fetching you. Yes, mutiny. Court-martial me later."

Soberness followed: "I have a cable around my waist, with the end free for you. Feel around till you find it. There's a lump at the end, a knot I made beforehand and covered with solder so the buckyballs can't get in and make it work loose. You can use that to make a hitch that will hold for yourself, can't you? Then I'll need your help. I have two geologist's hammers with me. Secured them by cords so they can't be lost. Wrapped tape around the handles in thick bands, to give a grip in spite of no friction. Used the pick ends to chip notches in the rock, and hauled myself along. But I'm exhausted now, and it's an uphill pull, even though gravity is weak. Take the hammers. Drag me along behind you. You have the strength."

"The strength—oh, my God, you talk about *my* strength?" he cried.

—The cable was actually heavy-gauge wire from the electrical parts locker, lengths of it spliced together till they reached. The far end was fastened around a great boulder beyond the treacherous part of the slope. Slipperiness had helped as well as hindered the ascent, but when he reached safety, Saxtorph allowed himself to collapse for a short spell.

He returned to Laurinda's earnest tones: "I can't tell you how sorry I am. I should have guessed. But it didn't occur to me—such quantities gathered together like this—I simply thought 'nebular dust,' without stopping to estimate what substance would become dominant over many billions of years—"

He sat straight to look at her. In the level red light, her face was palely rosy, her eyes afire. "Why, how could you have foreseen, lass?" he answered. "I'd hate to tell you how often something in space has taken me by surprise, and that was in familiar parts. You did realize what the problem was, and figured out a solution. We needn't worry about your breaking orders. If you'd failed, you'd have been insubordinate; but you succeeded, so by definition you showed initiative."

"Thank you." Eagerness blazed. "And listen, I've had another idea—"

He lifted a palm. "Whoa! Look, in a couple of minutes we'd better hike back to *Shep*, you take your station again, I get a drive unit and fly across to *Rover*. But first will you please, please tell me what the mess was that I got myself into?"

"Buckyballs," she said. "Or, formally, buckminsterfullerene. I didn't think the pitful of that you'd slid down into could be very deep or the bottom very

large. Its walls would surely slope inward. It's really
just a . . . pothole, though surely the formation process was different, possibly it's a small astrobleme—"
She giggled. "My, the academic in me is really taking over, isn't it? Well, essentially, the material is
frictionless. It will puddle in any hole, no matter
how tiny, and it has just enough cohesion that a
number of such puddles close together will form a
film over the entire surface. But that film is only a
few molecules thick, and you can't walk on it or
anything. In this slight gravity, though—and the metal-
poor rock is friable—I could strike the sharp end of a
hammerhead in with a single blow to act as a kind of
. . . piton, is that the word?"

"Okay. Splendid. Dorcas had better look to her
standing as the most formidable woman in known
space. Now tell me what the—the hell buckyballs
are."

"They're produced in the vicinity of supernovae.
Carbon atoms link together and form a faceted spheri-
cal molecule around a single metal atom. Sixty car-
bons around one lanthanum is common, galactically
speaking, but there are other forms, too. And with
the molecule closed in on itself the way it is, it acts
in the aggregate like a fluid. In fact, it's virtually a
perfect lubricant, and if we didn't have things easier
to use you'd see synthetic buckyballs on sale everywhere." A vision rose in those ruby eyes. "It's thought
they may have a basic role in the origin of life on
planets—"

"Damn near did the opposite number today,"
Saxtorph said. "But you saved my ass, and the rest of
me as well. I don't suppose I can ever repay you."

She got to her knees before him and seized his
hands. "You can, Robert. You can fetch me back my
man."

22

Ponderously, *Rover* closed velocities with the iron asteroid. She couldn't quite match, because it was under boost, but thus far the acceleration was low.

Ominously aglow, the molten mass dwarfed the spacecraft that toiled meters ahead of it; yet *Sun Defier*, harnessed by her own forcefield, was a plowhorse dragging it bit by bit from its former path; and the dwarf sun was at work, and Secunda's gravity was beginning to have a real effect. . . .

Arrived a little before the ship, the boat drifted at some distance, a needle in a haystack of stars. Laurinda was still aboard. The tug had no place to receive *Shep*, nor had the girl the skill to cross safely by herself in a spacesuit even though relative speeds were small. The autopilot kept her accompanying the others.

In *Rover*'s command center, Saxtorph asked the image of Dorcas, more shakily than he had expected to, "How are you? How's everything?"

She was haggard with weariness, but triumph rang:

"Kam's got our gear packed to transfer over to you, and I—I've worked the bugs out of the program. Compatibility with kzin hardware was a stumbling block, but—Well, it's been operating smoothly for the past several hours, and I've no reason to doubt it will continue doing what it's supposed to."

He whistled. "Hey, quite a feat, lady! I really didn't think it would be possible, at least in the time available, when I put you up to trying it. What're you going to do next—square the circle, invent the perpetual motion machine, reform the tax laws, or what?"

Her voice grew steely. "I was motivated." She regarded his face in her own screen. "How are you? Laurinda said something about your running into danger on the moon. Were you hurt?"

"Only in my pride. She can tell you all about it later. Right now we're in a hurry." Saxtorph became intent. "Listen, there's been a change of plan. You and Kam both flit over to *Shep*. But don't you bring her in; lay her alongside. Kam can help Laurinda aboard *Rover* before he moves your stuff. I'd like you to join me in a job around *Shep*. Simple thing and shouldn't take but a couple hours, given the two of us working together. Though I'll bet even money you'll have a useful suggestion or three. Then you can line out for deep space."

She sat a moment silent, her expression bleakened, before she said, "You're taking the boat to Prima while the rest of us ferry *Rover* away."

"You catch on quick, sweetheart."

"To rescue Juan and Carita."

"What else? Laurinda's hatched a scheme I think could do the trick. Naturally, we'll agree in advance where you'll wait, and *Shep* will come join you there. If we don't dawdle, the odds are pretty good that the kzinti won't locate you first and force you to go hyperspatial."

"What about them locating you?"

"Why should they expect anybody to go to Prima? They'll buzz around Secunda like angry hornets. They may well be engaged for a while in evacuating survivors from the warship; I suspect the shuttles aren't terribly efficient at that sort of thing. Afterward they'll have to work out a search doctrine, when *Rover* can have skitted in any old direction. And sometime along about then, they should have their minds taken off us. The kzinti will notice a nice big surprise bound their way, about which it is then too late to do anything whatsoever."

"But you— How plausible is this idea of yours?"

"Plausible enough. Look, don't sit like that. Get cracking. I'll explain when we meet."

"I can take *Shep*. I'm as good a pilot as you are."

Saxtorph shook his head. "Sorry, no. One of us has to be in charge of *Rover*, of course. I hereby pull rank and appoint you. I am the captain."

23

The asteroid concealed the ship's initial boost from any possible observers around Secunda. She applied her mightiest vector to give southward motion, out of the ecliptic plane; but the thrust had an extra component, randomly chosen, to baffle hunter analysts who would fain reduce the volume of space wherein she might reasonably be sought. That volume would grow fast, become literally astronomical, as she flew free, generator cold, batteries maintaining life support on a minimum energy level. Having thus cometed for a time, she could with fair safety apply power again to bring herself to her destination.

Saxtorph let her make ample distance before he accelerated *Shep*, also using the iron to conceal his start. However, he ran at top drive the whole way. It wasn't likely that a detector would pick his little craft up. As he told Dorcas, the kzinti wouldn't suppose a human would make for Prima. It hurt them less, losing friends, provided the friends died bravely; and few of them had mastered the art of putting oneself in the head of an enemy.

Mainly, though, Carita and Juan didn't have much time left them.

Ever circling, the planets had changed configuration since *Rover* arrived. The navigation system allowed for that, but could do nothing to shorten a run of 30-odd hours. Saxtorph tried to compose his soul in peace. He played a lot of solitaire after he found he was losing most of the computer games, and smoked a lot of pipes. Books and shows were poor distraction, but music helped him relax and enjoy his memories. Whatever happened next, he'd have had a better life than 90 percent of his species—99 percent if you counted in everybody who lived and died before humankind went spacefaring.

Prima swelled in his view, sallow and faceless. The recorded broadcast came through clear from the night side, over and over. Saxtorph got his fix. *Fido* wasn't too far from the lethal dawn. He established a three-hour orbit and put a curt message of his own on the player. It ended with "Acknowledge."

Time passed. Heaviness grew within him. Were they dead? He rounded dayside and came back across darkness.

The voice leaped at him: "Bob, is that you? Juan here. We'd abandoned hope, we were asleep. Standing by now. Bob, is that you? Juan here—"

Joy surged. "Who else but me?" Saxtorph said. "How're you doing, you two?"

"Hanging on. Living in our spacesuits this past—I don't know how long. The boat's a rotted, crumbling shell. But we're hanging on."

"Good. Your drive units in working order?"

"Yes. But we haven't the lift to get onto a trajectory which you can match long enough for us to come aboard." Unspoken: It would be easy in atmosphere, or in free space, given a pilot like you. But what a vessel can do above an airless planet, at suborbital speed, without coming to grief, is sharply limited.

"That's all right," Saxtorph said, "as long as you can go outside, sit in a lock chamber or on top of the wreck, and keep watch, without danger of slipping off into the muck. You can? . . . Okay, prepare yourselves. I'll land in view of you and open the main personnel lock."

"Hadn't we better all find an area free of the material?"

"I'm not sure any exists big enough and flat enough for me. Anyhow, looking for one would take more time than we can afford. No, I'm coming straight down."

Carita cut in. She sounded wrung out. Saxtorph suspected her physical strength was what had preserved both. He imagined her manhandling pieces of metal and plastic, often wrenched from the weakened structure, to improvise braces, platforms, whatever would give some added hours of refuge. "Bob, is this wise?" she asked. "Do you know what you're getting into? The molecule might bind you fast immediately, even if you avoid shining light on it. The decay here is going quicker all the while. I think the molecule is . . . learning. Don't risk your life."

"Don't you give your captain orders," Saxtorph replied. "I'll be down in, m-m, about an hour. Then get to me as fast as you prudently can. Every minute we spend on the surface does add to the danger. But I've put bandits on the jacks."

"What?"

"Footpads," he laughed childishly. "Okay, no more conversation till we're back in space. I've got my reconnoitering to do."

Starlight was brilliant but didn't illuminate an unknown terrain very well. His landing field would be minute and hemmed in. For help he had optical amplifiers, radar, data-analysis programs which projected visuals as well as numbers. He had his skill.

Fear shunted from his mind, he became one with the boat.

Location . . . identification . . . positioning; you don't float around in airlessness the way you can in atmosphere . . . site picked, much closer to *Fido* than he liked but he could manage . . . coordinates established . . . down, down, nurse her down to touchdown. . . .

It was as soft a landing as he had ever achieved. It needed to be.

For a pulsebeat he stared across the hollow at the other boat. She was a ghastly sight indeed, a half-hull pocked, ragged, riddled, the pale devourer well up the side of what was left. Good thing he was insured; though multi-billionaire Stefan Brozik would be grateful, and presumably human governments—

Saxtorph grinned at his own inanity and hastened to go operate the airlock. Or was it stupid to think about money at an hour like this? To hell with heroics. He and Dorcas had their living to make.

Descent with the outer valve already open would have given him an imbalance: slight, but he had plenty else to contend with. He cracked it now without stopping to evacuate the chamber. Time was more precious than a few cubic meters of air. A light flashed green. His crewfolk were in. He closed the valve at once. A measure of pressure equalization was required before he admitted them into the hull proper. He did so the instant it was possible. A wind gusted by. His ears popped. Juan and Carita stumbled through. Frost formed on their spacesuits.

He hand-signalled: Grab hold. We're boosting right away.

He could be gentle about that, as well as quick.

Or need he have hastened? Afterward he inspected things at length and found Laurinda's idea had worked as well as could have been hoped, or maybe a little better.

Buckyballs scooped from that sink on the moon.

(An open container at the end of a line; he could throw it far in the low gravity.) Bags fashioned out of thick plastic, heat-sealed together, filled with buckyballs, placed around the bottom of each landing jack, superglued fast at the necks. That was all.

The molecule had only eaten through one of them while *Shep* stood on Prima. Perhaps the other jacks rested on sections where most of the chemical bonds were saturated, less readily catalyzed. It didn't matter, except scientifically, because after the single bag gave way, the wonderful stuff had done its job. A layer of it was beneath the metal, a heap of it around. The devourer could not quickly incorporate atoms so strongly interlinked. As it did, more flowed in to fill the gaps. *Shep* could have stayed for hours.

But she had no call to. Lifting, the tension abruptly off him, Saxtorph exploded into tuneless song. It wasn't a hymn or anthem, though it was traditional, "The Bastard King of England." Somehow it felt right.

24

Rover drove though hyperspace, homeward bound.

Man and wife sat together in their cabin, easing off. They were flesh, they would need days to get back the strength they had spent. The ship throbbed and whispered. A screen gave views of Hawaii, heights, greennesses, incredible colors on the sea. Beethoven's Fifth lilted in the background. He had a mug of beer, she a glass of white wine.

"Honeymoon cruise," she said with a wry smile. "Laurinda and Juan. Carita and Kam."

"You and me, for that matter," he replied drowsily.

"But when will we get any proper work done? The interior is a mess."

"Oh, we've time aplenty before we reach port. And if we aren't quite holystoned-perfect, who's going to care?"

"Yes, we'll be the sensation of the day." She grew somber. "How many will remember Arthur Tregennis?"

Saxtorph roused. "Our kind of people will. He was

. . . a Moses. He brought us to a scientific Promised Land, and . . . I think there'll be more explorations into the far deeps from now on."

"Yes. Markham's out of the way." Dorcas sighed. "His poor family."

The tug, rushing off too fast for recovery after it released the asteroid to hurtle toward Secunda—if all went as planned, straight at the base— Horror, a scramble to flee, desperate courage, and then the apparition in heaven, the flaming trail, Thor's hammer smites, the cloud of destruction engulfs everything and rises on high and spreads to darken the planet, nothing remains but a doubled crater plated with iron. It was unlikely that any kzinti who escaped would still be alive when their next starship came.

At the end, did Markham cry for his mother?

"And of course humans will be alerted to the situation," Saxtorph observed superfluously.

It was, in fact, unlikely that there would be more kzin ships to the red sun. Nothing was left for them, and they would get no chance to rebuild. Earth would have sent an armed fleet for a look-around. Maybe it would come soon enough to save what beings were left.

Dorcas frowned. "What will they do about it?"

"Why, uh, rebuild our navies. Defense has been grossly neglected."

"Well, we can hope for that much. We're certainly doing a service, bringing in the news that the kzinti have the hyperdrive." Dorcas shook her head. "But everybody knew they would, sooner or later. And this whole episode, it's no *casus belli*. No law forbade them to establish themselves in an unclaimed system. We should be legally safe, ourselves—self-defense—but the peace groups will say the kzinti were only being defensive, after Earth's planet grab following the war, and in fact this crew provoked them into overreacting. There may be talk of reparations due the pathetic put-upon kzinti."

"Yah, you're probably right. I share your faith in the infinite capacity of our species for wishful thinking." Saxtorph shrugged. "But we also have a capacity for muddling through. And you and I, sweetheart, have some mighty good years ahead of us. Let's talk about what to do with them."

Her mood eased. She snuggled close. The ship fared onward.

INCONSTANT STAR

1

A hunter's wind blew down off the Mooncatcher Mountains and across the Rungn Valley. Night filled with the sounds of it, rustling forest, remote animal cries, and with odors of soil, growth, beast. The wish that it roused, to be yonder, to stalk and pounce and slay and devour, grew in Weoch-Captain until he trembled. The fur stood up on him. Claws slid out of their sheaths; fingers bent into the same saber curves. He had long been deprived.

Nonetheless he walked steadily onward from the guard point. When Ress-Chiuu, High Admiral of Kzin, summoned, one came. That was not in servility but in hope, fatal though laggardness would be. Something great was surely afoot. It might even prove warlike.

Eastward stretched rangeland, wan beneath the stars. Westward, ahead, the woods loomed darkling, the game preserve part of Ress-Chiuu's vast domain. Far and high beyond glimmered snowpeaks. The chill that the wind also bore chastened bit by bit the lust in Weoch-Captain. Reason fought its way back. He reached the Admiral's lair with the turmoil no more than a drumbeat in his blood.

The castle remembered axes, arrows, and spears. Later generations had made their changes and additions but kept it true to itself, a stony mass baring battlements at heaven. After an electronic gate identified and admitted him, the portal through which he passed was a tunnel wherein he moved blind. Primitive instincts whispered, "Beware!" He ignored them. Guided by echoes and subtle tactile sensations, his pace never slackened. Ress-Chiuu always tested a visitor, one way or another.

Was it a harder test that waited in the courtyard? No kzin received Weoch-Captain. Instead hulked a kdatlyno slave. It made the clumsy gesture that was as close as the species could come to a prostration. However, then it turned and lumbered toward the main keep. Obviously he was expected to follow.

Rage blazed in him. Almost, he attacked. He choked emotion down and stalked after his guide, though lips remained pulled off fangs.

Echoes whispered. Corridors and rooms lay deserted. Night or no, personnel should have been in evidence. What did it portend? Alertness heightened, wariness, combat readiness.

A door slid aside. The kdatlyno groveled again and departed. Weoch-Captain went in. The door closed behind him.

The room was polished granite, austerely furnished. A window stood open to the wind. Ress-Chiuu reclined on a slashtooth skin draped over a couch. Weoch-Captain came to attention and presented himself. "At ease," the High Admiral said. "You may sit, stand, or pace as you wish. I expect you will, from time to time, pace."

Weoch-Captain decided to stay on his feet for the nonce.

Ress-Chiuu's deceptively soft tones went on: "Realize that I have offered you no insult. You were met by a slave because, at least for the present, extreme confidentiality is necessary. Furthermore, I require not only a Hero—they are many—but one who possesses an unusual measure of self-control and forethoughtfulness. I had reason to believe you do. You have shown I was right. Praise and honor be yours."

The accolade calmed Weoch-Captain's pride. It also focused his mind the more sharply. (Doubtless that was intended, said a part of his mind with a wryness rare in kzinti.) His ears rose and unfolded. "I have delegated my current duties and am instantly available for the High Admiral's orders," he reported.

Shadows dappled fur as the blocky head nodded approval. "We go straight to the spoor, then. You know of Werlith-Commandant's mission on the opposite side of human-hegemony space." It was not a question. "Ill tidings: lately a human crew stumbled upon the base that was under construction there. They came to investigate the sun, which appears to be unique in several ways."

Monkey curiosity, thought Weoch-Captain. He was slightly too young to have fought in the war, but he had spent his life hearing about it, studying it, dreaming of the next one. His knowledge included terms of scorn evolved among kzinti who had learned random things about the planet where the enemy originated.

Ress-Chiuu's level words smote him: "Worse, much worse. Incredibly, they seem to have destroyed the installations. Certain is that they inflicted heavy casualties, disabled our spacecraft, and went home nearly unscathed. You perceive what this means. They conveyed the information that we have developed the hyperdrive ourselves. All chance of springing a surprise is gone." Sarcasm harshened the voice. "No doubt the Patriarchy will soon receive 'representations' from Earth about this 'unfortunate incident.' "

Over the hyperwave, said Weoch-Captain's mind bleakly. Those few black boxes that the peace treaty provided for, left among us, engineered to self-destruct at the least tampering.

Well did he know. Such an explosion had killed a brother of his.

Understanding leaped. If the humans had not yet communicated officially—"May I ask how the Patriarchs learned?"

"We have our means. I will consider what to tell you." Ress-Chiuu's calm was giving way ever so little. His tail lashed his thighs, a pink whip. "We must find out exactly what happened. Or, if nothing else, we must establish what the situation is, whether anything of our base remains, what the Earth Navy is doing there. Survivors should be rescued. If this is impossible, perhaps they can be eliminated by rays or missiles before they fall into human grasp."

"Heroes—"

"Would never betray our secrets. Yes, yes. But can you catalogue every trick those creatures may possess?" Ress-Chiuu lifted head and shoulders. His eyes locked with Weoch-Captain's. "You will command our ship to that sun."

Disaster or no, eagerness flamed. "Sire!"

"Slow, slow," the older kzin growled. "We require an officer intelligent as well as bold, capable of agreeing that the destiny of the race transcends his own, and indeed, to put it bluntly—" he paused—"one who is not *afraid* to cut and run, should the alternative be valiant failure. Are you prepared for this?"

Weoch-Captain relaxed from his battle crouch and, inwardly, tautened further. "The High Admiral has bestowed a trust on me," he said. "I accept."

"It is well. Come, sit. This will be a long night."

They talked, and ransacked databases, and ran tentative plans through the computers, until dawn whitened the east. Finally, almost jovially, Ress-Chiuu asked, "Are you exhausted?"

"On the contrary, sire, I think I have never been more fightworthy."

"You need to work that off and get some rest. Besides, you have earned a pleasure. You may go into my forest and make a bare-handed kill."

When Weoch-Captain came back out at noontide, jaws still dripping red, he felt tranquil, happy, and, once he had slept, ready to conquer a cosmos.

2

The sun was an hour down and lights had come aglow along streets, but at this time of these years Alpha Centauri B was still aloft. Low in the west, like thousands of evening stars melted into one, it cast shadows the length of Karl-Jorge Avenue and set the steel steeple of St. Joachim's ashimmer against an eastern sky purpling into dusk. Vehicles and pedestrians alike were sparse, the city's pulsebeat quieted to a murmur through mild summer air—day's work ended, night's pleasures just getting started. Munchen had changed more in the past decade or two than most places on Wunderland. Commercial and cultural as well as political center, it was bound to draw an undue share of outworlders and their influence. Yet it still lived largely by the rhythms of the planet.

Robert Saxtorph doubted that that would continue through his lifetime. Let him enjoy it while it lasted. Traditions gave more color to existence than did any succession of flashy fashions.

He honored one by tipping his cap to the Liberation Memorial as he crossed the Silberplatz. Though the sculpture wasn't old and the events had taken place scarcely a generation ago, they stood in history with Marathon and Yorktown. Leaving the square, he sauntered up the street past a variety of shop windows. His destination, Harold's Terran Bar, had a certain venerability, too. And he was bound there to meet a beautiful woman with something mysterious to tell him. Another tradition, of sorts?

At the entrance, he paused. His grin going sour, he well-nigh said to hell with it and turned around. Tyra Nordbo should not have made him promise to keep this secret even from his wife, before she set the rendezvous. Nor should she have picked Harold's. He hadn't cared to patronize it since visit before last. Now the very sign that floated luminous before the brown brick wall had been expurgated. *A World On Its Own* remained below the name, but *humans only* was gone. Mustn't offend potential customers or, God forbid, local idealists.

In Saxtorph's book, courtesy was due everyone who hadn't forfeited the right. However, under the kzinti occupation that motto had been a tiny gesture of defiance. Since the war, no sophont that could pay was denied admittance. But onward with the bulldozer of blandness.

He shrugged. Having come this far, let him proceed. Time enough to leave if la Nordbo turned out to be a celebrity hunter or a vibrobrain. The fact was that she had spoken calmly, and about money. Besides, he'd enjoyed watching her image. He went on in. Nowadays the door opened for anybody.

As always, a large black man occupied the vestibule, wearing white coat and bow tie. What had once made some sense had now become mere costume. His eyes widened at the sight of the newcomer, as big as him, with the craggy features and thinning reddish hair. "Why, Captain Saxtorph!" he exclaimed in fluent English. "Welcome, sir. No, for you, no entry fee."

They had never met. "I'm on private business," Saxtorph warned.

"I understand, sir. If somebody bothers you, give me the high sign and I'll take care of them." Maybe the doorman could, overawing by sheer size if nothing else, or maybe his toughness was another part of the show. It wasn't a quality much in demand any more.

"Thanks." Saxtorph slipped him a tip and passed through a beaded curtain which might complicate signaling for the promised help, into the main room. It was dimly lit and little smoke hung about. Customers thus far were few, and most in the rear room gambling. Nevertheless a fellow at an obsolete model of musicomp was playing something ancient. Saxtorph went around the deserted sunken dance floor to the bar, chose a stool, and ordered draft Solborg from a live servitor.

He had swallowed a single mouthful of the half liter when he heard, at his left, "What, no akvavit with, and you a Dane?" The voice was husky and female; the words, English, bore a lilting accent and a hint of laughter.

He turned his head and was startled. The phone at his hotel had shown him this face, strong-boned, blunt-nosed, flaxen hair in a pageboy cut. That she was tall, easily 180 centimeters, gave no surprise; she was a Wunderlander. But she lacked the ordinary low-gravity lankiness. Robust and full-bosomed, she looked and moved as if she had grown up on Earth, nearly two-thirds again as heavy as here. That meant rigorous training and vigorous sports throughout her life. And the changeable sea-blue of her slacksuit matched her eyes. . . .

"American, really. My family moved from Denmark when I was small. And I'd better keep a clear head, right?" His tongue was speaking for him. Angry at himself, he took control back. "How do you do." He offered his hand. Her clasp was firm, cool, brief. At least she wasn't playing sultry or exotic. "Uh, care for a drink?"

"I have one yonder. Please to follow." She must have arrived early and waited for him. He picked up his beer and accompanied her to a privacy-screened table. Murky though the corner was, he could make out fine lines at the corners of her eyes and lips; and that fair skin had known much weather. She wasn't quite young, then. Late thirties, Earth calendar, he guessed.

They settled down. Her glass held white wine. She had barely sipped of it. "Thank you for that you came," she said. "I realize this is peculiar."

Well, shucks, he resisted admitting, I may be seven or eight years older than you and solidly married, but any wench this sightly rates a chance to make sense. "It is an odd place to meet," he countered.

She smiled. "I thought it would be appropriate."

He declined the joke. "Over-appropriate."

"Ja, saa?" The blond brows lifted. "How so?"

"I never did like staginess," he blurted. His hand waved around. "I knew this joint when it was a raffish den full of memories from the occupation and the tag-end of wartime afterward. But each time I called at Wunderland and dropped in, it'd become more of a tourist trap."

"Well, those old memories are romantic; and, yes, some of mine live here, too," she murmured. Turning straightforward again: "But it has an advantage, exactly because of what it now is. Few of its patrons will have heard about you. They are, as you say, mostly tourists. News like your deeds at that distant star is sensational but it takes a while to cross interstellar space and hit hard in public awareness on planets where the societies are different from yours or mine. Here, at this hour of the day, you have a good chance of not being recognized and pestered. Also, because people here often make assignations, it is the custom to ignore other couples."

Saxtorph felt his cheeks heat up. What the devil! The schoolboy he had once been lay long and deeply buried. Or so he'd supposed. It would be a ghost he could well do without. "Is that why you didn't want my wife along?" he asked roughly.

She nodded. "You two together are especially conspicuous, no? I found that yesterday evening she would be away, and thought you would not. Then I tried calling you."

He couldn't repress a chuckle. "Yah, you guessed right. Poor Dorcas, she had no escape from addressing a meeting of the *Weibliche Astroverein*." He'd looked forward to several peaceful hours alone. But when the phone showed this face, he'd accepted the call, which he probably would not have done otherwise. "After she got back, I took her down to the bar for a stiff drink." But he'd kept his promise not to mention the conversation. Half ashamed, he harshened his tone. "Why'd you do no more than talk me into a, uh, an appointment?" He hadn't liked telling Dorcas that he meant to go for a walk, might stop in at some pub, and if he found company he enjoyed— male, she'd taken for granted—would maybe return late. But he'd done it. "Could you not have gone directly to the point? The line wasn't tapped, was it?"

"I did not expect so," Tyra answered. "Yet it was possible. Perhaps a government official who is snoopish. You have legal and diplomatic complications left over, from what happened at the dwarf star."

Don't I know it, Saxtorph sighed to himself.

"There could even be undiscovered kzinti agents like Markham, trying for extra information that will help them or their masters," she continued. "You are marked, Captain. And in a way, that I am also."

"Why the secrecy?" he persisted. "Understand, I am not interested in anything illegal."

"This is not." She laid hold of her glass. Fingers grew white-nailed on its stem, and trembled the least bit. "It is, well, extraordinary. Perhaps dangerous."

"Then my wife and crew have got to know before *we* decide."

"Of course. First I ask you. If you say no, that is an end of the matter for you, and I must try elsewhere. I will have small hope. But if you agree, and your shipmates do, best that we hold secret. Otherwise certain parties—they will not want this mission, or they will want it carried out in a way that gives my cause no help. We present them a *fait accompli*. Do you see?"

Likewise tense, he gulped at his beer. "Uh, mind if I smoke?"

"Do." The edges of her mouth dimpled. "That pipe of yours has become famous like you."

"Or infamous." He fumbled briar, pouch, and lighter out of their pockets. Anxious to slack things off: "The vice is disapproved of again on Earth, did you know? As if cancer and emphysema and the rest still existed. I think puritanism runs in cycles. One periodicity for tobacco, one for alcohol, one for—Ah, hell, I'm babbling."

"I believe men smoke much on Wunderland because it is a symbol," she said. "From the occupation era. Kzinti do not smoke. They dislike the smell and seldom allowed it in their presence. I grew up used to it on men." She laughed. "See, I can babble, too." Lifting her glass: "*Skaal.*"

He touched his mug to it, repeating the word before remembering, in surprise: "Wait, you people generally say, '*Prosit*,' don't you?"

"They were mostly Scandinavians who settled in Skogarna," Tyra explained. "We have our own dialect. Some call it a patois."

"Really? I'd hardly imagine that was possible in this day and age."

"We were always rather isolated, there in the North. Under the occupation, more than ever. Kzinti, or the collaborationist government, monitored all traffic and communications. Few people had wide contacts, and those were very guarded. They drew into their neighborhoods. Keeping language and customs alive, that was one way they reminded themselves that humans were not everywhere and forever slaves of the ratcats." Speaking, Tyra had let somberness come upon her. "This isolation is a root of the story I must tell you."

Saxtorph wanted irrationally much to lighten her mood. "Well, shall we get to it? You'd like to charter the *Rover*, you said, for a fairly short trip. But that's all you said, except for not blanching when I gave you a cost estimate. Which, by itself, immediately got me mighty interested."

Her laugh gladdened him. "I'm in luck. Is that your American folk-word? Exactly when I need a hyperdrive ship, here you come with the only one in known space that is privately owned, and you admit you are broke. I confess I am puzzled. You took damage on your expedition—" Her voice grew soft and serious. "Besides that poor man the kzinti killed. But the harm was not else too bad, was it? And surely you have insurance, and I should think that super-rich gentleman on We Made It, Brozik, is grateful that you brought his daughter back safe."

Saxtorph tamped his pipe. "Sure. Still, losing a boat is fairly expensive. We haven't replaced *Fido* yet. Plus lesser repairs we needed, plus certain new equipment and refitting we decided have become necessary, plus the fact that insurance companies have never in history been prompt and in-full about anything except collecting their premiums. Brozik's paid us a generous bonus on the charter, yes, but we can't expect him to underwrite a marginal business like ours. His gratefulness has reasonable limits. After all, we were saving our own hides as well as

Laurinda's, and she had considerable to do with it herself. We aren't really broke, but we have gone through a big sum, on top of normal overhead expenses, and meanwhile haven't had a chance to scare up any fresh trade." He set fire to tobacco and rolled smoke across his palate. "See, I'm being completely frank with you." As he doubtless would not have been, this soon, were she homely or a man.

Again she nodded, thoughtfully. "Yes, it must be difficult, operating a tramp freighter. You compete with government lines for a market that is—marginal, you said. When each planetary system contains ample raw materials, and it is cheapest to synthesize or recycle almost everything else, what actual tonnage goes between the stars?"

"Damn little, aside from passengers, and we lack talent for catering to them." Saxtorph smiled. "Oh, it might be fun to carry nonhumans, but outfitting for it would be a huge investment, and then we'd be locked into those rounds."

"You wish to travel freely, widely. Freighting is your way to make it possible." Tyra straightened. Her voice rang. "Well, I offer you a voyage like none ever before!"

Caution awoke. He'd hate to think her dishonest. But she might be foolish—no, already he could dismiss that idea—she might be ill-informed. Planetsiders seldom had any notion of the complications in spacefaring. Physical requirements and hazards were merely the obvious ones. In addition, you had to make your nut, and avoid running afoul of several admiralty offices and countless bureaucrats, and keep every hatch battened through which the insurers might slither. "That's what we're here to talk about," Saxtorph said. "Only talk. Any promises come later."

The high spirits that evidently were normal to her sank back down. They must have been struggling against something stark. She raised her glass for a drink, gulp rather than swallow, and stared into the

wine. "My name means nothing to you, I gather,"
she began, hardly louder than the music. "I thought
you would know. You have told how you are often in
this system."

"Not that often, and I never paid much attention
to your politics. I've got a hunch that that's what this
is about." Her fingers strained together. "Yah. Politics, a disease of our species. Maybe someday they'll
develop a vaccine against it. Grind politicians up and
centrifuge the brains. Though you'd need an awful
lot of politicians per gram of brains."

A smile spooked momentarily over her lips. "But
you must have heard a great deal lately. You are now
in politics yourself."

"And working free as fast as we can, which involves declining to get into arguments. Look, we
came to Alpha Centauri originally because this is
where the Interworld Space Commission keeps headquarters, with warehouses full of stuff we'd need for
Professor Tregennis' expedition. We returned from
there to here because Commissioner Markham had
revealed himself to be a kzinti spy and we figured we
should take that news first to the top. It plunked us
into a monstrous kettle of hullaballoo. Seeing as how
we couldn't leave before the investigations and depo-
sitions and what-Godhelpus-not else were finished,
we got the work on our ship done meanwhile at
Tiamat. At last they've reluctantly agreed we didn't
break any laws except justifiably, and given us leave
to go. In between wading through that swamp of
glue and all the mostly unwanted distractions that
notoriety brought us, we kept hoping our brokers
could arrange a cargo for whenever we'd be able to
haul out. Understandably, no luck. We were pretty
much resigned to returning empty to Sol, when you—
Well, you can see why we discouraged anything,
even conversation, that might possibly have gotten
us mired deeper."

"Yes." She tensed. "I shall explain. The Nordbos belonged to the Freuchen clan."

"Hm? You mean you're of the Nineteen Families?"

"We *were*," she said in a rush, overriding the pain he heard. "Oh, of course today the special rights and obligations are mostly gone, the titles are mostly honorary, but the honor does remain. After the liberation, a court stripped his from my father and confiscated everything but his personal estate. He was not there to defend himself. The best we were able, my brother and I and a handful of loyal friends, was to save our mother from being tried for treasonable collaboration. We resigned membership in the clan before it could meet to expel her."

Saxtorph drew hard on his pipe. "You believe your father was innocent?"

"I swear he was!" Her breath went ragged. "At last I have evidence—no, a clue— A spaceship must go where he went and find the proof. Civilian hyperdrive craft are committed to their routes, and their governments control them in any case, except for yours. Our navy— My brother is an officer. He has made quiet inquiries. He actually got a naval astronomer to check that part of the sky, as a personal favor, not saying why. Nothing was found. He tells me the Navy would not dispatch a ship on the strength of a few notes that are partial at best."

And that could well have been forged by a person crazy-desperate for vindication, Saxtorph thought. She admits the instrumental search drew a blank.

Tyra had won to a steely calm. "Furthermore, thinking about it, I realized that if the Navy should go, it would be entirely in hopes of discovering something worthwhile. They would not care about the honor of Peter Nordbo, who was condemned as a traitor and is most likely long dead."

"But you have your own reputation to rescue," Saxtorph said gently.

The fair head shook. "That doesn't matter. Neither

Ib, my brother, nor I was accused of anything. In fact, at the liberation, he was among those who tried to storm the Ritterhaus where the kzinti were holding out, and was wounded. I told you, he has since become a naval officer. And I . . . helped the underground earlier, in a very small way, for I was very young then, and during the street fighting here I worked at a first aid station. *Ach*, the court said how they sympathized with us. We must have been one reason why they never formally charged my mother. That much justice got we, for she was innocent, too. She could not help what happened. But except for those few real friends, only Ib and I ever again called on her, at that lonely house on Korsness."

The musicomp man set his instrument to violin mode with orchestral backing and played a tune that Saxtorph recognized. Antique indeed, from Earth before spaceflight, sugary sentimental, yet timeless, *"Du kannst nicht treu sein."* You can't be true.

Tyra's gaze met his. "Yes, certainly we wish to rejoin the Freuchens, not as a favor but by birthright. And that would mean restoring us the holdings, or compensation for them; a modest fortune. But it doesn't matter, I say. What does is my father's good name, his honor. He was a wonderful man." Her voice deepened. "Or is? He could maybe be alive still, somewhere yonder, after all these years. Or if not, we could—maybe avenge him."

The wings of her pageboy bob stirred. He realized that she had laid her ears back, like a wolf before a foe, and she was in truth of the old stock that conquered this planet for humankind.

"Easy, there," he said hastily. "*Rover's* civilian, remember. Unarmed."

"She should carry weapons. Since you discovered the kzinti have the hyperdrive—"

"Yah. Agreed. I wanted some armament installed, during this overhaul. Permission was denied, flat. Against policy. Bad enough, a hyperdrive ship operating as a free enterprise at all. Besides, I was reminded, it's twenty years since the kzinti were driven from Alpha Centauri, ten years since the war ended, and they've learned their lesson and are good little kitties now, and it was nasty of us to smash their base on that planet and do in so many of them. If they threatened our lives, why, mightn't we have provoked them? In any event, the proper thing for us to have done was to file a complaint with the proper authorities—" Saxtorph broke off. "Sorry. I feel kind of strongly about it."

He avoided describing the new equipment that was aboard. Perfectly lawful, stuff for salvage work or prospecting or various other jobs that might come Rover's way. He hoped never to need it for anything else. But he and his shipmates had chosen it long-sightedly, and made certain modifications. Just in case. Moreover, a spacecraft by herself carried awesome destructive potentialities. The commissioners were right to worry about one falling into irresponsible hands. He simply felt that the historical record showed governments as being, on the whole, much less responsible than humans.

"Anyway," he said, "under no circumstances would we go looking for a fight. I've seen enough combat to last me for several incarnations."

"But you are serious about going!" she cried.

He lifted a palm. "Whoa, please. First describe the situation. Uh, your brother's in the Navy, you said, but may I ask what you do?"

Her tone leveled. "I write. When liberation came, I had started to study literature at the university here. Afterward I worked some years for a news service, but when I had sold a few things of my own, I became a free-lance."

"What do you write? I'm afraid I don't recognize your byline."

"That is natural. Hyperdrive and hyperwave have not been available so long that there goes much

exchange of culture between systems, especially when
the societies went separate ways while ships were
limited by light speed. I make different things. Books,
articles, scripts. Travel stuff; I like to travel, the
same as you, and this has gotten me to three other
stars so far. Other nonfiction. Short stories and plays.
Two novels. Four books for young children."

"I want to read some . . . whatever happens."
Saxtorph forbore to ask how she proposed to pay him
on a writer's income. He couldn't afford a wild gamble that she might regain the family lands. Let the
question wait.

Pride spoke: "Therefore you see, Captain, Ib and I
are independent. My aim—his, if I can persuade
him—is for our father's honor. Even about that, I
admit, nothing is guaranteed. But we must try, must
we not? We might become what the Nordbos used to
be. Or we might become far more rich, because
whatever it is out yonder is undoubtedly something
strange and mighty. But such things, if they happen,
will be incidental."

Or *we* might come to grief, maybe permanently,
Saxtorph thought. Nonetheless he intended to hear
her out. "Okay," he said. "Shall we stop maneuver-
ing and get down to the bones of the matter?"

Her look sought past him, beyond this tavern and
this night. Her muted monotone flowed on beneath
the music. "I give you the background first, for by
themselves my father's notes that I have found are
meaningless. Peter Nordbo was twelve years old,
Earth reckoning, when the kzinti appeared. He was
the only son of the house, by all accounts a bright
and adventurous boy. Surely the conquest was a still
crueler blow to him than to most dwellers on
Wunderland.

"But folk were less touched by it, in that far-off
northern district, than elsewhere. Travel restrictions,
growing shortages of machines and supplies, everything forced them into themselves, their own re-

sources. It became almost a . . . manorial system, is that the word? Or feudal? Children got instruction from what teachers and computer programs there were, and from their parents and from life. My father was a gifted pupil, but he was also much for sports, and he roamed the wilderness, hunted, took his sailboat out to sea—

"Mainly, from such thinly peopled outlying regions, the kzinti required tribute. The Landholders must collect this and arrange that it was delivered, but they generally did their best to lighten the burden on the tenants, who generally understood. Kzinti seldom visited Gerning, our part of Skogarna, and then just to hunt in the forests, so little if any open conflict happened. When my father reached an age for higher education, the family could send him to Munchen, the university.

"That was a quiet time also here. The humans who resisted had been hunted down, and the will to fight was not yet reborn in the younger generation. My father passed his student days peacefully, except, I suppose, for the usual carousals, and no doubt kzin-cursing behind closed doors. His study was astrophysics. He loved the stars. His dream was to go to space, but that was out of the question. Unless as slaves for special kzinti purposes, no Wunderlanders went any longer. The only Centaurian humans in space were Belters, subjugated like us, and Resistance fighters. And we never got real news of the fighters, you know. They were dim, half-real, mythic gods and heroes. Or, to the collaborationists and the quietists, dangerous enemies.

"Well. My father was . . . twenty-five, I think, Earth calendar . . . when my grandfather died a widower and Peter Nordbo inherited the Landholdership of Gerning. Dutiful, he put his scientific career aside and returned home to take up the load. Presently he married. They were happy together, if not otherwise.

"The position grew more and more difficult, you see. First, poverty worsened as machinery wore out and could not be replaced. Folk must work harder than ever before to stay alive, while the kzinti lessened their demands not a bit, which he must enforce. Resentment often went out over him. Then later the kzinti established a base in Gerning. It was fairly small, mainly a detector station against raids from space, for both the Resistance and the Solarians were growing bolder. And it was off in the woods, so that personnel could readily go hunting in their loose time. But it was there, and it made demands of its own, and now folk met kzinti quite commonly, one way or another.

"That led to humans being killed, some of them horribly. Do you understand that my father *must* put a stop to it? He must deal with the ratcats, make agreements, be useful enough that he would have a little influence and be granted an occasional favor. Surely he hated it. I was just eight years old on your calendar when he left us, but I remember, and from others I have heard. He began to drink heavily. He became a bad man to cross, who had been so fair-minded, and this made him more enemies. He worked off a part of the sorrow in physical activity, which might be wildly reckless, steeplechasing, hunting tigripards with a spear, sailing or skindiving among the skerries. And yet at home he was always kind, always loving—the big, handy, strong, sympathetic man, with his songs and jokes and stories, who never hurt his children but got much from them because he awaited they would give much."

Saxtorph was smoking too hard; his mouth felt scorched. He soothed it with beer. Tyra proceeded:

"I think he turned a blind eye on whatever underground activities arose in Gerning, or that he got wind of elsewhere. He could not risk joining them himself. He was all that stood between his folk and the kzinti that could devour them. Instead, he must

be the subservient servant, and never scream at the
devils gnawing in his soul.

"But I believe the worst devil, because half an
angel, was the relationship that developed between
him and Yiao-Captain. This was the space operations
officer at the defense base in Gerning. Father found
he could talk to him, bargain, persuade, better than
with any other kzin. Naturally, then, Yiao-Captain
became the one he often saw and . . . cultivated. I
am not sure what it was about him that pleased
Yiao-Captain, although I can guess. But Ib remem-
bers hearing Father remark to Mother, more than
once, that they were no longer quite master and
slave, those two, or predator and prey, but almost
friends.

"Of course folk noticed. They wondered. I, small
girl at home, was not aware of anything wrong, but
later I learned of the suspicions that Father had
changed from reluctant go-between to active collaborationist. It was in the testimony against him, after
liberation."

Tyra fell silent. The long talk had hoarsened her.
She drank deep. Still she looked at what Saxtorph
had never beheld.

Gone uneasy, he shifted his weight about, minor
though it was on this planet, and sought his stein.
The beer was as cool and strong as her handshake
had been. He found words. "What do you think that
pair had in common?" he asked.

She shook herself and came back to him. "Astrophysics," she answered. "Father's abiding interest,
you know. It turned into one of his consolations. He
built himself an observatory. Piece by piece, year by
year, he improvised equipment." Humor flickered.
"Or scrounged it. Is that your American word? Scientists under the occupation were as expert scroung-
ers as everybody else." Once more gravely: "He
spent much time at his instruments. When he had
gotten that relationship with Yiao-Captain—remember,

he mostly used it to help his tenants, shield them—he arranged for a link to a satellite observatory the kzinti maintained. It had military purposes, but those involved deep scanning of the heavens, and Father was allowed a little time-sharing." Her voice went slightly shrill. "Was this collaboration?"

"I wouldn't say so," replied Saxtorph, "but I'm not a fanatic." Nor was I here, enduring the ghastlinesses. I was an officer in the UN Navy, which was by no means a bad thing to be during the last war years. We managed quite a few jolly times.

With a renewed steadiness that he sensed was hard-held, Tyra continued: "It seems clear to me that Yiao-Captain shared Father's interest in astrophysics. As far as a kzin would be able to. They are not really capable of disinterested curiosity, are they? But Yiao-Captain could not have foreseen any important result. I think he gave his petty help and encouragement—easy to do in his position—for the sake of the search itself.

"And Father did make a discovery. It was important enough that Yiao-Captain arranged for a ship so he could go take a look. Father went along. They were never seen again. That was thirty Earth years ago."

By sheer coincidence, the musician changed to a different tune, brasses and an undertone of drums. Saxtorph knew it also. It too was ancient. The hair stood up on his arms. *"Ich hat' einen kameraten."* I had a comrade. The army song of mourning.

"He did not tell us why," Tyra said. The tears would no longer stay captive. "He was forbidden. He could only say he must go, and be gone a long time, but would always love us. We can only guess what happened."

3

The air was rank with kzin smell. The whole compound was, but in this room Yiao-Captain's excitement made it overwhelming, practically to choke on. He half leaned across his desk, claws out, as if it were an animal he had slain and was about to rip asunder. Sunlight through a window gleamed off eyes and wet fangs. Orange fur and naked tail stiffened erect. The sight terrified those human instincts that remembered the tiger and the sabertooth. Although Peter Nordbo had met it before and knew that no attack impended—probably—he must summon his courage. He was big and muscular, Yiao-Captain was short and slender, yet the kzin topped the man by fifteen centimeters, with a third again the bulk and twice the weight.

Words hissed, spat, snarled. "Action! Adventure! Getting away from this wretched outpost. Achievement, honor, a full name. Power gained, maybe, to end this dragged-on war at last. And afterward—afterward—" The words faded off in an exultant growl.

When he thought he saw a measure of calm, Nordbo dared say, in Wunderlander, "I don't quite understand, sir. A very interesting astronomical phenomenon, which should be studied intensively. I came to request your help in getting me authorization to— But that is all. Isn't it, sir?" While he knew the Hero's Tongue, he was not allowed to defile it by use, especially since his vocal organs inevitably gave it a grotesque accent. When he must communicate with a kzin ignorant of his language, he used a translator or, absent that, wrote his replies.

Yiao-Captain sat down again and indicated that Nordbo could do likewise. "No, humans are slow to perceive such possibilities," he said. With characteristic rapid mood shift, he went patronizing. "I supposed you might. You are bold for a monkey. Well, think as best you can. A mysterious source of tremendous energy. Study of the stars deepened knowledge of the atom, and thus became a key to the development of nuclear weapons. What now have you come upon?"

Nordbo shook his head. His mouth bent upward ruefully in the bushy brown beard that was starting to grizzle, below the hook nose. "Scarcely an unknown law of nature in operation, sir. What it may be I'd rather not try to guess before we have much more data. It does suggest— No, how could it have appeared so suddenly, if it were what has crossed my mind? In any case, not every scientific discovery finds military applications. Most don't. I can't imagine how this one could, five light-years off."

"*You* cannot. We shall see."

"Well, sir, if I get the kind of support I need for further research—" Nordbo stopped. Appalled, he stared at the possibility that his eagerness had camouflaged from him. Might this really mean a weapon to turn on his folk? No. It must not. Please, God, make it impossible.

"You will have better than that," Yiao-Captain purred. "We shall go there."

Have I misheard? Nordbo thought. Even for a kzin, it is crazy. "What?"

"Yes." Yiao-Captain rose again. His tail switched, his bat's-wing ears folded and lay back. He gazed out the window into the sky. "If nothing else, maybe that energy source can be transported. Maybe we can fling it at the enemy. They may have noticed, too. If they have, they are bound to send an expedition sometime. Their peering, prying curiosity— But Alpha Centauri is closer to it than Sol by . . . three light-years, is that a good guess? We shall forestall. I can readily persuade the governor, given the information you have brought. And I will be in command."

Nordbo had risen, too, less out of deference, for he realized that at present the kzin wouldn't notice or care, than because he couldn't endure being towered over by those devils. It struck him, not for the first time, that the reason few households on Wunderland kept cats any longer was that their faces were too much like a kzin's. Well, that was far from being the only happy thing the conquest had ruined.

"I, I wish you would reconsider, sir," he said.

"Never." The bass voice grew muted. "Our ancestors tamed their planet and went to the stars because they had learned that knowledge brings might. Shall we dishonor their ghosts?"

Nordbo moistened his lips. "I mean you personally, sir. We will . . . miss you."

It twisted in him: The damnable part is that that is true. Yiao-Captain has never been gratuitously cruel, nor let others be when he had any control over them. By his lights, he is kindly. He has helped us directly or intervened on our behalf when I showed him the need was dire and there would be no loss to his side. He has received me as hospitably as a Hero can receive a monkey, and, yes, we have had some fascinating talks, where he listened to what I said and thought about it and gave answers that approached being fair. Why, he got me to teach him chess, and if he loses he doesn't fly into a murderous rage, only curses and goes outside to work it off in hand-to-hand combat practice. He likes me, after his fashion, and, confess it, I like him in a crooked sort of way, and—what will happen to us in Gerning if he leaves us?

Yiao-Captain turned his head. Something akin to mirth rasped through his words. "Lament not. You are coming along."

Nordbo took a step backward. The horror was too vast for him to grasp immediately. He felt as if he were in a cold maelstrom, whirling down and down. His hands lifted. "No," he implored. "Oh, no, no."

Yiao-Captain refrained from slashing him for presuming to contradict a kzin. "Assuredly. You will keep total silence about this, of course." Lest a rival, rather than an enemy spy, learn, and move to get the coveted task himself. "Hr-r, you may return home, tell your household that you are going on a lengthy voyage, and pack what you need for your personal use. Then report back here for sequestration until we leave. I want your scientific skills." Laughter was a human thing, but a gruff noise vibrated. "And how can I do without my chess partner?"

Nordbo sagged against the wall. He seldom wept, never like this.

"What, you are reluctant?" Yiao-Captain teased. "You care nothing for struggle, glory, or your very curiosity? Take heart. Your time away shall be minimal. I am sure all arrangements can be completed within days."

A kzin's way of challenge is to scream and leap.

4

Tyra wiped furiously at her eyes. "I am, am sorry," she stammered. "I did not plan to cry at you."

No more than a few drops had glistened along those cheekbones. Saxtorph half reached to take her hand. No. She might resent that; and after snapping once or twice for air, she had regained her balance. Best stay prosy. "You think the kzin honcho forced your father to go," he deduced.

She shrugged, not quite spastically. "Or ordered him. What was the difference? He could not tell us anything. If he had, and the kzinti had found out—"

Uh-huh, Saxtorph knew. Children for dinner at the officers' mess. Mother to a hunting preserve, unless they didn't reckon she'd make good sport and decided on a worse death as a public example. "This implies the ratcats considered the object important," he said. "Even more does the item that it involved an interstellar journey, in those days before hyperdrive and with a war under way. It was interstellar, wasn't it?"

"Yes. Father spoke of . . . long years. Also, after the war, investigators got two or three eyewitness accounts by humans who worked for the kzinti. They had only seen requisition orders, that sort of thing, but it did establish that Yiao-Captain and a small crew left for some unrevealed destination in a vessel of the Swift Hunter class. Hardly anything else was learned."

Saxtorph laid his pipe on the ashtaker rack and rubbed his chin. "You're right, kzinti don't do science for the sake of pure knowledge, the way humans sometimes do. They want it to help them cope with a universe they see as fundamentally hostile, or to win them power. In this case, surely, they thought of military potential."

Tyra nodded. "That is clear." She braced herself. "Father had been excited, almost happy. He spoke to several people of a marvelous discovery he had made from his observatory. I do not remember that, but I was little, and maybe I did not happen to be there. Mother was not interested in science and did not understand what he talked of, nor recall it afterward well enough to be of any use. Likewise for what servants or tenants heard. Ib was at school, he says. Everybody agrees that Father said he must see Yiao-Captain about having a thorough study made; the kzinti had the powerful instruments and computers, of course. He came home from that and—I have told you." She bit her lip. "The accusation later was that he deliberately put the kzinti on the trail of something that might have led them to a new weapon, and accompanied them to investigate closer, in hopes of wealth and favors."

"Forgive me," Saxtorph said softly, "but I've got to ask this. Could it possibly be true?"

"No! We, his family, *knew* him. Year by year we had heard as much of his pain as he dared utter, and felt the rest. He loved us. Would he free-willingly have left us, for years stretching into decades, whatever the payment? No, he simply never thought in terms of helping the kzinti in their war, until they did and it was too late for him. But the hysteria immediately after liberation—there had been many real collaborators, you know. And there were people who paid off grudges by accusing other people, and— It was what I think you call a witch hunt.

"The fact that Peter Nordbo had cooperated, that was not in itself to be held against him. Most Landholders did. Taking to the bush was maybe more gallant, but then you could not be a thin, battered shield for your folk. Just the same, this was part of the reason why the new constitution took away the special status of the Nineteen Families. And in retrospect, that Peter Nordbo gave knowledge to the kzinti and fared off with them, that was made to make his earlier cooperation look willing, and like more than it actually was." Tyra's grip on the table edge drove the blood from her fingertips. "Yes, it is conceivable that in his heart he was on their side. Impossible, but conceivable. What I want you to find for me, Captain Saxtorph, is the truth. I am not afraid of it."

After a moment, shakily: "Please to excuse me. I should be more businesslike." She finished her wine.

Saxtorph knocked back his beer and rose. "Let me get us refills," he suggested. "Care for something stronger?"

"Thank you. A double Scotch. Water chaser." She managed a smile. "You may take you an akvavit this time. I have not much left to tell."

When he brought the drinks back, she was entirely self-possessed. "Ask whatever you want," she invited. "Be frank. I believed my wounds were long ago scarred over. What made them hurt again tonight was hope."

"Don't get yours too high," he advised. "This looks mighty dicey to me. And, like your dad, I've got other people to think about before I agree to anything."

"Naturally. I would not have approached you if the story of your adventures had not proved you are conscientious."

He attempted a laugh. "Please. Call 'em my experiences. Adventures are what happen to the incompetent." He sent caraway pungency down his throat and a dollop of brew in pursuit. "Okay, let's get cracking again. I gather no details about that expedition ever came out."

"They were suppressed, obliterated. When the human hyperdrive armada arrived and it became clear that the kzinti would lose Alpha Centauri, they destroyed all their records and installations that they could, before going forth to die in battle. Prisoners and surviving human witnesses had little information. About Yiao-Captain's mission, nobody had any, except what I mentioned to you. It was secret from the beginning; very few kzinti, either, ever knew about it."

"No report to the home world till success was assured. Nor when Wunderland was falling. They were smart bastards; they foresaw our new craft would hunt for every such beam, overtake it, read it, and jam it beyond recovery."

"I know. Ib has described to me the effect of faster-than-light travel on intelligence operations."

Her grasp of practical things was akin to Dorcas', Saxtorph thought. "When did the ship leave?" he asked.

"It was— Now I am forgetting your calendar. It was ten Earth-years before liberation."

"And whatever messages she'd sent back were wiped from the databases at that time, and whatever kzinti knew the content died fighting. She never returned, and after the liberation no word came from her."

"The general explanation was—is—that it and the crew perished." In bitterness, Tyra added, "Fortunately, they say."

"But if she did not, then she probably got news of

the defeat. A beam cycled through the volume of her possible trajectories could be read across several light-years, and wasn't in a direction humans would likely search. What then would her captain do?" Saxtorph addressed his beer. "Never mind for now. I'd be speculating far in advance of the facts. You say you have come upon some new ones?"

"Old ones." Her voice dropped low. "Thirty years old."

He waited.

She folded her hands on the table, looked at him straight across it, and said, "A few months ago, Mother died. She was never well since Father left. As surrogate Landholder, she was not really able to cope with the dreadful task. She did her best, I grew up seeing how she struggled, but she had not his skills, or his special relationship with a ranking kzin, or just his physical strength. So she . . . yielded . . . more than he had done. This caused her to be called a collaborator, when the kzinti were safely gone, and retrospectively it blackened Father's name worse, but—she was let go, to live out her life on what property the court had no legal right to take away from us. It is productive, and Ib found a good supervisor, so she was not in poverty. Nor wealthy. But how alone! We did what we could, Ib and I and her true friends, but it was not much, and never could we restore Father to her. She was brave, kept busy, and . . . dwindled. Her death was peaceful. I closed her eyes. The physician's verdict was general debility leading to cardiac failure.

"Ib has his duties, while I can set my own working hours. Therefore it was I who remained at Korsness, to make arrangements and put things in order. I went through the database, the papers, the remembrances, and at the bottom of a drawer, under layers of his clothes that she had kept, I found Father's last notebook from the observatory."

Air whistled in between Saxtorph's teeth. "Including the data on that thing? Jesu Kristi! Didn't he know how dangerous it was for his family to have?"

"He may have forgotten, in his emotional storm. I think likelier, however, he hid it there himself. No human would have reason to go through that drawer for many years. He knew Mother would not empty it."

"M-m, yah. And if nothing made them suspicious, the kzinti wouldn't search the house. Beneath their dignity, pawing through monkey stuff. And they never have managed to understand how humans feel about their families. Yah. Nordbo, your dad, he may very well have left those notes as a kind of heritage; because if you've given me a proper account of him, and I believe you have, then he had not given up the hope of freedom at last for his people."

A couple of fresh tears trembled on her lashes but went no farther. "*You* understand," she whispered.

Enthusiasm leaped in him. "Well, what did the book say?"

"I did not know at once. It took reviewing of science from school days. I dared not ask anybody else. It could be—undesirable."

Okay, Saxtorph thought, if he turned out to have been a traitor after all, why not suppress the information? What harm, at this late date? I don't suppose it'd have changed your love of him and his memory. You're that kind of person.

"What he found," Tyra said, "was a radiation source in Tigripardus." Most constellations bear the same names at Alpha Centauri as at Sol—four and a third light-years being a distance minuscule in the enormousness of the galaxy—but certain changes around the line between them have been inevitable. "It was faint, requiring a sensitive detector, and would have gone unnoticed had he not happened to study that exact part of the sky. This was in the course of a systematic, years-long search for small anomalies. They might indicate stray monopoles, or antimatter concentrations, or other such peculiarities, which in turn might give clues about the evolution of the whole— But I explain too much, no?"

"The radiation seemed to be from a point source. It consisted of extremely high-energy gamma rays. The spectrum suggested particles were being formed and annihilated. This indicated an extraordinary energy density. With access to the automated monitors the kzinti kept throughout this system, Father quickly got the parallax. The object was about five light-years away. That meant the radiation at the source was fantastically intense. I can show you the figures later, if you wish."

"I do," Saxtorph breathed. "Oh, I do."

"He checked through the astronomical databases, too," she went on. "Archival material from Sol, and studies made here before the war, showed nothing. This was a new thing, a few years old at most."

"And since then, evidently, it's turned off."

"Yes. As I told you, Ib got a Navy observer to look at the area, on a pretext. Nothing unusual."

"Curiouser and curiouser. Any idea what it might be, or have been?"

"I am a layman. My guesses are worthless."

"Don't be humble. I'm not. Hm-m-m . . . No, this is premature, at least till I've seen those numbers. Clearly, Yiao-Captain guessed at potentialities that made it worth taking a close look, and persuaded his superiors."

Saxtorph clutched the handle of his mug and stared down as if it were an oracular well. "Ten years plus, either way," he muttered. "That's what I'd estimate trip time as, from what I recall of the Swift Hunter class and know about kzinti style. Sparing even a single ship and crew for twenty-odd years, when every attack on Sol was ending in expensive defeat and we'd begun making our own raids—uh-huh. A gamble, but maybe for almighty big stakes."

"And the ship never came back," Tyra reminded

him. "A ten-year crossing, do you reckon? It should
have reached the goal about when the hyperdrive
armada got here to set us free. Surely the kzinti sent
it word of that. The news would have been received
five years later. Sooner, if the ship was en route
home." Or not at all if the ship was dead, Saxtorph
thought. "Then what? I cannot imagine a kzin commander staying on course, to surrender at journey's
end. He might have tried to arrive unexpectedly and
crash his ship on Wunderland, a last act of terrible
vengeance, but that would have happened already."

"More speculation," Saxtorph said. "What's needed
is facts."

A sword being drawn could have spoken her "Yes."

"Who've you told about this, besides your brother
and me?" Saxtorph asked.

"Nobody, and I swore him to secrecy. If nothing
else, we must think first, undisturbed, he and I. He
sounded out high officers, and decided they would
not believe our father's notes are genuine, when
their observatory contradicts."

"M-m, I dunno. They know the kzinti went after
something."

"It can have been something quite different."

"Still, these days a five-light-year jaunt is no great
shakes. Include it in a training cruise or whatever."

"And as for finding out the truth about our father,
which is Ib's and my real purpose—they would not
care."

"Again, I wonder. I want to talk with Ib."

"Of course, if you are serious. But can you not see,
if we give this matter over to the authorities, it goes
entirely out of our hands? They will never allow us to
do anything more."

"That is fairly plausible."

"If you, though, an independent observer, if you
verify that this is real and important, then we cannot
be denied. The public will insist on a complete
investigation."

A decent cause, and a decent chunk of much-needed money. Too many loose ends. However, Saxtorph flattered himself that he could recognize a genuine human being when he met one. "I'll have to know a lot more, and ring in my partners, et cetera, et cetera," he declared. "Right now, I can just say I'll be glad to do so."

"It is a plenty!" Her tone rejoiced. "Thank you, Captain, a thousand thanks. *Skaal!*" When they had clinked rims, she tossed off an astonishing draught.

It didn't make her drunk. Perhaps it helped bring ease, and a return of vivacity. "I had my special reason for meeting you like this," she said. Her smile challenged. "Before entrusting you with my dream, I wanted we should be face to face, alone, and I get the measure of you."

Yes, occasionally he had made critical decisions in which his personal impression of somebody was a major factor.

"We shall hold further discussion, and you bring your wife—your whole crew, if you wish," Tyra said. "Tonight, I think, we have talked enough. About this. But must you leave at once?"

"Well, no," he answered, more awkwardly than was his wont.

They conversed, and listened to the music that most of humankind had forgotten, and swapped private memories, and drank, and she was a sure and supple dancer. Nothing wrong took place. Still, it was a good thing for Saxtorph that when he got back to his hotel, Dorcas was awake and in the mood.

5

Swordbeak emerged from hyperspace and accelerated toward the Father Sun. A warcraft of the Raptor class, lately modified to accommodate a superluminal drive, it moved faster than most, agilely responsive to the thrust of its gravity polarizers. Watchers in space saw laser turrets and missile launchers silhouetted against the Milky Way, sleek as the plumage of its namesake, overwhelmingly deadlier than the talons. It identified itself to their satisfaction and passed onward. Messages flew to and fro. When the vessel reached Kzin, a priority orbit around the planet was preassigned it. Weoch-Captain took a boat straight down to Defiant Warrior Base. Thence he proceeded immediately to the lair of Ress-Chiuu. A proper escort waited there.

The High Admiral received him in the same room as before. Now, however, a table had been set with silver goblets of drink and golden braziers of sweet, mildly psychotropic incense. In the blood trough at the middle a live *zianya* lay bound. Its muzzle had been taped shut to keep it from squealing, but the smell of its fear stimulated more than did the smoke.

"You enter in honor," Ress-Chiuu greeted.

From his rank, that was a pridemaking compliment. Nevertheless Weoch-Captain felt he should demur. "You are generous, sire. In truth I accomplished little."

"You slew no foes and saved no friends. We never, realistically, expected you would. To judge by your preliminary report as you returned, you did well against considerable odds. But you shall tell me about it in person, at leisure. Afterward Intelligence will examine what is in your ship's database. Recline—" in this presence, another great distinction "—and take refreshment." —an extraordinary one.

As he talked, interrupted only by shrewd questions, memories more than drink or drug restored to Weoch-Captain his full self-confidence. If he had not prevailed, neither had he lost, and his mission was basically successful.

The story unfolded at length: Voyage to the old red dwarf. Cautious, probing approach to the planet on which Werlith-Commandant's forces had been at work. Detection and challenge by humans. Dialogue, carefully steered to make them think that the kzinti had no foreknowledge of anything and this was a routine visit. Refusal to let the kzinti proceed farther, orders for *Swordbeak* to depart. ("So they show that much spirit, do they?" Ress-Chiuu mused. "The official communications have been as jelly-mild as I predicted. Well, maybe it was just this individual commander.") *Swordbeak*'s forward plunge. An attack warded off, except for a ray that did no significant damage before the ship was out of range. Three more human vessels summoned and straining to intercept. Weoch-Captain's trajectory by the planet, wild, too close in for the pursuit to dare, instruments and cameras recording that the kzinti installation had been annihilated, the kzinti warcraft that had been

on guard orbited as a mass of cold wreckage, the
likelihood of any survivors was essentially nil. Running a gauntlet of enemy fire on the way out. Another bravado maneuver, this around the larger gas
giant, that could have thrown *Swordbeak* aflame into
the atmosphere but left its nearest, more heavily
armed chaser hopelessly behind. Swatting missiles
on the way out to hyperspacing distance. A jeering
message beamed aft, and escape from 3-space.

"It is well, it is well." Ress-Chiuu rolled the words
over his tongue as if they were the fine drink in his
goblet.

Weoch-Captain gauged that he had asserted himself as much as was advisable. He had his future to
think of, the career that should bring him at last a
full name and the right to breed. "If the High Admiral is pleased, that suffices. But it was mere information we captured, which the monkeys may in time
have given us freely."

"Vouchsafed us," Ress-Chiuu snarled. "Condescended to throw to us."

"True, sire." It had indeed been in the minds of
Weoch-Captain and his crew, a strong motivation to
do what they did.

"Nor could we be certain they would not lie."

"True, sire. Nonetheless—" The utterance was dis-
tasteful but necessary, if Weoch-Captain was to maintain the High Admiral's opinion of him as an officer
not only valiant but wise. "They will resent what
happened. We have barely begun to modernize and
re-expand the fleet. Theirs is much stronger. How
may they react? I admit to fretting about that on the
way home."

"The Patriarchs considered it beforehand," Ress-
Chiuu assured him. "The humans will bleat. Perhaps
they will even huff and puff. We shall point out that
they have registered no territorial claim on yonder
sun and its planets, therefore they had no right to
forbid entry to a peaceful visitor, and you did noth-

ing but save yourselves after they opened fire. Arh, your restraint was masterly, Weoch-Captain. We will demand reparation, they will make a little more noise, and that will be the end of the matter. Meanwhile you have learned a great deal for us, about their capabilities and about what to expect, what to prepare for, when we start pushing at them in earnest. You deserve well of us, Weoch-Captain."

He leaned forward. His voice became music and distant thunder. "You deserve the opportunity to win more glory. You may earn the ultimate reward."

Energy thrilled along nerves and into blood. "Sire! I stand ready!"

"I knew you would." Ress-Chiuu sipped, rather than lapped, from his cup. His gaze went afar, his tone deceptively meditative. "We have our sources of information among the humans. They are limited in what they can convey but on occasion they have proven useful. For the present, you need know no more than that. Let me simply say that not everything the hyperwave brings us is known to the human *government*." Perforce he attempted to pronounce the English word. Weoch-Captain recognized, if not exactly understood it.

"For relevant example," Ress-Chiuu continued, "we got early news of the disaster at the red sun, well before they contacted us officially about it. This you recall, of course. What you do not recall, because it happened while you were gone, is that we have received fresh intelligence, conceivably of the first importance."

Stoic, as became a Hero, Weoch-Captain waited. His ribs ached with tension. His heart slugged.

"Briefly put—we will go into details later," he heard, "a Wunderland resident has come upon a lost record from the time of the war. It appears that, some years before the enemy got the hyperdrive, an astronomer observed a cosmic phenomenon, about five light-years from Alpha Centauri. It was inexplicable, but involved enormous energies. The possibility of military uses caused the high command of the occupation to dispatch a ship to investigate. If the ship sent any messages back, those were expunged when the human armada appeared, and all kzinti who had knowledge of the mission died. Any beams that arrived afterward were never received, the tuned and programmed apparatus being destroyed; they are dissipated, lost. The ship has not been heard of again. Recent search has failed to detect anything remarkable in that part of the Wunderland sky.

"Regardless, for reasons not quite clear to me, humans are trying to organize an expedition to that region. Humans, I say, individuals, not *the* humans. Their patriarchs are, as yet, unaware of it.

"We have obtained the astronomical data. They are sufficient basis for an investigation. Perhaps nothing is there, or nothing of interest. Yet it is imaginable that those kzinti were justified who decided, three decades ago, that this was worth sending a high-velocity vessel.

"We must know. If it is anything of value, we must win it ourselves. The way is considerably longer from here than from there. Are you and your crew prepared to leave again quite soon?"

"Sire," blazed Weoch-Captain, "you need not ask!"

"And I say, to your honor, that I am unsurprised." Ress-Chiuu showed fangs. "I give you an added incentive. If the humans do mount their expedition, it will apparently consist of a single ship, unarmed, commanded by one . . . S-s-saxtor-r-rph, the designation is. The ship, commander, and crew that wrought the havoc you beheld."

Weoch-Captain roared.

They spoke together, ran computations and simulations, speculated, envisioned, dreamed their fierce dreams, until past sundown. Much remained to do when they stopped for a feast of celebration. The first flesh ripped from the *zianya*, before it died, was especially savory.

6

While the government ground ponderously through its motions, Juan Yoshii and Laurinda Brozik were as trapped on Wunderland as their friends. Released, they could not get early passage to We Made It; as yet, few ships plied that route. When a sudden opportunity came by, they grabbed. The others took no offense. Laurinda's parents were eager to get her home and legally married. Her father had already promised his prospective son-in-law an excellent job, no sinecure but still one that would allow him to pursue his literary interests on the side. You don't dawdle over such things. However, the situation gave scant notice or time for a sendoff. Preoccupied as they were with the Nordbo business, skipper and mate could merely offer their best wishes. Kamehameha Ryan and Carita Fenger made what arrangements they were able, and the foursome took off for the pair of days available before departure.

Though Gelbstein Park is popular in summer, visitors to that high country are few when winter has fallen over the southern hemisphere of Wunderland. These got romantic near-solitude. A walk amidst the scenery preceded dinner back at the lodge, drinks before the fireplace, and a long goodnight.

"Brrr-hooee!" Ryan hugged himself. Breath smoked from his round brown countenance. "I'm glad I'm not a brass monkey."

Carita took his arm. The Jinxian's own skin seemed coal-black against the snowscape, in which Laurinda's albino complexion showed ghostly. "Keep reminding yourself that not all your ancestors were kanakas," she suggested.

"Or that it gets pretty cold on top of Mauna Kea, too, yeah." The quartermaster snuggled his chin under the collar of his jacket.

"You could've insisted we go to Eden or the Roseninsel or wherever tropical."

"Naw, I'm okay. Juan opted for here, and this's his last chance."

Yoshii seemed indeed lost in his surroundings. Was a poem brewing? Overhead the sky stood huge, cloudless, as deeply blue as the shadows cast by sun A across the snows. Paler were those from B, an elfin tracery mingled with the frost-glitter. A kilometer ahead, the trail ended at a hot springs area. The greens and russets of pools were twice vivid in the whiteness elsewhere; the steam that rose from them was utter purity. Beyond, the Lucknerberg gleamed in its might. The sounds of seething carried this far through the silence, but muffled, as if it were the underground working of the planet that one heard.

"You are so kind," Laurinda said. "We'll miss you so much."

Yoshii shivered, left his reverie, and caught his girl's gloved hand. They were walking in front of their companions. He glanced back. "Yes, and we'll worry about you," he added. "Headed into the . . . the unknown—"

"You'll have better things to do," Ryan laughed.

"And we'll be fine," Carita put in.

"Shorthanded," Yoshii said. They had not found a satisfactory replacement for him. "I can't help feeling guilty, like a deserter."

"Juan, boy," Carita replied, "if you left this lass behind now, even for a month's jaunt, I'd turn you over my knee and spank you till you took first prize at the next baboon show." Quite possibly she meant it. Her short, massive frame certainly had the capability.

"I might have gone, too—" Laurinda's words trailed off. No, she would not have done that to her parents. "If we could only stay in touch!"

Ryan shrugged. "Someday they'll miniaturize hyperwave equipment to the point where it'll fit in a spaceship."

"Why haven't they already?" she protested. "Or why didn't it come with the hyperdrive?"

"We can't expect to understand or assimilate a nonhuman technology overnight," Yoshii told her in his soft fashion. "As was, it took skull sweat to adapt what the Outsiders sold your world to our uses. I'm surprised that you, of all people, should ask such a question."

"A woman needs to spring an occasional surprise," Carita said.

Laurinda gulped. "But not a stupid remark. I'm sorry. My thinking had gone askew. I *am* afraid for you two and the Saxtorphs."

"Nonsense," Ryan said. "It'll be *aheahe*, a breeze, a well-paid junket." Into reaches that had swallowed a kzinti warcraft. "You don't get ol' Bob haring right off on impulse. If we should meet difficulties we can't skip straight away from, we're equipped like an octopus to handle 'em."

"No weapons." She had not been concerned with the refitting, but she knew this.

"Oh, he and I saw quietly to our stash of small arms, explosives, and all."

Yoshii's mouth tightened. "What use against the universe?"

"As for that," Carita stated, "you know full well what we've got." Mainly to Laurinda: "A beefed-up grapnel field system. We can lock onto a fair-sized asteroid and shift its orbit, if we want to spend the fuel. Our new main laser can bore a hole from end to end of it. Our robot prospector-lander can boost at as high as a hundred Earth gees, for a total delta *v* of a thousand KPS. Plus the stuff we carried before, except for the second boat—radars, instruments, teleprobes, you name it. Oh, we'd be no match for a naval vessel, but aside from that, we're loaded like a *verguuz* drinker."

"Now will you joyful honeymooners kindly reel in your faces and start singing and dancing as the drill calls for?" Ryan snorted.

The couple traded a look, which rapidly grew warm. Smiles radiated between them. "Makes me feel downright lecherous," Carita murmured to Ryan. "How 'bout you?"

With a rumbling roar, a geyser erupted among the springs. Higher and higher it climbed against the gentle gravity, until the tower of it reached a hundred meters aloft. Light sharded to bows and diamonds in its plume. Thence it flung a fine rain which fell stinging hot, smelling of sulfur and tasting of iron, violence broken loose from rocks far below. Abruptly the humans felt very small.

7

Waves move more slowly on Wunderland than on Earth and strike less hard, but the seas that beat against the cliffs of Korsness were heavy enough. The noise of them reached the old house on the headland as a muted throb, drums beneath the wind-skirl. Gray, green, and white-maned, they heaved out to a horizon vague with scud. The clouds flew low, like smoke. The room overlooking the view seemed full of their twilight, despite its fluoros. That glow lost itself in swartwood furniture, murky carpet, leatherbound codices and ancestral portraits. Above the stone mantel hung a crossed pair of oars, dried and cracked. The first Nordbo who settled here had used them after the motor in his boat failed, to fetch a son wrecked on Horn Reef.

Saxtorph liked this place. It spoke to something in his blood. "You've got roots," he remarked. "Not many folks do these days."

Seated on his left, Tyra nodded. Her hair was the sole real brightness. "The honor of the house," she said, then grimaced. "No, forgive me, I do not mean to be pretentious."

"But you shouldn't be afraid of speaking about what truly matters," said Dorcas on her far side.

"I am not. Your husband knows. But—" The com that they confronted chimed and blinked. Tyra stiffened. "Accept," she snapped.

The full-size image of a man appeared, and part of the desk behind which he sat, and through the window at his back a glimpse of the Drachenturm in Munchen. "Good day," he greeted. Half rising to make a stiff little bow: "Frau Saxtorph, at last I got the pleasure of your acquaintance." He must have worked to flatten out of his English the accent his sister retained.

Dorcas inclined her head. The mahogany-hued crest and tail of her Belter hairstyle rippled. "How do you do, Herr," she answered as formally. The smile on the Athene visage was less warm than usual. "Someday I may have the pleasure of shaking your hand."

Ib Nordbo took the implied reproof impassively. He was in his mid-forties, tall and low-gee slim, smooth-chinned, bearing much of Tyra's blond handsomeness but none of her verve and frequent merriment. At least, during his previous two short encounters with Saxtorph he had been curt and somber. Insignia on the blue uniform proclaimed him a lieutenant commander of naval intelligence.

"Why would you not come in person today?" burst from Tyra. "I tell you, this is the one spot on Wunderland where we can be sure we are private."

"Come, now," her brother replied. "My office was and is perfectly secure, there is no reason to imagine your town apartment or the Saxtorphs' hotel room were ever under surveillance, and I assure you, this circuit is well sealed."

Anxious to avoid a breach, for the earlier scenes had gotten a bit tense, Saxtorph said, "You'd know, in your job. Actually, my wife and I were glad of

Tyra's invitation because we were curious to see the homestead."

"We hoped to get some feel for your father, some insight or intuition," Dorcas added.

"What value can that have, on a search through space?" Nordbo's question would have been a challenge or a gibe if it had been uttered less flatly.

"Perhaps none. You never can tell. If nothing else, this was an interesting visit; and to hold his actual notebook in our hands was . . . an experience."

"I fear nobody else would agree, Frau." Nordbo's attention went to his sister. "Tyra, I hesitate to say you have become paranoiac on this subject, but you have exaggerated it in your mind out of all proportion. What cause does anyone have to spy on you? How often must I repeat, the Navy—no part of officialdom—will concern itself?"

Saxtorph stirred. "And *I* repeat, if you please, that I have trouble believing that," he said. "Okay, one kzinti ship was lost thirty years ago, among hundreds. There was an avalanche of matters to handle in the years right after liberation. This business was forgotten. Sure. But if we did show them your father's notes and reminded them that the kzinti reckoned it worthwhile dispatching a ship—"

"Nothing special is now in that part of the sky," Nordbo retorted. "What he detected must have been a transient thing at best, an accident leaving no trace, perhaps the collision of a matter and an antimatter body."

"That'd have been plenty weird. Who's ever found so much loose antimatter? But we've still got that infrared anomaly." Saxtorph had insisted on Nordbo's retrieving the entire record of the naval observation.

"Meaningless. Its intensity against the cosmic background falls within probable error." The officer stirred where he sat. "We need scarcely go over this ground again for your lady wife's benefit. We have trodden it bare, and you must have relayed the arguments to her. But to complete the repetition, Frau Saxtorph, I have pointed out that the kzinti may well have had some entirely different destination, and took my father along merely because his noticing this phenomenon put them in mind of him as an excellent observer. They quite commonly employed human technicians, you know. Our species has more patience for detail work than theirs."

He paused before finishing: "This is how they will think in the Navy if we tell them. I have sounded out various high-ranking persons, at Tyra's request. Besides, I am Navy myself; I ought to know, ought I not? It *might* be decided to go take a look, on the odd chance that my father did stumble on something special. But they would not care about him or his fate. Nor would they want civilians underfoot. You, Captain Saxtorph, would be specifically forbidden to enter that region."

"I understand that," Tyra said. "At least, it is possible. Therefore *Rover* must go first, before anything has been revealed. What information it brings back can jumpstart some real action."

"Frau Saxtorph, I appeal to you," Nordbo said. "My sister has involved me —"

"It was your right to know," Tyra interjected, "and I thought you would help."

"She wants me, if nothing else, to withhold from my service word about this ill-advised space mission of yours. Can you not see what a difficult position that creates for me?"

"I agree your position is delicate," Dorcas murmured.

Did Nordbo wince or flinch? If so, he clamped control back down too fast for Robert Saxtorph to be sure. Either way, the captain felt momentarily sorry for what had happened of late.

Not that the *Rover* crew were at fault. They'd had no way of foreseeing. They simply carried back to Alpha Centauri the news that Commissioner Markham had been a spy for the kzinti. It provoked a

hunt for others. And—soon after liberation, when Ib
Nordbo was a young engineer working in the asteroids, Ulf Reichstein Markham, still out there settling
assorted affairs, had befriended him. They returned
to Wunderland together, Nordbo enlisting, Markham going unsuccessfully into politics and later rather
brilliantly into astronautics administration. Markham's
prestige, the occasional overt recommendation or con-
versational suggestion, helped Nordbo rise. They met
fairly often.

Well, but suspicion found no grounds. "It must
die away altogether," Tyra had pleaded to Saxtorph.
"Must it not? Ib fought for freedom—not like Markham, only in one uprising, that crazy try of young
men to take back the Ritterhaus, but he did suffer
injuries. And Markham was in fact a hero of the
Resistance, maybe its greatest. He did not change
till long afterward. How could Ib tell? Yes, they did
things together, dining, hunting, talking. What does
that mean? They were both lonely. They have—they
had not sociable personalities. Ib was always of dark
spirit. He has never married. I think he still carries
the torment of our father inside him. Remember, he
is seven Earth-years older than me. He lived through
more of it, and then through the years alone with our
mother, at that impressionable age. Now he is fine in
his work. He would have risen higher if he had a
wife who knew all the unspoken social rules, or if he
could just be smooth. But he is too honest. He does
not share those filthy dictatorial ideas you told me
Markham held. I am his sister, I would know if he
did. We are not close, he is not close to anyone, but
we are the children of Peter Nordbo."

Dorcas, who was tactful when she cared to be,
went directly on: "However, nothing illegal or un-
ethical is involved. We plan a scientific mission.
Amateurs, yes, but if we get in trouble, nobody will
be harmed except us. That kind of personal risk is

not prohibited by any statute or regulation I know of—"

Thus far, Saxtorph thought.

"—nor do the terms of our insurance and mortgage require more than 'informed prudence,' the interpretation of which clause is a matter for the civil courts. You are merely assisting an undertaking that may prove beneficial to your nation."

Nordbo shook his head. "I am not," he answered. "I have given it the serious thought I promised. Today I tell you that I will have no further part of it."

"Ib!" Tyra cried. Her hand went to her mouth.

"It is lunatic," he stated. "If we turned those notes over to my service, at least any investigation would be competently handled. My apologies, Captain and Mate Saxtorph. I am sure you command your ship well. You have been persuaded to enter a field outside your competence. Please reconsider."

Tyra said something unsteadily in her childhood dialect. He replied likewise. In English: "Yes, I will keep my promise, my silence about this, unless circumstances force me. But I will not make any contribution to your effort, nor lend any more aid or counsel, except my earnest advice that you abandon it. That is final."

His tone softened. "Tyra, you sit in what we have left of our inheritance, our father's and mother's and ancestors' heritage. Will you really throw it away?"

"No," she whispered. Her shoulders straightened. "But I will do what is my right."

Korsness was no Landholding, only a freehold, shared by the heirs. She had arranged to hypothecate her half of the equity, to pay for the charter. The agreement lay awaiting her print. In the odds-on event that *Rover* found nothing of monetary value, her income from the property ought to pay off the debt, though not before she was well along in years. It would have helped if Ib had joined in.

Saxtorph didn't feel abashed. He had a living to

make. If Tyra wanted his capabilities this badly, why, her profession supported her. For his part, and Dorcas', Kam's, Carita's, they'd be putting their necks on the line. Still, he admired her spirit.

"Then best I say farewell," Nordbo sighed. "Before we quarrel. I will see you in a few days, Tyra, and we will speak of happier things."

"I am not sure where I will be," she replied. "I cannot sit idle while— It will be research for a new piece of writing. But of course I will get in touch when I can." Her words wavered. "We shall always be friends, *Broder min*."

"Yes," he said gravely. "Fare you ever well." His image vanished.

The surf and the wind resounded through silence. After a while Dorcas said low, "I think that was why he chose to call, instead of coming in person as you asked. So he could leave at once."

They barely heard Tyra: "Dealings like this are hard for him. He knows not well how to cope with humans."

She sprang to her feet. "But I am not crushed." Her stance, her voice avowed it. "I had small hope for better, after our talks before. Poor soul, he took more wounds than I did, and fears they might come open. I gave him his chance." Louder yet: "We can proceed. Robert, you have told me very little of what you intend."

Dorcas cast a glance at her man and also raised her lean length from the chair.

"Uh, yah, I s'pose we are on first-name terms by now," he said fast, fumbling after pipe and tobacco. They had in fact been for a while, when by themselves. "I've had my thoughts, and discussed them with Dorcas, but we figured we'd best wait with you till the contract was definite. It is, isn't it?"

"Yes, in all except our prints," Tyra told him. "You have seen it, have you not, Frau—m-m, Dorcas?"

Rover's mate smiled and nodded. "I rewrote two

of the clauses," she said. "Evidently, next time you met Bob, you agreed."

"But what do you propose to *do*?" Tyra demanded.

Saxtorph busied his hands. "A lot will depend on what we find." He had explained earlier, but sketchily. "What Dorcas and I have drawn up is not a plan but a set of contingency plans, subject to change without notice. However, it makes sense to start by trying for that whatever-it-is that your father spotted. Presumably the kzinti ship got there, and what the crew found became a factor in determining what they did afterward."

"Have you any idea about it?"

"None, really," Dorcas admitted. "Your brother may well be right, it was a freak of no special significance."

"Except, we believe, Yiao-Captain thought otherwise," Saxtorph pointed out. "And he got his superiors to agree it was worth a shot. Of course, from a human viewpoint, kzinti are natural-born wild gamblers." He thumbed tobacco down into bowl. "Well, this is a secondary mystery. What you've engaged us for is to learn, if we can, what happened to your father. Yonder objective is a starting point."

Tyra went to a window and gazed out across sea and wrack. A burst of rain spattered on the glasyl. "You have mentioned intercepting radio waves in space," she said slowly. "Could you get any from that ship?"

"We'll try. I'm not optimistic. Space is almighty big, and if a beam wasn't very tightly collimated to start with, I doubt we could pick it out of the background noise after this many years, supposing we could locate it at all. Shipboard transmitters aren't really powerful. But I do have some notions as to what the kzinti may have done."

"*Ja?*" she exclaimed, and swung around to stare at him.

He got his pipe going. "What do you know about the Swift Hunter class?"

"Almost nothing. I see now that I should have looked it up, but—"

"No blame. You had a lot else to keep track of, including the earning of your daily bread and peanut butter. I remembered things from the war, and retrieved more from the naval histories in the Wunderland library system."

Saxtorph blew a smoke ring. "I don't know if the kzinti still use Swift Hunters. Who knows for sure what goes on in their empire? Any that remain in service will certainly be phased out as hyperdrive comes in, because it makes them as obsolete as windjammers. In their time, though, they were wicked.

"Good-sized, but skimpy payload, most of what they carried being mass for conversion. Generally they took special weapons, or sometimes special troops, on ultra-quick missions followed by getaways faster than any missile could pursue. Total delta v of about two and a half c, Newtonian regime. Customarily, during the war, they'd boost to one-half c and go ballistic till time to decelerate. Anything higher would've been too inefficient, as relativity effects began getting large. This means that they'd strike and return, with the extra half light-speed available for high-powered maneuvers in between. The gravity polarizer made it all possible. Jets would never have managed anything comparable. At that, the Swift Hunters were so energy-hungry that the kzinti saved them for special jobs, as I said. Obviously they figured this was one such."

"Nevertheless, ten years to their goal," Dorcas murmured.

"But in stasis, apart from standing watch," Saxtorph reminded her. "Or, rather, the kzinti version of time-suspension technics, in those days. You can be pretty patient if you get to lie unconscious and unaging during most of the voyage."

It had been in Tyra's awareness, of course, but she tautened and breathed, "My father—" Seen from indoors, she was a shapely shadow against the silver-gray in the window, save for the light on her hair.

Saxtorph nodded. "Uh-huh," he said around puffs. "Do not, repeat, do not get your hopes up. But it just could be. Bound back here with word of something tremendous—or without, for that matter—the kzinti captain catches a beam that tells him Wunderland is falling to humans who've acquired a faster-than-light drive. What's he going to do? He's got a half *c* of delta *v* left to kill his forward vector, and another half *c* to boost him to the kzinti home sun."

"But when he got there, he could not stop," she said, as if against her will.

"He might wager they could do something about that at the other end," Saxtorph answered. "Or he might travel at one-fourth *c* and take about 120 years, instead of about sixty, to arrive. In stasis he wouldn't notice the difference. But I doubt that, especially if he was carrying important information which he couldn't reliably transmit by radio. And kzinti always do go balls-out. If he could not be recovered at his new destination, at least he'd die a hero.

"Anyway, this is a possibility that we'll investigate as best we can, within the bounds of due caution."

Once again, as on that evening in the tavern, Tyra stared beyond him and the room and this world. "To find my father," shuddered from her. "To waken him back to life."

Dorcas gave her a hard look. The same unease touched Saxtorph. He rose. "Uh, wait a minute," he said, "you're not supposing you—"

Tyra returned to them. Total calm was upon her. "Oh, yes," she stated. "I am going with you."

"Hey, there!"

He saw her grin. "Nothing is in the contract to deny me." Grimly: "If you refuse, I do not give it my print and you have no charter. Then I must see what if anything the Navy will do."

"But—"

Dorcas laid a hand over his. "She is determined," she said. "I don't imagine it can do any harm, if we write in a waiver of liability."

"You may have that, but you won't need it," Tyra promised. "I take responsibility for myself. Did you imagine I would stay behind while you hunted for my father? Well, Ib does, so I suppose it is natural for you. Let him. If he knew, he might feel he must release the truth and get the authorities to stop us. As for me—" sudden laughter belled "—after all, I am a travel writer. What a story!"

Saxtorph chuckled and dismissed his objections. She could well prove an asset, and would indisputably be an ornament.

Dorcas stood pensive. When she spoke, it was so quietly that he knew she was thinking aloud. "In relativity physics, travel faster than light is equivalent to time travel. We use quantum rules. And yet what are we trying on this voyage but to probe the past and learn what happened long ago?"

8

When the kzinti drew Peter Nordbo into time, his first clear thought was: Hulda, Tyra, Ib. Oh, unmerciful God, it's been ten years now.

"Up, monkey," growled the technician and cuffed him, lightly, claws sheathed, but with force to rock his head. "The commander wants you."

Nordbo crept from his box. He shivered with the cold inside him. Weight dragged at his bones, an interior field set higher than Earth's. Around him, huge forms were likewise stirring, crew revived. Their snarls and spits ripped at the gloom. He stumbled from them, down a remembered passageway. His second clear thought was: What would I give for a cup of coffee!

Noticing, he barked a laugh at himself. Full awareness seeped back into him, and warmth as he moved and unstiffened. Even in this, his exile, eagerness kindled. *Snapping Sherrek* had arrived. What had it reached?

Yiao-Captain waited in the observation turret. It

was illuminated only by the images of the stars, he a shadow blotting out that constellation in which Alpha Centauri and Sol must lie. The light of their legions gleamed off an eyeball when he glanced about. "Arh, Speaker for Humans," he greeted, brusque but not hostile, as in days that were suddenly old. "I know you are still somewhat numb. However, behold."

He turned a dial. A section of the view seemed to rush toward them. Magnification stabilized. Nordbo stood an instant dumbfounded, then a low whistle passed his lips. "What *is* that thing?"

Against frosty star-clouds floated a sphere. Shapes encrusted it here and there, a dome in the form of half a dodecahedron, three concentric helices bent into a semicircle, several curving dendritic masts or antennae, objects less recognizable. The hue was dull gray, spotted with shadows filling countless pocks and scratches. Erosion by spatial dust, Nordbo thought dazedly, by near-vanishingly rare interstellar mete-oroids, and, yes, by cosmic rays. *How long has this derelict drifted?*

"Diameter about sixteen kilometers," he heard Yiao-Captain say, using kzinti units. "We have taken a parallel trajectory at a goodly distance."

"Where is . . . the energy I detected . . . at home?" *At home.*

"On the other side. We who were on watch in the terminal stages of approach saw it from far. It was what decided us to stay well away until we know more. Now we commence the real investigation. The first observer capsule leaves in a few minutes."

Already, before most of the crew were properly roused. Kzin style.

Yiao-Captain's fingers crooked, his tail flicked. "I envy that Hero," he said. "The first, the first. But I must stay in command until . . . *I* am the first to set foot there."

In spite of everything, Nordbo was curiously touched, that the other should, consciously or not, reveal that much to a human. Well, doubtless Nordbo was the sole such human in existence.

A question came to him. "Have you measured the infrared emission?"

"Not yet. Why?"

"Maybe whatever is inside that thing sends its output through a single spot. If not, if it emits in all directions, then the remaining energy has to go somewhere. Presumably the shell reradiates it in the infrared. But given the size of the shell, that must be at a low temperature, so it's not readily distinguished from the galactic background."

"And the integrated emission over the entire surface will give us the total power. Good. Our scientists would have thought of it, but perhaps not at once. Yes-s-s, you will be useful."

"If the shell rotates—"

"It does, on three axes. Tumbles. Quite slowly, but it does. We established that upon arrival."

"Then the bright spot would only point at Alpha Centauri, or any given star, for a short span of time, a few years at most. No wonder it wasn't noticed before. Sheer chance that I did." And condemned myself.

A thump shivered through metal and Nordbo's anguish. "The capsule is on its way," Yiao-Captain said with glee.

Nordbo understood. He had heard about the arrangement before the expedition departed. The intensity of the hard radiation here was such that nothing else would serve for a close passage. The screen fields that had protected the ship from collision with interstellar gas at half the speed of light were insufficient; near this fire, enough stray particles and gamma ray photons would get through to wreck her electronics and give the crew a lethal dose. Her two boats were laughably more vulnerable.

Room and mass were at a premium in a Swift

Hunter, but *Sherrek* carried a pair of thickly armored spheroids which contained generators for ultrastrong fields. Wunderlanders before the war had used them in flyby studies of their suns. The kzinti had quickly modified them to accommodate a single crew member; when dealing with the unknown, a live brain overseeing the instruments might well prove best. Besides an air and water recycler, life support included a gravity polarizer. It was necessarily small, its action confined to the interior, but at such close quarters it could counteract possible accelerations that would kill even a kzin, up to fifty or sixty Terran gravities.

The capsule whipped through the magnified part of the turret view. Its metal gleamed hazy-bright, a nucleus cocooned in shimmering forces. Nordbo imagined the rider voicing an exuberant screech. It vanished from his sight.

More sounds followed, quieter and longer-drawn. A boat was not thrown out by a machine; it launched itself. The lean form glided by on its way to a rendezvous point at the far side of the mystery. There it would seize the capsule in a grapnel field, haul it inboard, and bring it back.

Yiao-Captain stared yonder. "What might the thing be?" he mumbled.

"Artificial, obviously," Nordbo answered, just as low.

"Yes, but for what? Who built it?"

"And when? It's extremely old, I'm sure. Just look at it."

Yiao-Captain's fur bristled. "Billions of years?"

"Not a bad guess."

"The Slavers—"

"The tnuctipun. They were engineers to the Slavers, the thrintun, you know, till they revolted." And the war that followed exterminated both races, back while the ancestors of man and kzin were microbes in primordial seas.

Yiao-Captain's ears lay flat. He shivered. "Haunted weapons. We have tales about things ancient and accursed—" Resolution surged. "Aowrrgh!" he shouted. "Whatever this be, we'll master it! It's ours now!"

Time crept. Nordbo realized he was hungry. Was that right? Why hadn't grief filled him to the brim? He had lost his loves, twenty-odd years of their lives at least, and he felt hungry and ragingly curious.

Well, but they wouldn't expect him to wallow in self-pity, would they? Despicable emotion. Let him take whatever anodyne that work offered. He could do nothing else about his situation.

Yet.

It was actually no long spell until the boat, at a safe distance, snared the capsule. Although its screen fields had degraded incoming data, a shipboard computer could restore much. Transmission commenced at once. In minutes numbers and images were appearing on screens.

Blue-white hell-flame streamed from a ragged hole in the shell, meters wide. The color was nothing but ghost-flicker, quanta given off by excited atoms. The real glow was the gamma light of annihilation, matter and antimatter created, meeting, perishing in cascade after curious cascade until the photons flew free in search of revenge.

"Yes," Nordbo whispered, "I think the source does emit in all directions. The output—fantastic. On the order of terawatts, no, I suspect magnitudes higher than that. The material enclosing it, though, that is what's truly incredible. It stops those hard rays, it's totally opaque to them, damps them down to infrared before it lets them go. . . . But after billions of years, even it has worn thin and fragile. Something, a large meteoroid or something, finally punched through at one point, and there the radiation escapes unchecked. Elsewhere—"

"Can we make contact?" Yiao-Captain screamed. "Can we land and take possession?"

"I don't know. We'll have to study, probe, set up models and run them through the computer. My guess at the moment is that probably we can, if we choose the place well and are careful. No promises, understand, and not soon."

"Get to work on it! Immediately! Go!"

Nordbo obeyed, before Yiao-Captain should lose his temper and give him the claws.

He'd been granted a comparatively free hand to carry on research, with access to a laboratory and the production shop, assistance if necessary, provided of course that he remained properly servile. On a ship like this, those facilities were improvised, tucked into odd corners, so cramped that as a rule only one individual at a time could use them. That suited Nordbo fine.

First he required nourishment. He made for the food synthesizer. What it dispensed was as loathsome to the kzinti as to him, albeit for different reasons. Irritable at the lack of fresh meat, a spacehand kicked the man aside. Nordbo crashed against a bulkhead. The bruises lasted for days. "Keep your place, monkey! You'll swill after the wakened Heroes have fed."

"Yes, my master. I am sorry, my master." Nordbo withdrew on hands and knees, as became an animal.

A thought that he had borne along from Wunderland crystallized. He'd be modifying apparatus, or making it from scratch, as occasion arose. Contemptuous, the kzinti, including the scientists, would pay scant heed. Yiao-Captain might be the exception, but he'd have plenty of other demands on his attention. With caution, patience, piecemeal labor, it should be possible to fashion some kind of weapon—a knife, if nothing else—and keep it concealed under a jumble of stuff in a cabinet or box.

Chances were he'd never use it. What could he win? But the simple knowledge of its existence would help him get through the next months. If he could at last endure no longer, if nothing whatsoever remained to lose, maybe he could wreak a little harm, and die like a man.

9

Having left Alpha Centauri far enough behind, *Rover* phased into hyperspace and commenced the long haul. "We'll go about four and a half light-years, emerge, and see what our instruments can tell us at that distance," Saxtorph had decided. "When we've got a proper fix on the whatchamacallit, we'll approach by short jumps, taking new observations after each one."

"Jamais l'audace," Dorcas had laughed.

"Huh? Oh. Oh, yah. Caution. Finagle knows what we're letting ourselves in for, but I'll bet my favorite meerschaum that Murphy will take a strong interest in the proceedings."

In the galley, on the second day under quantum drive, Ryan exclaimed, "Hey, you really are handy with the tools."

Tyra trimmed the last creamfruit and dropped it in a bowl. "One learns," she said. "I am not a bad cook, either. Maybe sometime you will let me make us a meal."

"M-m, you cook for yourself a lot?"

She nodded. "Eating out alone very much is depressing. Also, some of the places I have been, nobody but a local person or a berserker would go into a restaurant. Or else it is machines programmed for the same menus that bore me everywhere in known space."

"Adventurous sort. Well, sure, I'd be glad to take a chance on you, if you'd like to try being more than the bull cook." Ryan cocked his head and ran his glance up, down, and sideways across her. "For which job, strictly speaking, you lack certain qualifications anyway. Not that I object, mind you."

The blue eyes blinked. "What?" Now and then an English idiom eluded her.

"Never mind. For the moment. Uh, you are quite sweet, helping out like this. You aren't obliged to, you know, our paying passenger."

"What should I do, sit yawning at a screen? I wish I could find more to keep me busy."

"I'd be delighted to see to that, after hours," he proposed.

She colored slightly, but her tone stayed calm and her smile amicable. "I suspect Pilot Fenger would complain. It could be safer to offend a keg of detonite."

"You've noticed, have you?" he replied, unembarrassed. "I guess in your line of work you develop a Sherlock Holmes kind of talent. Well, yes, Carita and I do have a thing going. Have had for years. But it's just friendly, no pledges, no claims. She's not possessive or jealous or anything." He edged closer. "This evenwatch after dinner? Your cabin or mine, whichever you prefer. I'll bring a bottle of pineapple wine, which I s'pose you've never had. Good stuff, dry, trust me. We'll talk and get better acquainted. I'd love to hear about your travels."

"No, thank you," she said, still good-humored. "Entanglements, innocent or not, on an expedition like this, they are unwise, don't you agree? And I

have . . . private things to think about when I am by
myself." She clapped him on the shoulder. "Tomorrow, besides the galley, can I assist in other of your
duties?"

Since his hopes had not been especially high, they
were not dashed. He beamed. " *'Auwē nō ho'i ē!'* By
all manner of means."

Tyra left him and went down a corridor. The ship
throbbed around her, an underlying susurrus of ventilators, mechanisms, power. Dorcas came the opposite way. They halted. "How do you do," the mate
greeted. Her expression was reserved.

"Hallo," Tyra responded. "Are you in a hurry?"

Dorcas unbent to the extent of a lopsided grin. "In
space we have time to burn, or else bare microsec-
onds. What can I do for you?"

"You were so busy earlier, you and Robert, there
was no opportunity to ask. A minute here, please. I
want to be useful aboard. Kam lets me help him, but
that takes two or three hours a daycycle at most. Can
I do anything else?"

Dorcas frowned. "I can't think of anything. Most
of our work is highly skilled."

"I could maybe learn a little, if somebody will
teach me. I do have some space experience."

"That will be up to the somebody, subject to the
captain's okay. We have an ample supply of books,
music, shows, games."

"I brought my own. Finally, I thought, I shall read
War and Peace. But—well, thank you. Don't worry,
I will be all right."

"Feel free. But do not interfere." Dorcas stared
unblinkingly into Tyra's gaze. "You understand, I'm
sure."

"Of course. I will try to annoy nobody. Thank
you." They parted.

Those on mass detector watch didn't count, unless
something registered in the globe. Then anyone else
got out of the chamber fast. Tyra found Carita seated

there, smoking a cigar—the air was blue and acrid—while she played *go* with the computer. "Well, hi!" the Jinxian cried. Teeth flashed startling white in her midnight visage. "On free orbit, are you? C'mon in."

"I thought you might care to talk," said the Wunderlander, shyer than erstwhile. "But it is not needful."

"Oh, Lord, for me it's a breath of fresh beer. Dullest chore in the galaxy, this side of listening to an Ecotheist preacher. And the damn machine always beats me. Hey, don't look near that unshuttered port. We'd have to screw your eyeballs back in and hang your brain out to dry."

"I know about hyperspace." Tyra flowed into the second chair.

"Yes, you have knocked around a fair amount, haven't you?"

"Part of my work."

"I globbed a disc of yours before we left. Put it through the translator and read it yesterday. In English, *Astrid's Purple Submarine.*"

"That is for children."

"What of it? Fun. When I got to the part where the teddy bear has to sit on the safety valve of the steam telephone, I laughed my molars loose. I'll keep the book for whatever kids I may eventually have."

"Thank you." A silence fell.

Carita blew a smoke ring and said softly, "You're a cheerful one, aren't you? That takes grit, in a situation like yours. Because you've never put aside what happened to your parents, have you? I imagine you always dreamed of going out on your father's trail."

Tyra shrugged. "The tragedy is in the past. Whatever comes of it is in the future. Meanwhile, he would be the last person who wanted me to mope."

"And you've more life in you than most. Yank me down if I pry, but I can't help wondering why you've never married."

"Oh, I did. Twice."

Carita waited.

Tyra glanced past her. "I may as well tell you. We shall be shipmates for a time that may grow long and a little dangerous. I married first soon after the liberation. It was a mistake. He was born in space, he had spent his life as a Resistance fighter. I was young and, and impulsive and worshipped him for a hero." She sighed. "He was, is not a bad man. But he was too much used to violence and to being obeyed."

"Yeah, you wouldn't take kindly to that."

"No. My second husband was several years later. An engineer, who had traveled and done great things in space before he settled on Wunderland. A good man, he, strong, gentle. But I found—we discovered together, time by time, that he no longer cared to explore things. He was content with what he had, with his routines. I grew restless until—there was someone else. That ended, but by then it had broken the marriage." Tyra sighed. "Poor Jonas. He deserved better. But he was not too sad. I was his third wife. He is now happy with his fourth."

"So you've had other fellows in between and afterward."

"Well, yes." Tyra flushed. "Not many. I do not hunt them."

"No, no, I never said you do. Besides, I'd look silly perched on a moralistic fence. Still," Carita murmured, "older men generally, eh?"

"Do you care for puppies?" Tyra snapped.

"I'm sorry. I mean well, but Kam says that for me 'tact' is a four-letter word. 'Fraid he's right. Uh, you here after anything in particular, or just to chat? You're welcome either way."

Tyra relaxed somewhat. "Both. I would like to know you folk better."

Carita grinned. "To put us in a book?"

Tyra smiled back. "If you permit. This journey will become big news when we return. I think I can tell it in such a way that your privacy is protected but it gives you publicity that will help your business."

"Which could sure use help. Don't feel guilty about any risks. You're paying, and we went in with our eyes wide open, radiating the light of pure greed." Carita paused. "Yes, I guess you are the right writer for us."

"I want more to know you as, as human beings."

"And we to know you. Okay. We've got a couple weeks ahead of us before the trip gets interesting, except for whatever we can stir up amongst ourselves. What else is on your agenda today?"

"I would liefer have a part in this ship than be idle and passive. You know I help Kam. M-m, do you mind?"

"Finagle, no!" Carita chortled. "Why should I? No claims. I warn you, he'll try to get you in his bunk. Or is that a warning? He's pretty good."

"Thank you, but I shall . . . respect your territory." Tyra hastened onward. "The thought came to me, another thing I might help with. This watch you are keeping. It demands very little, no?"

"If only it did demand. Hours and hours of nothing. And till we replace Juan Yoshii, the spells are longer than ever." Carita's cigar jabbed air. "You're volunteering? I wish you could. Unfortunately, it's not quite as easy as it appears."

"I know. I did research for a script, a while ago, and remember. In the unlikely event that the detector registers a significant mass, the person must know exactly what to do, and do it at once. But the list of actions that may be required is short and rather simple. Give me instructions and some simulator practice, and I believe I could pass any test." Tyra smiled again. "I would want you should be satisfied first I can handle the job. This ship carries something precious, namely me."

Thick hand tugged heavy chin. "It tempts, it tempts. . . . But no. I learned how. That doesn't mean I'm qualified to teach how. Same for Kam. You see, the academies require that an instructor have experience of command. They're right. This is a psionic dingus. The trainee needs close exposure to a personality who knows how everything aboard a ship bleshes together." Carita brightened. "Ask Bob or Dorcas. Either of them could. And hoo-ha, do I want them to!"

"Thank you, I will." Tyra's voice vibrated.

"Fine. But let's get sociable, okay? For me right now, that's a big service. Care for a seegar? I thought not. Well, here's a box of Kam's excellent cookies."

Reminiscences wandered. Inevitably they led to the present enterprise, the wish that drove it. By then the women felt enough at ease that Carita could murmur, "Every girl's first sweetheart is her daddy, but you were only eight when you lost yours. And nevertheless—he must have been one hell of a man."

"He was," Tyra answered as low. "I dare to hope he is."

A while later, she left. Bound for the cubicle known as her stateroom, this time she encountered Saxtorph. He waved expansively at her. She stopped. He did, too. "Anything you want, Tyra?" he inquired.

She met his look. "Robert, will you teach me to stand mass detector watch?"

10

From a hundred-kilometer distance, *Rover* sent her robot prospector around the thing she had tracked down. The little machine circled close, taking readings, storing data. When behind the sphere, it steered itself, with sufficient judgment to stay well clear of the radiation streaming forth from one site there. Otherwise Saxtorph kept in radio rapport, his computer helping him devise the orders he issued. From time to time the prospector transmitted, downloading what it had gathered. At length Saxtorph had it land on the surface. Capable of hundred-gravity acceleration, the robot could also make feather-soft contact. Presently he ventured to have it apply its dynamic analyzer, attempting sonic, electronic, and radiation soundings plus measurements of several different moduli.

Mostly it drew blank. This material was nothing like the asteroids and moons that it was meant to study. A few experiments yielded values, but with ridiculously large probable errors. Nor was the robot

well suited for a tour of inspection. Saxtorph recalled
it to his ship.

"At any rate, the side away from the firebeam
should be safe for people," he said. "Okay, I'm on
my way."

" 'Should be' isn't quite the same as 'is,' " Ryan
objected.

The captain ignored him. "I could use a partner."
He glanced at Carita. She nodded avidly.

After some unavoidable argument and essential
preparations, they left. Saxtorph deemed that taking
the boat, a comparatively large and ungainly object,
was hazardous. They flitted in spacesuits.

The nearer they drew to the objective, the more
the mystery deepened for them. Its horizon arcing
across nearly half their sky, the starlit surface became a pitted bare plain on which crouched outland-
ish bulks, soared skeletal spires, sprawled shadowy
labyrinths. Soon *Rover* seemed as remote as Earth.
Breath sounded harsh in helmets, pulsebeats loud in
motors, pumps, and bloodstreams.

The man pressed the control for a radar reading.
Numbers appeared. He made his command carefully
prosaic: "Brake, hold position, and wait for further
instructions. I'm going down."

"I still say I should," Carita answered. "We can't
spare you."

"Sure you can, while you've got Dorcas." That was
why his wife stayed behind, though he'd had to pull
rank to make her do it.

"Your vectors are correct for landing," she informed him from her post aboard. The ship tracked
the flyers with a precision they themselves could not
match. Probably he alone heard the tremor in her
voice.

It filled Tyra's: "Be careful, Robert, oh, be careful!"

"Quiet," Dorcas snapped. She hadn't wanted the
Wunderlander in the circuit. Ryan wasn't; he kept
lookout at the main observation panel. But Tyra had

appealed to Saxtorph. Not sniveling or anything; a simple request. When she wanted to, though, she could charm the stripes off a skunk.

"I'm sorry," she said.

The captain set his thrusters and boosted. Acceleration tugged briefly. As he turned and slowed, giddiness whirled through him. He was used to it, his reflexes compensated, it passed. His bootsoles touched solidity and he stood on the thing.

Rather, he floated. A few tens of millions of tons, concentrated some eight kilometers below him, exerted no gravity worth mentioning. He directed thruster force upward and increased it until he was pressed down hard enough that he could stand or walk low-gee fashion. This adjustment he made most slowly and cautiously, a fraction at a time. Untold ages had eroded the hollow shell, wearing away its strength until a rock traveling at mere KPS could drive a hole through. Of course, that might mean resistance equal to ordinary armor plate, but it might be considerably less, if not everywhere then at certain points; and he could have happened to land at one of those points.

Otherwise the stuff kept unbelievable properties. Measurements taken on the escaping radiation showed what an inferno raged inside. Yet on this opposite hemisphere, a glance at instruments on his vambrace confirmed the findings made by the robot. Nothing was coming off but infrared at a temperature hardly above ambient.

Saxtorph realized he had been holding his breath. He let it out in a gust. His ribs ached, his sweat stank. Why had he undertaken the flit, anyway?

Well, it was irresistible. Nobody felt able to leave without exploring just a little bit more. And after all, you never knew; a search could turn up a clue to Peter Nordbo's fate.

Saxtorph made for a surrealistic jumble of pipes, reticulations, and clustered globules. Dust, millimeters thick, scuffed up in ghost-wisps wherever his boots struck. After several leaps, he halted. "Okay, Carita, come join the fun. Don't land, remember. Stay a few meters above and behind me, on the alert."

"You're afraid maybe I'll take a nap?" the crewman gibed. Edged with their luminance, her spacesuit arrowed across the stars.

I suppose we shouldn't crack jokes in the presence of something ancient and inscrutable, Saxtorph thought. *We should be duly awed, reverent, and exalted. To hell with that. We've got a job to do. I hope Tyra will understand, when she writes this up.*

Of course she will. She's our own sort. If her whole life didn't prove it already, the past couple of weeks sure did.

Saxtorph neared the complex. At hover, Carita directed a search beam as he desired, supplementing his flash. Undiffused, the brightness flowed like water over a substance that was not rock nor metal nor anything the humans knew. They both operated cameras as well as instruments, while their suits transmitted to the ship. Saxtorph's eyes strained.

"I think the microcraters everywhere were formed in the last hundred million years, plus or minus x," he said. "Otherwise we'd see much more overlap."

"You're supposing the construction is older than that, then," Carita deduced.

"It certainly is," Dorcas told them from the ship. "The computer just finished evaluating our data on the dust. Isotope ratios prove it's been collecting for a minimum of two billion years, likely more." After a moment: "Incidentally, that suggests cosmic radiation isn't what weakened the shell to the point where impacts started leaving pockmarks and at last a big one broke through. The radiation inside must be mainly responsible. But if *it* hasn't done more damage, well, the thing was built to last."

"Besides," Saxtorph said, "if I've got any feeling

for machinery, this bears every earmark of tnuctipun work."

"How can you tell?" Carita asked. Her words sounded thin. Ordinarily she would have kept silence, except for business and an occasional wise-crack, but the weirdness had shaken her a bit, roused a need to talk. Saxtorph sympathized. "What do we know about the Slaver era? What little the bandersnatchi remember, or believe they do, and what got learned from the thrint that came out of stasis for a short while, before they got it bottled again."

"That includes a smidgin of technical information, and a lot of thinking has been done about it ever since," he reminded her. "I've studied the subject some. It interests me. Come on."

He bounded ahead to the next aggregation and examined it as best he cursorily could.

And the next and the next and the next. Time ceased to exist. He drank from his water tube, stuffed rations through his chowlock, excreted into his disposer, without noticing. He had become pure search. Sturdily, Carita followed. She made no attempt to call halt, nor did anyone aboard ship. The quest had seized them all.

Monkey curiosity, Saxtorph thought once, fleetingly. The kzinti would sneer. But they'd examine this, too, in detail, till they used up every possibility of discovery that was in their equipment and their brains. Because to them it'd spell power.

The knowledge was chill: It is a terrible weapon.

"I suspect it's one of a kind," he said. "Humans and their acquaintances haven't found any mini-black holes yet, and that hasn't been for lack of looking. They're bound to be uncommon."

"Yes," Dorcas agreed. "The tnuctipun doubtless came on this one by chance. I'd guess that was after they'd rebelled. They saw how to use it against the Slavers. Otherwise, if they'd built the machine around it earlier, the Slavers would have been in possession, and might have quelled the uprising early on. They might be alive today."

Carita shuddered audibly. "A black hole—"

It could only be that. Mass, dimensions, radiation spectrum, everything fitted astrophysical theory. Peter Nordbo had recorded the idea in his notes, but he couldn't reconcile it with the sudden apparition in the heavens. The tumbling shell and the meteoroid gap accounted for that. Perhaps while they were here the kzinti, under his guidance, had found indirect ways to study the interior, the eerie effects of so mighty a gravitation on space-time. But *Rover*'s crew already had ample data to be confident of what it was they confronted.

Burnt out, a giant star collapses into a form so dense, infinitely dense at the core singularity, that light itself can no longer escape its grip. The minimum mass required is about three Sols. Today. In the first furious instants of creation, immediately after the Big Bang, immeasurably great forces were at play. Where they chanced to concentrate, they had the power to compress any amount of mass, however small, into the black hole state. It must have happened, over and over. Countless billions must have formed, a few large, most diminutive.

In the universe of later epochs, they are not stable. Quantum tunneling causes them to give off particles, matter and antimatter, which mutually annihilate. For a body of stellar size, the rate of evaporation is negligible. But it increases as the body shrinks. Ever faster and more fiercely does the radiation go, until in a final supernal eruption the remnant vanishes altogether. Nearly every black hole made in the beginning has thus, long since, departed.

This one had been just big enough to survive to the present day. Applying what theory the ship's database contained, Dorcas had made some estimates. Three or four billion years ago it was radiating with about half its current intensity. Its mass, equal to a minor asteroid's, was now packed inside an event horizon with a diameter less than that of an atomic nucleus. Another 50,000 years or so remained until the end.

Carita rallied. "A weapon?" she asked. "How could that be?"

"Your mind isn't as nasty as mine," Saxtorph replied absently. His attention was on high lattices, surrounding a paraboloid (?), which grew out of the shell where he stood. Their half-familiarity chewed at him. Almost, almost, he knew them.

"What else could it be?" Dorcas said. "A power source for peaceful use? Awkward and unnecessary when you have fusion, let alone total conversion. As a weapon, though, the thing is hideous. Invulnerable. Open a port, and a beam shoots out that no screen can protect against. At a minimum, electronics are scrambled and personnel get a lethal dose. No missile can penetrate that defense; if it manages to approach, it will be vaporized before it strikes. Sail through an enemy fleet, with death in your wake. Pass near any fort and leave corpses manning armament in ruins. Cruise low around a planet and sterilize it at your leisure."

"Then why didn't the tnuctipun win?"

"We'll never know. But they can only have had this one. That was scarcely decisive. And . . . the war exterminated both races. Perhaps the crew here heard they were the last of their kind, and went elsewhere to die."

Saxtorph caught Tyra's whisper: "While the black hole, the machine, drifted through space for billions of years—" The Wunderlander raised her voice: "I am sorry. I should not interrupt. But do you not overlook something?"

"What?" Dorcas sounded edgy. As well she might be after these many hours, Saxtorph told himself.

"How could the tnuctipun bring the weapon to bear?" Tyra asked. "The black hole was orbiting free

in interstellar space, surely, light-years from anywhere. The mass is huge to accelerate."

"They could have harnessed its own energy output
to a polarizer system."

"Really? Is that enough, to get it to a destination
fast enough to be useful?"

Smart girl, Saxtorph thought. She hasn't got the
figures at her fingertips, but those fingers have a
good, firm, sensitive hold on reality.

"Through hyperspace," Dorcas clipped.

"Forgive me," Tyra said. "I do not mean to be a
nuisance. You must know more about tnuctipun technology than I do. But I studied what I was able. Is it
not true that their hyperdrive was crude? It would
not work before the vessel was moving close to light
speed. This *Genstand* has ordinary velocity, in the
middle of empty space."

"That is a shrewd question," Dorcas admitted.

"A real fox question," Saxtorph said. He was coming out of his preoccupation, aware how tired he was
but also exuberant, full of love for everybody. Well,
for most beings. Especially his comrades. "It could
stonker our whole notion. Except I believe I've found
the answer. There is in fact a hyperdrive engine. It's
not like anything we know or much like any of the
hypothetical reconstructions I've seen of tnuctipun
artifacts. But I believe I can identify it for what it is,
or anyhow what it does. My guess is that, yes, they
could take this black hole through hyperspace, emerg-
ing with a reasonable intrinsic velocity that a gravity
drive could then change to whatever they needed for
combat purposes."

"How, when every ship must first move so fast?"
Tyra wondered.

"I am only guessing, mind you. But think." Despite physical exhaustion, Saxtorph's brain had seldom run like this. Talking to her was a burst of
added stimulation. "Speed means kinetic energy,
right? That's what the Slaver hyperdrive depended

on, kinetic energy, not speed in itself. Well, here you've got a terrific energy concentration, so-and-so fantastically many joules per mean cubic centimeter. If the tnuctipun invented a way to feed it to their quantum jumper, they'd be in business."

"I see. Yes. Robert, you are brilliant."

"Naw. I may be dead wrong. The tech boys and girls will need months to swarm over this gizmo before they can figure it out for sure. They better be careful. Considering how well preserved the apparatus is, in spite of everything that the black hole inside and the universe outside could do, I wouldn't be surprised but what that hyperdrive is still in working order."

"More powerful than ever," Dorcas breathed. "The black hole has been evolving."

"Brrr!" Carita exclaimed. "Knock it off, will you? If the ratcats got hold of it—" She yelped. "But they were here! Weren't they? How much did they learn? How come they didn't whoop home to Alpha Centauri with this thing and scrub our fleet out of space?"

"Even taking its time, what a single expedition could find out would be limited, I should think," Dorcas said. Her tone went metallic. "We, though, the human species, we'd better make certain."

"Yah," Saxtorph concurred. He shook himself in his armor. "Listen, I decree we're past the point of diminishing returns today. Let's head back, Carita, have a hot meal and a stiff drink, and sleep for ten or twelve hours. Then I have some ideas about our next move."

"Wow-hoo!" his companion caroled, uneasiness shoved aside. "I thought you'd decided to home-stead. Say, ever consider how lucky the tnuctip race was, not speaking English? Spell the name backwards—"

"Never mind," Saxtorph sighed. "Compute your vectors and boost."

Bound for *Rover*, he felt as if he were awakening

from a dream. In the time lately past, he had experienced in full something that had rarely and barely touched him before, the excitement of the scientist. It had been a transcendence. How did that line or two of poetry go? "Some watcher of the skies, when a new planet swims into his ken." Or a new star, small and strange, foredoomed, yet waxingly radiant; and the archaeology of a civilization vast and vanished. Now he returned to his ordinary self.

He ached, his tongue was a block of wood, his eyelids were sandpaper, but he rejoiced. By God, he had seen Truth naked, and She took him by the hand and led him beyond himself, into Her own country! It wouldn't happen again, he supposed; and that was as well. He wasn't built for it. But this once it did happen.

When he and Carita completed airlock cycle, their shipmates were waiting for them. Dorcas embraced him. "Welcome, welcome," she said tenderly.

"Thanks." He looked past her shoulder. How bright was Tyra's hair against the bulkhead. His brain hadn't yet stopped leapfrogging. "We've got facts to go on," he blurted. "Knowing what the kzinti found, we can make a pretty good guess at what they did. And where they are. With your dad."

"O-o-oh—" the Wunderlander gasped.

He disengaged. She sprang forward, seized, and kissed him.

11

When the kzinti again drew Peter Nordbo into time, his first clear thought was: Hulda, Tyra, Ib. More than twenty years now. Do you live? I almost wish not, I who come home after helping our masters arm themselves for the enslavement of all humanity. Forgive me, my darlings. I had no choice.

"Up," growled the one that hulked above him. "The commander wants you. Why, I don't know."

Nordbo blinked, bewildered. Through the gloom in the chamber he recognized the kzin. It wasn't the technician in charge of such tasks, it was one of the fire-control ratings. Their designation translated roughly as "Gunner." What had gone on? A fight, a killing? The crew were disciplined and the discoveries at the black hole had kept them enthusiastic; nevertheless, after months in close quarters, tempers grew foul and quarrels flared.

Well he knew. He bore several scars from the claws of individuals who took anger out on him. They were punished, though no disabling injury was inflicted. Nor had torture left him crippled, being carefully administered. He was too useful to damage without cause.

"Move!" Gunner hauled him from the box and flung him to the deck. There was mercy in the wave of physical pain that swept from the impact. For a moment it drowned every other awareness.

It faded, Nordbo remembered anew, he crept to his feet and hobbled off.

The corridor stretched empty and silent. How utterly silent. The rustle of ventilators sounded loud. Dread sharpened in him and cut the last dullness away. A-shiver, he reached the observation turret and entered. Only the heavens illuminated it.

No suns of Alpha Centauri shone before him, no constellations whatsoever. Around a pit of lightlessness, blue stars clustered thinly. As he stared aft he saw more, whose colors changed through yellow to red; but behind the ship yawned another darkness rimmed with embers.

Aberration and Doppler effect, he recognized. We haven't slowed down yet, we're flying ballistic at half the speed of light. Why have they revived me early? They didn't expect to. I'd served my purpose. No, their purpose. I could merely pray that when their scientists on Wunderland finished interrogating me, I'd be released to take up any rags of my life that were left. Unless it makes more sense to pray for death.

Yiao-Captain poised athwart the stranger sky. Its radiances gleamed icy on eyeballs and fangs. His ears stood unfolded but his tail switched. "You are not where you think you are," he rumbled. "Twenty-two years have passed,"—Nordbo's mind automatically rendered the timespan into human units—"and we are bound for our Father Sun."

The shock was too great. It could not register at once. Nordbo heard himself say, "May I ask for an explanation?"

Did Yiao-Captain's curtness mask pain of his own? "We were about three years en route back to Alpha Centauri." After half a year at the black hole. "A message came. It told of a fleet from Sol, invading the system and shattering our forces. Somehow the humans have gained a capability of traveling faster than light. No ship without it can win against the least of theirs. We must inevitably lose these planets. It must already have happened when *Snapping Sherrek* received the beam.

"When I was roused and informed, naturally I did not propose to continue there, bringing my great news to the enemy. I ordered our forward velocity quenched and the last of our delta v applied to send us home."

At one-half c, a trip of nearly six decades. Nordbo's thoughts trickled vague and slow. Can't stop at the far end. Hurtle on till the last reserve mass has been converted, the screen fields go out, and the wind of our passage through the medium begins to crumble us. Unless first another ship matches speed and takes us off. I daresay they'll try, once they have an idea of what this crew can tell.

It jolted: Faster than light? We had no means, nothing but some mathematical hints in quantum theory and the knowledge that the thrintun could do it, billions of years ago—knowledge that led this expedition to conclude that the artifact is indeed a gigantic hyperdrive spacecraft powered by the black hole it surrounds. But how did the means come so suddenly to my race?

A thunderbolt: Wunderland is free! My folk have been free for eighteen years!

Nightfall: While I am captive on the Flying Dutchman among the demons that sail it.

Yiao-Captain's voice rolled on: "If the humans do not find what we did, and if we can inform the Patriarchy of it, victory may yet be ours. Not from the alien vessel alone, irresistible though it be, but from what our engineers will learn."

Was he boasting, or trying to reassure himself? Certainly the words were unnecessary. Even without Nordbo's intellectual cooperation, the kzin known as Chief Physicist and his team had traced circuits, computed probable effects, inferred that the most plausible purpose was to achieve the relationship of wave functions which theory said *might* throw matter into a hypothetical hyperspace. They had actually identified an installation that appeared to be an activator of the entire system. Yiao-Captain had had to exert authority to keep three young members of the group from throwing what they thought was the main switch. Much more study was called for, a complete plan of the whole, before any such action was justifiable. Else they could well lose the whole treasure, construct and knowledge alike.

"We are continuously transmitting, over and over, the entire set of data we did acquire, together with our ideas about it, on a beam directed forward," the commander proceeded.

The merest fraction of what is there to discover, commented the remote part of Nordbo, yet an enormous load of information, words, numbers, equations, diagrams, pictures, everything we got at a cost of seven kzinti lives and the price I paid. But perhaps the beam, dopplered though its waves are, will register on someone's communicator.

"The likelihood of its being noticed, even when it reaches Kzin, is very small, of course," Yiao-Captain said. "We send it because it does go faster than we, and may perchance convey our word, should we perish along the way. Otherwise, we shall surely be detected as we near the home planets, and receivers will be adjusted to hear what we then broadcast. Meanwhile we stand three-month watches in pairs. More would be intolerable, would lead to hatred and deadly clashes, over so long a voyage. It is again my turn. Gunner is poor company. That is best; we need not see each other much, as I would have to do were he of a rank entitled to courtesy. But the time grows wearisome. Finally I have had you wakened. Maybe we can talk. Certainly we can play chess."

Realization was draining downward from Nordbo's forebrain, along the nerves, into blood and marrow. He barely swallowed his vomit. It burned gullet and belly.

Almost, he screamed aloud: Yes, whistle your pet monkey to you. Get what amusement you can out of the sorry creature. In the end, after he begins to bore you, disembowel him with a swipe of claws and eat the fresh, dripping meat. Enjoy.

Did you enjoy watching me under the torture? Your eyes shone, ears lay back, tongue ran over lips. No, it was not for pleasure in itself. It was to make me recant my refusal to work any more for you, after it became clear that what we were investigating was a monstrous weapon. You may have regretted it a little. But naturally the spectacle spoke to your instincts.

I cheated them, Yiao-Captain. I yielded within minutes. As for your contempt, inwardly I laughed. It was not the pain that changed my mind, nor the threat of mutilation and death. It was the hope of returning home, to stand once more between you and my Hulda, my children, my folk. Yes, also the crazy hope that somehow I might smuggle a warning off to Sol.

Afterward, yes, I worked for you again, but I told you of no more inspirations, insights, ideas worth trying. I did nothing, really, that a robot could not. What else can you expect from a slave, Yiao-Captain? Love?

The kzin's tone softened. "I know this is a stormwind upon you. You will need a while to regain balance. Go. Rest, think. Come back to me when you feel ready."

Nordbo stumbled from him.

Grief welled up: I have lost you for always, my beloved.

Bleak joy: You are free. We can outpace light. Surely our fleets went on to defeat the kzinti everywhere and ram peace down their throats.

Despair: But no secret has ever stayed long under lock and key. Someday, somehow, they too will gain the knowledge. This ship bears news that may well help them to it. We did conclude that the machine englobing the black hole is tnuctipun and is meant to pass it through hyperspace. We think we identified the activator. We could not puzzle out more than the likeliest-looking procedure for starting it up, and we have no idea how to set a course or stop a destination. But a later expedition, better equipped, with up-to-date physicists, ought to learn much more than we did.

Wrath: "We!" As if this were my band!

Shame: For a while it came near being so. I was captivated. In the work, I could forget my loss for hours at a time. But then I began to see what the thing must be—

Horror: A part of the arsenal that destroyed intelligent life throughout this galactic sector, those billions of years ago. Shall it fall into kzinti hands?

Logic: Oh, by itself it might not prove decisive, come (God take pity on us) the next war. But it would kill many. Worse, it would lead the kzinti to the hyperdrive; or, if they have that by now, it could well suggest improvements that make their ships irresistibly superior to ours. And who can be certain that that would be all it did?

Agony: And I am helpless, helpless.

Revelation: *NO!*

Through a time beyond time, Nordbo stood amidst lightnings. *And the remnant were slain with the sword of him that sat upon the horse—*

Apocalypse opened itself to metal, silence, and

unseen stars; but the hand of the Lord was upon him. Somewhere a voice quavered that he had better take nourishment, sleep, recover his full strength, while watching for the best chance. He scorned it into extinction. He would never be stronger than now. Surprise, and a will that had given doubt no days or weeks to corrode it, were his only allies.

With long strides he made his way to the workshop. Every sense thrilled preternaturally keen. A bulkhead bore furrows where a kzin in a rage had scratched the facing. Air from the ventilators blew warm, a tinge of ozone cleansing a ratcat taint become slight. His feet thudded on the deck, the impacts went up through his bones. His mouth was no longer dry, but hunter-wet. He had bitten his tongue and tasted the salt blood. His heart beat steady, powerful. His fingers flexed, making ready.

Though the shop was dark, cramful of stored equipment, he had no trouble finding his toolbox. Things clattered as he went after the knife he had made and left buried at the bottom. The kzinti had never suspected; else he would have become meat. He drew it forth. Heavy in his grasp, blade about thirty centimeters by two, it was crude, a piece of scrap surreptitiously sawed, hammered, and filed, a haft of plastic riveted to the tang; but patience had given it a microtome edge. He discarded the improvised sheath and held the steel behind his back when he went out. Barehanded, a kzin could take a man apart, and speed as well as strength was why. Nordbo didn't plan to waste time drawing.

Nor had he any qualms of conscience. The odds against him were huge enough without the beasts he hunted being prepared for him.

He found Gunner slumped sullen in the den that corresponded to a human ship's saloon. The kzin watched a drama which Nordbo recognized as classic. Maybe he'd seen the popular repertory too often and was desperate for entertainment. In the screen,

Chrung was attacking an enemy stronghold, wielding an ax on its parapet. Gunner was moderately interested. He did not notice the man who glided forward until Nordbo reached his shoulder.

The massive head turned. Lips pulled from fangs, irritation that might flash into murder frenzy, did the intruder not grovel and plead. Nordbo's hand came around, machine precise. He drove his knife through the right eye, upward into the brain.

Gunner bellowed. Nordbo cast himself against the great body. His left hand clung to the fur while his right twisted the knife. An arm scythed past him, reflex that would have laid him open were he in its path. He worked his blade to and fro. Abruptly he clutched limpness. The kzin sagged to the deck. Death-stench rose fetid.

Nordbo withdrew the knife and stepped aside. Not much blood ran from the socket at his feet. He had hoped for a silent kill. Well, that he had killed at all was remarkable. Next he must repeat it or die trying. He felt no fear, nor gladness or even anger. His mind was the control center of the mechanism that was himself.

He wouldn't get a second opportunity like this. A spear, a crossbow—a daydream. He glanced about. Their food being synthetic, these travelers had adopted the Wunderlander fashion of tablecloths. The gory play continued in the screen. It stirred memory of things watched or read at home, historical sociology and fiction. The trick he recalled must require long practice to be done right, but a man who had pitched tents and hoisted sails shouldn't be too inept. Heavy feet sped along the passageway outside. Nordbo took a corner of the napery in his left hand. He snapped the fabric, to gain some feeling for its behavior.

Yiao-Captain burst into the den. "What's wrong?" he roared while he slammed to a halt. His look blazed across the corpse and the man who stood beyond it, knife reddened. Insolent past belief, the man shook a rag at him and *grinned*.

For a whole second, sheer stupefaction held Yiao-Captain immobile. Then fury exploded. He screamed and leaped.

Nordbo swayed aside. The giant orange body arced across the space where the cloth rippled. It slipped aside. As the kzin passed, Nordbo hewed.

Yiao-Captain hit the bulkhead. It groaned and buckled. The kzin bounded off the deck and rushed. Nordbo was drifting toward the door. Again his capework saved him, though a leg brushed his and made him stagger. Yet he had gotten a stab into the neck.

He reached the corridor. "Blunderfoot!" he shouted in the kzinti language. "Eater of *sthondat* dung! Come get me if you dare!" His trick would soon fail him unless he kept his antagonist amok.

Yiao-Captain charged. Blood marked his trail, pumped out of the rents beneath ribs and jaws. Nordbo cut him. Leaping by, he closed teeth on fabric. Nordbo nearly lost it. He slashed it across and saved half.

Scarlet spouted. My God, I got a major vein, Nordbo realized. Yiao-Captain turned. He lurched and mewled, but he attacked. Nordbo retreated. Flick cape over eyeballs, once, twice, thrice. Blindly, Yiao-Captain went past. Nordbo sliced his tail off.

Yiao-Captain came back around. He crumpled to his knees, to all fours. Snarling, he crawled at the man. Nordbo backed up, easily keeping ahead of him.

Yiao-Captain stopped. He stared. The raw whisper held a sudden gentleness. Or puzzlement? "Speaker for Humans, I . . . I liked you. I thought . . . you liked . . . me. . . ." He collapsed. His death struggle took several minutes.

The ship is mine, said the computer in Nordbo's head. Not that I can do anything with it. Except, of course, shut off the beamcast. And wait. Recycling is operative; plenty of food and water. Including kzin steaks, if I want. I can break into the small arms locker and shoot them where they lie. But probably that's too ugly an act. I am not a kzin, I am a man.

Otherwise I wait. Forty or more years till I reach their sun. I will occupy myself, handicrafts, study of what's in the database, love letters to Hulda. Meditation, maybe. For something may yet happen to set me free. The one sure way to lose all hope is to give up all hope.

Rationality fell apart. He retched and began to shake, miserably cold. Reaction. Let him go sleep and sleep and sleep. Afterward he would eat something, and clean up this mess, and settle down into solitude.

12

In galactic space a sun is a mote, a planet well-nigh infinitesimal. How then to find a spacecraft falling through light-years?

"Ve haff our met'ods," boasted Saxtorph. Begin by reasoning. The kzinti would not stay longer at the black hole than it took to learn everything they were able; and they were doubtless not extremely well chosen or well outfitted for scientific research. Having shot a beam at Alpha Centauri, describing what they had done and recommending a proper expedition, they'd start after it. Presently they'd receive word that the system was falling to an armada from Sol. Consider the dates of events, assume they'd been some months at work before they set forth, figure in acceleration time, and you conclude that they got the news about a third of the way along their course. What would they then plausibly do? Why, make for 61 Ursae Majoris, the star that Kzin itself orbits, the world that spawned their breed. Just as likely, they'd spend their engine reserve boosting to a full half c, and now be moving at approximately that speed. Calculate the trajectory.

Your answer will reflect the uncertainties in your guesstimates. What you get is not a curve but a cone. The ship is somewhere near the top, which leaves you with a volume still so enormous that random search is a fool's errand.

However, space is not empty. The interstellar medium, mostly hydrogen with some helium and pinches of higher elements, has a mean density equivalent to about one proton per cubic centimeter. An object passing through it at 150,000 klicks per second hits a *lot* of stuff. The X-rays given off at these encounters would quickly fry the crew and their electronics, save that the screen fields keep the gas at a distance from the hull and guide it into a fairly smooth flow. Nevertheless, the perturbation is considerable. Atoms are excited and emit softer quanta. The tunnel of near-total vacuum left behind the vessel will take years to fill: which means it is correspondingly long. All this shows in the radio spectrum from that part of the sky. Sensitive instruments can detect it across quite a few parsecs.

The technique was not original with Saxtorph. The UN Navy had developed and employed it during the war. Since *Rover* was not specially equipped for it, he did have to devise modifications. In essence, he went via hyperspace from point to precalculated point. At each, his gang took readings. Dorcas had written a program that interpreted them. In due course, the seekers should get an identification. On that basis they could measure a parallax and obtain a fix.

Saxtorph and Tyra sat by themselves over beers in the saloon. Talk ransacked the past, for the future seemed like a wire drawn so taut that at any moment it would snap and the sharp ends recoil. "Oh, yes," she said, "I have been on Silvereyes. It is fascinating. A hundred lifetimes were too little for to understand those ecologies."

"You were writing about it?" he inquired.

"What else? One must pay for one's travel somehow. Of course, I knew better than to try squeezing a whole world into a book. I looked me around, but that which I made my subject was the Cyclops island."

"Really? I've got to read your book when we get back. You see, I was there myself once. A tourniquet vine damn near did for a shipmate, but we chopped her free in time, and otherwise it was, as you say, fascinating. I begrudged every minute I was on duty and couldn't explore."

"You have been everywhere, have you not?" she murmured.

"No, no, much though I'd like to. Besides, this wasn't my idea. Navy, tail end of the war, establishing a just-in-case base. Satellite, but initial supplies of air and water and such would come from the ground."

Reminiscence went on. "—boats, to check out the surrounding shoals. A simple mooring is a timber tethered to a rock. What I could've told those clowns, because I'd been in Hawaii, was that they'd picked a chunk of volcanic pumice. But I wouldn't've known either that the log was stonewood. So they took the ensemble to the mooring place and heaved it overboard, and the rock floated while the log sank."

He always liked the heartiness of Tyra's laughter.

"Here I've gone again, blathering on about me," he said. "You're a good listener—no, a great, a vintage listener—but honest, I set out to hear about you. And I really can listen, too."

She sobered. "I know. Not many men can, or will. You act very everyday, Robert, but in truth you are a deep and complicated person."

"Wrong, wrong. Never mind. I said we should talk about you. Uh, on Silvereyes, did you visit the Amanda Lakes region?"

"Of course." Tyra sighed. "Beauty that high comes near to hurt, no? At least when there is no one to share it with."

"You had nobody? You should have."

Her smile was rueful. "Well, I roomed with another woman. Although she was pleasant, finally we agreed what a shame that one of us was of the wrong sex."

"Yah, I daresay it'll become a favorite honeymoon resort." Saxtorph stared into his beer stein. "Tyra, none of my business, except we're friends. But you rate better than going through life alone the way you're doing."

She reached across the table and laid her hand on his. "You are kind." Her voice lowered. "On this journey I have discovered my father was not the only man who is a fine creature."

"Aw, hey—"

They turned their heads. Tyra pulled her hand back. Dorcas had entered. Her slenderness reared over them. "We have a decision to make about the next jump point," she said calmly. "It depends on what weight we give the last set of data. Will you come and consult, Bob?"

Saxtorph's chair scraped. " 'Scuse me, Tyra."

The Wunderlander smiled. "Why should I?" she replied. "What need? You go in my cause."

He tossed off his drink and left with his wife. When they were several meters down the corridor, she told him, "I lied, you realize. Not to make a scene."

"For Christ's sake!" he exclaimed. "Nothing was going on."

"I'd prefer to keep it that way."

"You, jealous?" He forced a chuckle. "Honey, you flatter me."

"Not exactly. I've watched where things are headed. No bad intentions on anybody's part. I continue to like her myself. But, Bob, I'd hate to see you hurt. And I've no reason—so far—to wish it on her. As for this team of ours—" She clutched his forearm. Had the muscle been less thick underneath, her fingers would have left marks.

13

Weoch-Captain was a thoughtful and self-controlled kzin. Much though he lusted to streak directly to his goal, first he pondered the implications of what he knew about it. Ideas came to him which he communicated to Ress-Chiuu. The High Admiral agreed that his flight plan should be changed.

Therefore *Swordbeak* cruised about, in and out of hyperspace, day after tedious day. It chewed on nerves. The crew grew restless. Quarrels exploded. A couple of times they led to fights. Weoch-Captain disciplined the offenders severely; they were long in sickbay and would bear the marks for the rest of their lives.

He had given his officers an explanation. The Swift Hunter that went to the unknown body had not been heard of again. If it found the thing, as was probable, this would have happened just about when the human armada entered the Alpha Centaurian System. That news would have taken five years to reach the ship, except that it was likely bound back. What then was its best course? Other kzin-held worlds might fall to the enemy before it could get to any of them. Wisest was to head directly for the Father Sun, especially if the expedition had made worthwhile discoveries. Assuming the crew still lived, they were now about a third of the way home. *Swordbeak* ought to search them out and learn what they could tell, before proceeding. Furthermore, such Heroes deserved to know as soon as possible that they were not forgotten.

Every basis for calculation was a matter of guessing. That included, especially, the location of the mystery object. The data that Ress-Chinn's informant had been able to pass on were fragmentary, maddeningly vague. Thus the Swift Hunter's cone of location was immense. But the High Admiral had ordered Weoch-Captain's vessel outfitted with the best radio spectrum detectors and analyzers that its hull could accommodate.

So at length his technicians identified a tunnel of passage and placed it approximately in space. Prudence dictated that *Swordbeak* not attempt immediate rendezvous. The precise trajectory and momentary position of the other craft remained unclear; and mass moving at half light-speed is dangerous. Weoch-Captain made for a point about two light-years behind. Inside the trail, the technicians could map it exactly and pinpoint his target.

There they picked up a message.

Weoch-Captain was not totally surprised. In a like situation, he did not think he would send a radio beam ahead. The slimy humans might come upon it, read it, and jam it. However, the idea of superluminal travel would have been unfamiliar to the expedition members. They would scarcely have thought of everything that it meant. If the possibility did occur to them, they might well have discounted it, since the probability of interception was slight, while the transmission increased by a little the likelihood that the

Patriarchs would eventually get the news they bore. At any rate, Weoch-Captain had provided for the contingency. When he reached the tunnel, receivers were open on a wide enough band that they would register anything, Doppler-diminished though the waves be.

They buzzed. A computer got busy. A part of the message unrolled on a screen before him.

He narrowed his eyes. What *was* this? "—*material unknown. Eroded but, except where pierced, impervious to radiation*—" His finger stabbed at the intercom. The image of Executive Officer appeared. "We have evidently come in in the middle of a sending," Weoch-Captain said. "Doubtless the Swift Hunter plays a recorded beamcast continuously. I want the entirety of it. Have an acquisition program prepared."

"Immediately, sire."

"Mock me not," purred the commander. "You know full well that we shall have to leap about, snatching pieces here and there, while reception will often be poor; and the whole must be fitted together in proper sequence, ungarbled where needful, until it is complete and coherent; and the highly technical content will make this a process difficult and slow. Do you suggest I am ignorant of communications principles?"

Executive Officer was a Hero, but he remembered the punishments. "Never, sire! I misspoke me. I abase myself before you."

"Correct." Weoch-Captain switched off. He had not actually taken offense. Because he was a cautious leader, he must snatch every opportunity to assert dominance.

Alone, he rose and prowled the control cabin. Its narrowness caged him. The real mockery came from the stars in the viewport, multitudes and majesty, a hunting ground unbounded. He bared fangs at them. *We shall range among you yet,* he vowed; *we shall do with you what we will.*

First the humans—

Excitement waxed. Clearly the expedition had caught something important, something of power. He would persist until he knew everything the message told. Then he would seek out the old ship, hear whatever might remain to hear, give whatever praise and reassurance were due. And then, informed and prepared, he would be off to the goal of all this voyaging.

His ears lay back. The hair stood up on his body. Let any monkeys that he might encounter beware. The kzinti had much to avenge.

14

Once more *Rover* came out of hyperspace, and there the fugitive was. A computer recognized the inputs to instruments; a chime sounded; an image leaped onto a screen. "That's it," said Saxtorph quietly in the command cabin. The intercom brought him a gasp from Tyra at the mass detector. Everybody else was at a duty station, too. "Got to be."

He increased magnification, and the spark crawling across the constellations waxed. Tyra saw the same, on the viewer where she was. Optics set limits to what could be reconstructed at a distance of some eighty million kilometers, but he made out a blurry lancehead shape amidst a comma of bluish light, which trailed aft like a tail, the visible part of photons from excited atoms and plasma around the screen fields and aft of them. The invisible part was greater, and deadly.

"The right class of vessel, and just about where she ought to be," Saxtorph added. "Uh, what's her name? I forget."

"*Khrach-Sherrek*," Dorcas supplied. It was in the bit of record and recollection that had survived. "A cursorial carnivore on their home planet." She didn't normally waste breath on trivia. Anticipated though it was, this culmination must have shaken her, too.

"Well, well," came Ryan's voice, overly genial. "That was fun. Now what shall we play?"

"*Dada-mann*," Tyra whispered. Saxtorph guessed it was unconscious, her pet name for her father when she was small. He imagined tears running down her cheeks, and wanted to go hold her hand and speak comfort. Her words strengthened, not yet quite steady. "Y-yes, that is the proper question. Isn't it? How shall we get him out? Have you had any more ideas, Robert?"

They had discussed it, of course, over and over, as watch after watch dragged by. Yonder vessel couldn't decelerate if the kzinti aboard wanted to, and *Rover* hadn't a decent fraction of the delta v necessary to match velocities. In the era of hyperdrive such capabilities were very nearly as obsolete as flint axes. If somebody took off in a boat, he'd still have that forward speed, and be unable to kill enough of it to help before his energy reserve was gone. Not that there'd be any point in trying. A boat's screens were totally inadequate against the level of radiation involved. He'd be doomed in a second, dead in an hour or two. The craft would become an instant derelict, electronics burned out.

The UN Navy kept a few high-boosters. They had marginal utility for certain kinds of research. "Besides," Saxtorph had observed, "all government agencies hoard stuff to a degree a squirrel or jaybird would envy. They've also got quite a lot else in common with squirrels and jaybirds."

Rigged with a hyperdrive, such a craft could theoretically come out here, spend months building up her vector, at last draw close, mesh fields, and extend a gang tube—if the kzinti cooperated. If they didn't, an operation already perilous would become insanely so, forcing an entry under those conditions in order to meet armed resistance. Either way, the expense would be staggering. Next year's budget might even have to cut back on a boondoggle or two. Would the top brass consider it, to rescue one man, a man convicted of treason? Saxtorph's bet was that they wouldn't. If they did anything, it would most likely be to order the ship destroyed—simple and safe; leave an undeflectably large mass ahead of her— before she brought home intelligence of the black hole.

He'd not had the heart to express his opinion as more than a possibility, nor did he now. After all, in the course of time Tyra might conceivably manage to rouse public sentiment and turn it into political pressure. She was a skilled writer, and beautiful. Never had he pointed out that her success must entail mortal hazard to a number of other lives. Once he'd thought Dorcas was about to say it, and had given her their private "steer clear" sign. "She's got grief aplenty as is," he explained later.

"We start by peering, don't we?" Carita put in. Good girl, Saxtorph thought. You can always count on her for nuts-and-bolts common sense.

"Right," he said. "Not that I expect we'll learn a lot. However, let's secure every loose end we can before we decide on any further moves."

"We shall c-call them," Tyra stammered. "Shall we not?"

"Well, I suppose we should, but I want to gang mighty warily. 'Twon't be easy, you know."

Indeed not. Aberration and Doppler effect complicated the task abundantly. The speed that caused them made matters worse yet. If *Rover* sent a message, by the time a response could arrive, *Sherrek* would have passed the point where *Rover* lay. Saxtorph meant to stay always well clear. It would be nice if he could fake matched velocity by popping in and out of hyperspace. Too bad that transition between relativistic and quantum modes required time to get the wave functions of atoms into the proper phase relationships. Late in the war the kzinti had figured this out and discovered what the neutrino emission pattern was when a drive prepared itself. Warned of impending attack from an unpredictable new direction, they'd actually won a couple of engagements.

Modern vessels changed state in minutes. The engineers talked about future models that would only take seconds. *Rover*'s antiquated engine needed almost half an hour. Ordinarily that made no difference. You'd be doing something else meanwhile anyway, such as completing your climb sufficiently high out of a gravity well. But here she'd better come no closer than a quarter billion klicks ahead of *Sherrek*. Preferably much more.

"Bloody hell!" cried Ryan. "Why are we glooming and dooming like this? We've *found* her! Let's throw a proper luau."

A sob caught in Tyra's throat. "Thank you, Kam. Yes. Let us."

When she's seen the ship and doesn't know whether her father is alive or dead or worse, thought Saxtorph. That's one gallant lass. "Okay," he said. "The computers can handle the observations. We'll put other functions on auto and relax. Aside from you, Kam. We expect something special for dinner this evenwatch."

"I will help," Tyra said. "I . . . need to."

"No, you don't," Saxtorph told her. "At least, not right off. Report to the saloon. What *I* need help with is downing two or three large schooners."

She smiled forlornly as he entered, but she did smile. Quickly, before the rest arrived, he took both her hands in his. Their eyes met and lingered. Hearing footfalls, they let go. He felt a little breathless and giddy.

Either Tyra put tension aside and cheered up in the course of the next eight hours, or she did a damn good job of acting. The party wasn't riotous, but it became warm, affectionate, finally sentimental. After they started singing, she gave them several ballads from her homeland. She had a lovely voice.

15

Effort upon effort succeeded ultimately in getting
through. The first partial, distorted reply croaked
forth. Dorcas heard and yelled. She, who had the
most knowledge of kzin xenology, was prepared to
speak through a translator for her band. What she
would say, she could not foresee; she must grope
forward. Could she bargain, could she threaten? To
her husband she admitted that her hopes were low.
He agreed, more grimly than the situation seemed to
warrant as far as they two were concerned.

She was not prepared for human words.

"*Sind Sie wirklich Menschen?*" And what must be
Tyra's own dialect: "*Gud Jesu, endelig! Hvor langt,
hvor langt—*" Interference ripped the cry asunder.
Static hissed and snarled like a kzin.

"Hang in there," Saxtorph said. "I'll be back." He
scrambled from his seat and out of the cabin. Dorcas'
gaze followed him.

Nobody else had been listening. To endure repeated failures is mere masochism, if you yourself

can do nothing about them. Saxtorph pounded on Tyra's door. "Wake up!" he bellowed. "We've contacted your father! He lives, he lives!"

The door flew open and she stumbled into his arms. She slept unclothed. He held her tightly until she stopped weeping and shivered only a little. She was warm and firm and silken. "We don't know more than that," he mouthed. Did desire shout louder in his blood than compassion? "It's going to take time. What'll come of it, we can't tell. But we're working on it, Tyra. We are."

She drew herself free and stood before him. Briefly, fists clenched at her sides. Then she remembered the situation, crossed arms over the fairness above and below, caught a ragged breath and blinked the tears away. "Yes, you will," she answered before she fled, "because you are what you are. I can abide."

She did, calmly, even blithely, while three daycycles passed and the story arrived in shreds and snatches. When at last the whole crew met, bodily, for they needed to draw strength from each other, she sat half smiling.

Saxtorph looked around the saloon table. "Okay," he said with far more steadiness than he felt, "Peter Nordbo is alive, well, and alone. Two years alone, but better that than the company he was keeping, and apparently he's stayed sane. The problem is how to debark him. I can be honest now and tell you that I don't expect any navy will do the job, nor anybody else that may have the capability."

"Why not?" Carita asked. "He's got important information, hasn't he, about the black hole? That expedition checked it over as thoroughly as they could."

The captain began filling his pipe. "Yah, but you see, their information's in the radio beam the ship was transmitting till he took over. A hell of a lot quicker, easier, and safer to recover than by matching velocity and boarding. Oh, I daresay what he's gone through and what he's done will stir up a wave of public sympathy, but unless it becomes a tsunami, that probably won't be enough."

"Among the considerations," Dorcas added in an impersonal tone, "*Sherrek* is approaching kzin-controlled space. Kzinti hyperships are bound to be sniffing about. A few of their kind did have valid reasons, from their viewpoint, to flee Alpha Centauri twenty years ago, rather than die fighting or get taken prisoner. The kzinti will search for any, as well as exploring on general principles. I agree the chance of their spotting *Sherrek*'s trail by accident is small, but it is finite, and every month that passes makes it larger. I can well imagine political objections to risking an unwanted incident, on top of every other argument."

"We can go home, report this, and agitate for help," Saxtorph said. "It's the sensible, obvious course. I won't veto it, if that's what you want."

Tyra gave him a sea-blue regard. "You have a different possibility," she said low.

His grin twisted. "You've gotten to know me, huh?"

She nodded. Light sheened across her hair.

"It's a dicey thing," he said. "Some danger to us, a lot to your father. But if it works, you'll have him back in days."

"Else years," she replied as softly as before, "or never." Only her fingernails, white where she gripped the tabletop, revealed more. "What think you on?"

"We've, uh, discussed it, him and Dorcas and me. In the jaggedy fashion you've observed. We didn't want to announce this earlier, because we had to do some figuring and would've hated to . . . disappoint you." Saxtorph put fire to pipe. "Yon ship carries a pair of flyby capsules, unpowered but made to withstand extremely heavy radiation. As much as you'd get at one-half *c*. He can get inside one and have its launcher toss him out." He puffed forth a cloud.

"You believe you can recover him," she said, and began to tremble ever so slightly.

"Yes. Our new grapnel field installation. If we get the configuration and timing just right—if not, you realize, he's gone beyond any catching—if we do, we can lock on. *Rover* has more mass by several orders of magnitude. We estimate that the combined momentum will mean a velocity of about 200 klicks per second, well within our delta v reserve."

"Down from . . . that speed? I should think—" she must struggle to utter it "—the acceleration overcomes your polarizers and tears your grappler out through the hull."

"Smart girl." How ludicrously inadequate that was for his admiration. "It would also reduce him to thin jelly. We can do up to fifty g. The capsules have interior polarizers with power to counteract a bit more, but we want a safety factor. Our systems can handle it, too. Do you know about deep-sea fishing? Your dolphins may have told stories of marlin and tarpon."

She nodded again. "I saw a documentary once. And in the Frisian Sea on Wunderland I have myself taken a dinotriton." Ardor flamed up. "I see! You let the capsule run, but never far enough to get away, and you play it, you pull it in a little at a time—"

"Right. The math says we can do it in three and a half daycycles, through a distance of 225 billion kilometers. In practice it'll doubtless be harder." He had to have a moment's relief. "Anderson's Law, remember: 'Everything takes longer and costs more.'"

Awe struck her. She sagged back in her chair. "The skill—"

"The danger," Dorcas said. "At any point we can fail. *Rover* may then suffer damage, although if we stand ready I don't expect it'll cripple us. But your father will be a dead man."

"What thinks he?"

"He's for it," Saxtorph replied. "Of course a buck like that would be. But he leaves the decision to us. With . . . his blessing. And we, Dorcas and I, we leave it to you. I imagine Kam and Carita will go along with whatever you choose."

Abruptly Tyra's voice wavered. "Kam," she said, "you have taught me a word of yours, a very good, brave word. I use it now." She leaped to her feet. "Go for broke!" she shouted.

The Hawaiian and the Jinxian cheered.

Thereafter it was toil, savage demands on brain and body, nerves aquiver and pulled close to breaking, heedless overuse of stimulants, tranquilizers, whatever might keep the organism awake and alert.

No humans could have done the task. The forces involved were immensely too great, changeable, complex. Nor could they be felt at the fingertips; over spatial reaches, the lightspeed that carried them became a laggard, and the fisher must judge what was happening when it would not manifest itself for minutes. The computer program that Dorcas wrote with the aid of the computer that was to use it, this held the rod and reeled the line.

Yet humans must be in the loop, constantly monitoring, gauging, making judgments. Theirs was the intuition, the instinct and creative insight, that no one has engineered into any machine. The Saxtorphs were the two best qualified. Carita could handle the less violent hours. The main burden fell on Dorcas. Ryan and Tyra kept them fed, coffeed, medicated. Often she rubbed a back, kneaded shoulders, ran a wet washcloth over a face, crooned a lullaby at a catnap. Mostly she did it for the captain.

From dead *Sherrek*, the cannonball that held the living shot free. Unseeable amidst the light of lethal radiation, a force-beam reached to lay hold. Almost, the grip failed. Needles spun on dials and Dorcas cast her man a look of terror. Things stabilized. The hook was in.

Gently, now, gently. Itself a comet trailing luminance, the capsule fled. The grapnel field stretched, tugging, dragging *Rover* along, but how slowly slow-ing it. As distance grew, precision diminished. The capsule plunged about. The Saxtorphs ordered compensating boosts. Ideally, they could maintain contact across the width of a planetary system. In fact, the chance of losing it was large.

They played their fish.

Hour by hour, day by day, the haste diminished, the gap closed. Worst was a moment near the end, when the capsule was visible in a magnifying screen, and suddenly rolled free. Somehow Dorcas clapped the grapnel back onto it. Then: "Take over for a while, Bob," she choked, put head in hands, and wept. He couldn't recall, at that point, when he had last seen her shed tears.

Ship and sphere drew nigh. A cargo port opened. The catch went in. The port shut and air roared into the bay. Some time yet must pass; at first that metal was too cold for flesh to approach. When at length its own hatch cracked, the warmth and stench of life long confined billowed out.

A man crept after. He rose unsteadily, tall, hooknosed, bushy-bearded, going gray, though still hard and lithe. He climbed a ladder. A door swung wide for him. Beyond waited his daughter.

16

The song of her working systems throbbed through *Rover*, too softly for ears to hear anything save rustles and murmurs, yet somehow pervading bones, flesh, and spirit. In Ryan's cabin Carita asked, "But *why* are we headed back to the black hole? Add a week's travel time at least, plus whatever we spend there. I've *seen* the damn thing. Why not straight to Wunderland?"

She had been asleep, exhausted, when her shipmates made the decision, and had only lately awakened, to eat ravenously and join her friend. The rest had spent their remnant strength laying plans and getting on hyperspatial course. Ryan took the first mass detector watch. Tyra had it now, drowsily; when relieved, she would doubtless seek her bunk again.

"We thought you'd agree, and in any case wouldn't appreciate being hauled out to cast a vote when the count could just go one way," Ryan answered. "Wherever we picked, it was foolish to linger. Nothing else to gain, and a small possibility that a ratcat *moku* might suddenly pop up and shout, 'Boo!' Care for a drink?"

"You know me. In several different meanings of the word." Carita propped a pillow between her and the bulkhead and lounged back, her legs twin pillars of darkness on the gaudy bedspread. Ryan stepped across to a cabinet above a minifridge. He'd crowded a great deal of sybaritism into his quarters. In the screen, a barely clad songstress sat under a palm tree near a beach, plucked a ukulele, and looked seductive as she crooned. He did esoteric things with rum and fruit juices.

Meanwhile he explained: "Partly it's a matter of recuperation. Nordbo's served a hitch in Hell, and we visited the forecourts of Purgatory, eh? When we return, the sensation and the official flapdoodle are going to make what happened after the red sun business seem like a session of the garden committee of the Philosophical Society. We'd better be well rested and have a lot of beforehand thinking done."

"M-m, yes, that makes sense. But I can tell you pleasanter places to let our brains simmer down in than that black hole. You know what the name means in Russian?"

Ryan laughed. "Uh-huh. So they call it a 'frozen star.' Pretty turn of phrase. Except that this one never really was a star, and is anything but frozen."

"It's turned into a kind of star, then." For a moment they were silent. The same vision stood before them, a radiance more terrible century by century, at last day by day, until its final nova-like self-immolation. For the most part spacefarers speak casually, prosaically about their work, because the reality of the universe is as daunting as the reality of death.

"Well, but we've got a reason," Ryan continued. "Nailing down a claim of discovery. The kzinti examined the artifact as thoroughly as they could, much more than our quick once-over. Especially, of course, with an eye to the military potentials. Nordbo was there. He knows fairly well what they learned. But as you'd expect, he needs to refresh his memory. He told us the kzinti ship beamcast a full description till he got control and shut it off. But we aren't equipped to retrieve it. Think how much trouble we had communicating with him. We could waste weeks, and not be sure of recording more than snatches. Let Nordbo revisit the actual thing, repeat a few measurements and such, and he can write that description himself, or enough of it to establish the claim."

Carita raised her brows. "What claim? The government's bound to swarm there, take charge, and stamp everything Incredibly Secret."

Ryan nodded. "Does a shark eat fish? They'll be plenty peeved at us for telling the *hoi polloi* that it exists at all. We've got to do that, if only as part of Nordbo's vindication, but I'll concede that it's probably best to keep quiet about the technical details. However, he'll have priority of discovery. For legal purposes, the kzinti and their beamcast can be ignored. They shanghaied him, among numerous other unlawful acts; they've forfeited any rights, not to mention that there is no court with jurisdiction. He'll be entitled to a discoverer's award. In view of the importance of the find, and the fact that public disputes would be very awkward for the government, that award will be plenty big—and we'll share it with him."

"Ah-ha!" Carita exulted. "I see. You were right, there was no need to roll me out of the sheets to vote."

"Same thing should apply to the kzinti ship, if the Navy elects to go recover it for intelligence purposes," Ryan said. "Not likely, though. My guess is they'll simply read the message and then jam it. The black hole is our real jackpot." He finished mixing the drinks and gave her one. *"Pōmaika'i."*

"Into orbit." Rims clinked. He sat down on the edge of the bunk.

Carita turned thoughtful. "That poor man. He will be, uh, vindicated, won't he?"

"Oh, yes. If necessary, he can take truth tests, but the story by itself, with the corroboration we can give, should do the trick. His name will be cleared, his family will be reinstated in its clan, and he'll get back the property that was confiscated, or compensation for it if reversion isn't practical. He won't need any award money. I suspect he's forcing himself, for our sake."

Carita stared before her. "How's he taking all this?"

Ryan shrugged. "Too early to tell. Excitement; exhaustion; the last scrap of endurance that stimulants could give, spent on making plans. But surely he'll be okay. He's a tough cookie if ever I bit into one."

Compassion gentled her voice. "He met his little girl-child, and she was a not-quite-young woman. She told him his wife has died."

"I think I saw grief, though he was fairly stoic throughout. However, it can't have been a huge surprise. And he wouldn't be human if, down underneath, he didn't feel a slight relief."

"Yes. She'd have been old. I bet he'd have stuck loyally by her till the end, but— Well, sheer pride in his daughter ought to help him a lot, emotionally."

"A rare specimen, her." Ryan let out an elaborate sigh. "And sexy as Pele, under that brisk, sprightly, competent surface. I'd give a lot to be in the path of the next eruption. No such luck, though. In a perfectly pleasant fashion, she's made that clear. It's the single fault I find in her."

Carita drank deep, frowned, and drank again. "Her eyes are on the skipper. And his on her. They can't hide it any longer, no matter how hard they try."

"I know, I know. I'm resigned. If anybody rates that fling—more than me, that is—Bob does."

"Dorcas."

"Aw, she shouldn't mind too much. She's as realistic a soul as our species has got."

Carita's lips tightened. "I'm afraid this wouldn't be just a fling."

"Huh? Come on, now."

"You've been giving Tyra your whole attention. I've paid some to him."

"You really think—?" Flustered, Ryan took a long drink of his own. "Well, none of our business." He relaxed, smiled, leaned over, laid an arm across her waist. "How about we attend to what does concern us, firepants? It's been a while."

For a little span yet Carita sat troubled, then she put her tumbler aside, smiled back, and turned to him. The ship sailed on through lightlessness.

17

"No, I must speak the truth," said Chief Communications Officer. "We will continue trying if the commander orders, but I respectfully warn it will be a total waste of time and effort. The commander knows we have beamed every kind of signal on every band available to us. Not so much as an automaton has responded. That vessel is dead."

Or sleeping beyond any power of ours to disturb, thought Weoch-Captain. He stared into the screen before him as if into a forest midnight. At its distance, the runaway was a thin flame, crawling across the stars. Imagination failed to feel the immensity of its haste and of the energy borne thereby.

"I concur," he said after a minute. "Deactivate your apparatus and stand by for further orders." Rage flared. "Go, you *sthondat*-licker! Go!"

The image blinked off. Weoch-Captain mastered his temper. Chief Communications Officer did not deserve that, he thought. This past time, locked in futility, has made me as irascible as the lowliest crew member.

What, do I regret taking it out on him? I am thinking like a monkey—also by looking inward and gibing at myself. No other Hero must ever know. Yes, we are badly overdue for some action.

Weoch-Captain cast introspection from him and concentrated on the future. Not that he had a large choice. He could not overhaul *Sherrek*, board, and learn its fate. He had repeatedly suppressed an impulse to have it destroyed, that object which mocked him with silence. The Patriarchs would decide what to do about it. He could return directly to them and report. A human shipmaster would do so as a matter of course, given the circumstances.

The High Admiral has granted me broad discretion. If I come back with my basic mission half-completed, someone else may take it from me and go capture the glory. Also, I do *not* think like a monkey.

He summoned Astronomer's image. "Does analysis suggest anything new about the perturbation you noticed?" he inquired without expectations.

"No, or I would have informed the commander immediately. The data are too sparse. Something roiled the interstellar medium besides *Sherrek*, a few light-days aft of where we found it, but the effect was barely noticeable. The commander recalls my idea that a stray rock encountered the screen fields, too small to penetrate but large enough to leave a trail as it was flung aside in fragments. Further number-crunching has merely reinforced my opinion that a search would be useless."

Yes, thought Weoch-Captain. The overwhelming size of space. And if we did retrieve a meteoroidal shard or two, what of it? An improbable encounter, but not impossible, and altogether meaningless. Whatever happened to *Sherrek* happened a light-year farther back, two years in the past, which is when we established that it ceased communicating.

And yet I have a hunter's intuition—

A cold thrill passed through him. He dismissed

Astronomer and called Executive Officer. "Prepare for hyperspace," he said. "We shall proceed to our primary goal."

"At once, sir!" the kzin rejoiced.

"En route, you will conduct combat drill with full simulations. The crew have grown edgy and ill-coordinated. You will make them again into an efficient fighting machine. Despite what we have learned from the beamcast, there is no foreseeing what we will find at the far end."

"Sire."

Humans? thought Weoch-Captain. Maybe, maybe. According to our information, the black hole was not their principal objective; but monkey curiosity, if nothing else, may hold them at it still. Or—I know not, I simply have a feeling that they are involved in *Sherrek*'s misfortune. They, the same who destroyed Werlith-Commandant and his great enterprise.

Be there, Saxtorph, that I may take the glory of killing you.

18

Stars crowded the encompassing night, wintry brilliant. Alpha Centauri was only one among them, and Sol shone small. The Milky Way glimmered around the circle of sight, like a river flowing back into its wellspring. Rifts in it were dustclouds such as veil the unknown heart of the galaxy. Big in vision, a worldlet hilled and begrown with strangeness, loomed the black hole artifact.

Rover held station fifty kilometers off the hemisphere opposite the radiation-spouting gap. "Below" her, Peter Nordbo, with Carita Fenger to help, examined a structure that he believed could throw the entire mass into hyperspace. Elsewhere squatted the robot prospector, patiently tracing a circuit embedded in the shell substance.

Aboard ship was leisure. Dorcas kept the bridge, mostly on general principles. If the robot signaled that it had finished, she would confer with Nordbo and order it to a different site. Ryan watched a show in his cabin; some people would have been surprised to know it was *King Lear*. Saxtorph and Tyra sat over coffee in the saloon. When Carita relieved him on the surface and he flitted back up, he had meant to sleep, but the Wunderlander met him and they fell to talking.

"Your dad shouldn't work so hard," he said. "Three watches out of four, daycycle after daycycle. He ought to take it easier. We've got as much time as we care to spend."

"He is impatient to finish and go home," Tyra said. "You can understand."

"Yes. Home to sadness, though."

"But more to hope."

Saxtorph nodded. "Uh-huh. He's that sort of man. Not that I have any close acquaintance, but—a great guy. I see now why you laid everything on the line to buy a chance of having him again." He paused before adding in a rush: "And with you once more in his life, he's bound to become happy."

She looked away. "You should not— Oh, Robert, you are too kind, always too kind to me. I shall miss you so much."

He reached across the table and took her hand. "Hey, there, little lady, don't borrow trouble. You know I'll be detained on Wunderland for a goodly spell, like it or not." He grinned. "Want to help me like it?"

Her eyes sought back to his. The blood mounted in her face. "Yes, we must see what we can—"

Dorcas' voice tore across hers. "Emergency stations! Kzinti ship!" Coming from every annunciator, it seemed to roll and echo down the corridors.

"Judas priest! To the boat, Tyra!" Saxtorph shouted. He was already on his way. His feet slapped out a devil's tattoo on the deck. As he ran, the enormity of the tidings crashed into him.

At the control cabin, he burst through its open door and flung himself into the seat by Dorcas'. In the forward viewport, the shell occulted the suns of their desire. Starboard, port, aft gleamed grandeur indifferent to them. The communicator, automatically switched on when it detected an incoming signal, gave forth the flat English of a translator: "—not attempt to escape. If we observe the neutrino signature of a hyperspatial drive starting up, we will fire."

Sweat shone on the woman's scalp, around her Belter crest. Saxtorph caught an acrid whiff of it, or was that his own, running down his ribs? Her fingers moved firm over a keyboard. "Ha, I've got him," she whispered. A speck appeared in the scanner screen. She magnified.

Toylike still, the other vessel appeared. Saxtorph followed current naval literature. He identified the lean length, the guns and missile tubes and ray projectors, of a Raptor-class warcraft. The meters told him she was about half a million klicks off, closing fast.

"Acknowledge!" the radio snapped.

"Message received," he said around an acid lump in his gorge. "What do you want? We're here legitimately. Our races are at peace." Yah, sure, sure.

"Oh, God, Bob," Dorcas choked while the beam winged yonder. "The call was the first sign I had. She may have emerged a long distance away. If we'd spotted her approaching—"

He squeezed her arm. "We didn't keep an alert, sweetheart. We didn't. The bunch of us. What reason had we to fear anything like this?"

"Weoch-Captain of Hero vessel *Swordbeak*, speaking for the Patriarchy." Now, behind the synthetic human tones, were audible the growls and spits of kzinti. "You trespass on our property, you violate our secrets, and I believe that in the past you have been guilty of worse. Identify yourself."

Saxtorph stalled. "Why do you ask that? According to you, no human has a real name."

Can we cut and run for it? he wondered. No. The question shows how kicked in the gut I am. She can

outboost us by a factor of five, at least. Not that she'd
need to. Even at this remove, her lasers can probably cripple us. A missile can cross the gap in a few
minutes, and we've nothing to fend it off. (Grab it
with our grapnel, no, too slow, and anyway, there'd
be a second or a third missile, or a multiple warhead,
or—) She herself, at her acceleration, she'll be here
in half an hour. But how can I think about flight?
Carita and Pete are down at the black hole.

It had flashed through him in the short seconds of
transmission lag. "Do as you are told, monkey! Give
me your designation."

No sense in provoking the kzin further by a refusal. He'd soon be able to read the name, jaunty
across these bows. "Freighter *Rover* of Leyport, Luna.
I repeat, our intentions are entirely honest and we
can't imagine what we may have done that you could
call wrong."

Silence crackled. Dorcas sat stiff, fists clenched.

"*Rover*. Harrgh! Saxtorph-Captain, is it? Give me
video."

Huh? The man sat numbed. The woman did the
obedience.

Weoch-Captain evidently chose to make it mutual.
His tiger head slanted forward in the screen, as if he
peered out of his den at prey. "So that is what you
look like," he rumbled. Eyes narrowed, tongue ran
over fangs. "How I hoped that mine would be this
pleasure."

"What do you mean?" Dorcas cried.

Silence. The heart drubbed in Saxtorph's breast.

"You know full well," said Weoch-Captain. "You
killed the Heroes and destroyed their works at the
red sun."

So the story had reached Kzin. Not too surprising,
as spectacular as it was. Saxtorph had been assured
that the Alpha Centaurian and Solar governments
had avoided being very specific in their official communications thus far. They wanted to test ratcat reac-

tions an item at a time. But spacefarers, especially nonhuman spacefarers with less of a grudge or none, traveling from Wunderland to neutral planets, might well have passed details on to their kzin counterparts in the course of meetings.

"Through my whole long voyage, I hoped I would find you," Weoch-Captain purred. His flattened ears lifted and spread. "A formidable opponent, a worthy one. If you behave yourselves and do as you are told, I promise you deaths quick and painless. . . . No, not quite that for you, Saxtorph. I think you and I shall have single combat. Afterward I will take your body for my exclusive eating, fit nourishment for a Hero, and give your head a place among my trophies."

Saxtorph braced himself. "You do us great honor, Weoch-Captain," he croaked. "We thank you. We praise your large spirit." What else could I say? Keep them happy. Kzinti don't normally torture for fun, but if this one got vengeful enough he might take it out on Tyra, Dorcas, Kam, Carita, Peter. At the least, he might bring them, us, back with him. Unless we kill ourselves first.

In the magnifying viewport the Raptor had perceptibly gained size, eclipsing more and more stars.

Weoch-Captain flexed claws out, in, out again. "Good," he said. "But I still will not talk at length to a monkey. Stand by. You will receive your final instructions when I arrive."

The screen blanked.

"Bob, darling, darling." Dorcas twisted about in her seat to cast her arms around him.

He hugged her. As always in crisis, confronting the worst, he had grown cool, watchful but half detached, a survival machine. Not that he saw any prospect of living onward, but— "We should bring the others up," he reminded her. "We can have a short time together." Before the kzinti arrive.

"Yes." He felt how she quelled her shuddering. Steady as he, she turned to the communicator and directed a broad beam at the sphere. "Carita, Peter, get straight back to the ship," she said crisply.

"*Was ist*—what is bad?" sounded Nordbo's hoarse bass.

"Never mind now. Move, I tell you!"

"*Jawohl.*" And: "Aye, aye, ma'am, we're off," from Carita.

Dorcas cut transmission. "I want to spare them while they flit," she explained. "They'll worry, but if they don't happen to make the enemy out in the sky, they won't be in shock."

"Until we meet again," Saxtorph agreed. "What about . . . Tyra and Kam? Shall we keep them waiting, too?"

"We may as well, or better."

"No. Maybe you weren't being kind after all. I think Tyra would want to know right away, so she can, well, she can—" kiss me goodbye?—"prepare herself, and meet the end with her eyes wide open. She's like that."

Dorcas bit her lip. "I can't stop you if you insist." Her words quivered a little. "But I thought you and I, these fifteen minutes or so we have left before we must tell them—"

He grinned, doubtless rather horribly. " 'Fraid I couldn't manage a quickie."

She achieved a laugh. "Down, boy." Soberly: "Not to get maudlin either. But let me say I love you, and thank you for everything."

"Aw, now, the thanks are all due you, my lady." He rose. She did. They embraced. He damned himself for wishing she were Tyra.

She kissed him long and hard. "That's for what we've had." The tears wouldn't quite stay put. "And for, for everything we were going to have—the kids and—"

Yah, he thought, our stored gametes. We never made provision for exogenesis, in case something clobbered us. They'll stay in the freeze, those tiny ghosts of might-have-been, year after year after year, I suppose, forgotten and forsaken, like our robot yonder.

Saxtorph lurched where he stood. *"Fanden i helvede!"* he roared.

Dorcas stepped back. She saw his face, and the breath whistled in between her teeth. "What?"

The Danish of his childhood, "The Devil in Hell," his father's favorite oath, yes, truly, for a devil did squat just outside the hell star awaiting his command. His revelation spilled from him.

Fierceness kindled in her, she shouted, but then she must ask, "What if we fail?"

"Why, we open our airlocks and drink space," he answered. He had dismissed the idea earlier because he knew she wouldn't want suicide while any chance of being cleanly killed remained. "Though most likely the kzinti will be so enraged they'll missile us on the spot. Come on, we haven't got time to gab, let's get going."

They returned to their seats and controls. An order went out. On the tnuctipun structure, the robot prospector stirred. Cautiously, at minimum boost, it lifted. When it was well clear, the humans accelerated it harder. They must work fast, to have the machine positioned before the enemy came so near that watchers at instruments might notice it and wonder. They must likewise work precisely, mathematically, solving a problem of vectors and coordinates in three-dimensional space. "—line integral of velocity divergence dS—" Dorcas muttered aloud to the computer while her fingers did the real speaking. There passed through the back of Saxtorph's awareness: If the scheme flops, this'll be how we spent our last moments together. Appropriate.

A telltale blinked. Nordbo and Carita had arrived. "Kam, our friends are back," the captain said through the intercom. "Cycle 'em through and have them sit tight. Tyra, I think we can cope with our visitors."

Except for Ryan's "Aye," neither of them responded. The quartermaster knew better than to distract the pair on the bridge. The woman must have understood the same on her own account. She isn't whimpering or hysterical or anything, Saxtorph thought —not her. Maybe, not being a spacehand, she won't obey my order and stay at the boat. It's useless anyway. But the most mutinous thing she might do is walk quietly, firmly through my ship to meet her dad.

"On station," Dorcas sighed. She leaned back, hands still on the keys, gaze on the displays. "It'll take three or four mini-nudges to maintain, but I doubt the kzinti will detect them."

The Raptor was big in the screen. Twin laser guns in the nose caught starlight and gleamed like eyes.

"Good." Saxtorph's attention skewered *Rover*'s control board. He'd calculated how he wanted to move, at full thrust, when things started happening. Though his present location was presumably safe, he'd rather be as far off as possible. Clear to Wunderland would be ideal, a sunny patio, a beer stein in his fist, and at his side—

"Go!" Dorcas yelled. She hit the switch that closed her last circuit. "*Ki-yai!*"

Afloat among stars, the robot prospector received the signal for which the program that she sent it had waited. It took off. At a hundred gravities of acceleration, it crossed a hundred kilometers of space in less than five seconds, to strike the shell around the black hole with the force of a boulder falling from heaven.

It crashed through. White light was in the radiation that torrented from the hole it left and smote the kzinti ship.

19

"Put me through again to the human commander," said Weoch-Captain.

"Yes, sire," replied Communications Officer.

Human, thought Weoch-Captain. Not monkey, whatever my position may require me to call him in public. A brave and resourceful enemy. I well-nigh wish we were more equally matched when I fight him. But no one must know that.

His optics showed *Rover*, an ungainly shape, battered and wayworn. Should he claim it, too, for a trophy? No, let Saxtorph's head suffice; and it would not have much meaning either, when he returned in his glory to take a full name, a seat among the Patriarchs, the right to found a house of his own. Still, his descendants might cherish the withered thing as a sign of what their ancestor did. Weoch-Captain's glance shifted to the great artifact. Power laired there, power perhaps to make the universe tremble. "Arrrh," he breathed.

The screens blanked. The lights went out. He tumbled through an endless dark.

"Ye-a-a-ach, what's this? What the venom's going on?" Screams tore at air that had ceased to blow from ventilators. Weoch-Captain recognized his state. He was weightless.

"Stations, report!" No answer except the chaos in the corridors. Everything was dead. The crew were ghosts flapping blindly around in a tomb. Nausea snatched at Weoch-Captain,

He fought it down. If down existed any more, adrift among stars he no longer saw. He shouldn't get spacesick. He never had in the past when he orbited free. He must act, take charge, uncover what was wrong, rip it asunder and set things right. He groped his way by feel, from object to suddenly unfamiliar object. "Quiet!" he bawled. "Hold fast! To me, officers, to me, your commander!"

The sickness swelled inside him.

He reached the door and the passage beyond. A body blundered into his. Both caromed, flailing air, rebounding from bulkheads, all grip on dignity lost. "My eyes, arh, my eyes," moaned the other kzin. "Did the light burn them out? I am blind. Help me, help me."

An idea took Weoch-Captain by the throat. He bared teeth at it, but it gave him a direction, a quarry. Remembrance was a guide. He pushed along corridors where noise diminished as personnel mastered panic. Good males, he thought amidst the hammerblows of blood in ears and temples. Valiant males. Heroes.

His goal was the nearest observation turret. It had transparent ports for direct viewing, backup in case of electronic failures, which he kept unshuttered during any action. He fumbled through the entry. A blue-white beam, too dazzling to look near, stabbed across the space beyond. It disappeared as *Swordbeak* floated past. Weoch-Captain reached a pane and squinted. Stars clustered knife-sharp. Carefully, fingers hooked on frames, he moved to the next.

A gray curve, a jutting tower, yes, the relic of the ancient lords, the end of his quest. *Swordbeak* slipped farther along. Weoch-Captain shrieked, clapped palms to face, bobbed helpless in midair.

Slowly the after-images faded. The glare hadn't blinded him. By what light now came in, he discerned metal and meters. He understood what had happened.

Somehow the humans had opened a new hole in the shell. Radiation tore the life from his ship.

Sickness overwhelmed him. He vomited. Foul gobbets and globules swarmed around his head and up his nostrils. He fled before they strangled him.

Yes, death is in my bones, he knew. How long can I fight it off, and why? You have conquered, human.

No! He shoved feet against bulkhead and arrowed forward. The plan took shape while he flew. "Meet at Station Three!" he shouted against night. "All hands to Station Three for orders! Pass the word on! Your commander calls you to battle!"

One by one, clumsily, many shivering and retching, they joined him. Officers identified themselves, crew rallied round them. Some had found flashlights. Fangs and claws sheened in the shadows.

He told them they would soon die. He told them how they should. They snarled their wrath and resolution.

Spacesuits were lockered throughout the ship. Kzinti sought those assigned them. In gloom and free fall, racked by waxing illness, a number of them never made it.

Air hung thick, increasingly chill. Recyclers, thrusters, radios in the spacesuits were inoperative. Well, but the pumps still had capacitor power, and you wouldn't have use for more air than your reserve tank held. You had your legs to leap with. You knew where you were bound, and could curse death by yourself.

Weoch-Captain helped at the wheel of his airlock, opening it manually. Atmosphere howled out, momentarily mist-white, dissipated, revealed the stars afresh. He followed it. *Rover* wasn't in sight. It must have scampered away. Maybe *Swordbeak*'s hull blocked it off. The artifact was a jaggedness straight ahead. He gauged distance, direction, and velocities as well as he was able, bunched his muscles, and leaped, a hunter at his quarry.

"Hee-yaa!" he screamed. The noise rattled feebly in his helmet. Blood came with it, droplets and smears.

Headed across the void, he could look around. Except for his breathing, the rattle of fluid in his lungs, he had fallen into a silence, an enormous peace. Here and there, glints moved athwart constellations, the spacesuits of his fellows. We too are star-stuff, he thought. Sun-stuff. Fire.

Hardly any of them would accomplish the passage, he knew. Most would go by, misaimed, and perish somewhere beyond. A lucky few might chance to pass in front of the furnace mouth and receive instant oblivion. Those who succeeded would not know where to go. There had been no way for Weoch-Captain to describe what he had learned from long days of study. A few might spy him, recognize him, seek him, but it was unlikely in the extreme.

No matter. Because of him they would die as warriors, on the attack.

Swordbeak receded. It had still had a significant component of velocity toward the sphere when the flame struck, though it was not on a collision course. It left him that heritage for his flight.

Rover hove into view. Saxtorph was coming back to examine the havoc he had wrought, was he? Well, he'd take a while to assess what his screens and instruments told him, and realize what it meant and then—what could he do? Unlimber his grapnel and collect dying kzinti?

He can try raying us, Weoch-Captain thought. He must have an industrial laser. I would certainly do it in his place. But as a weapon it's slow, unwieldy, and—I am almost at my mark.

The shell filled half of heaven. Its curve now hid the deadly light; only stars shone on spires, mazes, unknown engines. Weoch-Captain tensed.

A latticework seemed to spring at him. He grabbed a member. His strength ebbing, he nearly lost hold and shot on past. Somehow he kept the grip, and slammed to a halt. He clung while he got his wind back. Rags of darkness floated across his eyes.

Onward, though, lest he die unfulfilled. It was hard, and grew harder moment by moment as he clambered down. With nothing left him but the capacitor supplying the air pump and a little heat, he must by himself bend the joints at arms, legs, and fingers against interior pressure. With his mind going hazy, he must stay alert enough to find his way among things he knew merely from pictures, while taking care not to push so hard that he drifted away in space.

Nevertheless he moved.

A glance aloft. Yes, *Rover* was lumbering about. Maybe Saxtorph had guessed what was afoot. Weoch-Captain grinned. He hoped the human was frantic.

He'd aimed himself carefully, and luck had been with him. His impact was close to the activator. He reached it and went in among the structures and darknesses.

On a lanyard he carried a flashlight. By its glow he examined that which surrounded him. Yes, according to Yiao-Captain's report, this object like a lever and that object like a pedal ought to close a connection when pushed. The tnuctipun had scarcely intended any such procedure. Somewhere must be an automaton, a program, and shelter for whatever crew the black hole ship bore on its warfaring. But the tnuctipun too installed backup systems. Across billions of years, Weoch-Captain hailed them, his brother warriors.

This may not work, he cautioned himself. *I can but try to reave the power from the humans.*

I do not know where it will go, or if it will ever come back into our space. Nor will I know. I shall be dead. Proudly, gloriously.

A spasm shook him, but he had spewed out everything in his stomach before he left *Swordbeak*. Parched and vile-tasting mouth, dizziness, ringing ears, blood coughed forth and smeared over faceplate, wheezing breath, shaky hands, weakness, weakness, yes, it was good to die. He got himself well braced against metal—to be inside this framework was like being inside a canebrake at home, he thought vaguely, waiting for prey—and pushed with the whole force that remained to him.

Aboard *Rover*, shortly afterward, they saw their prize disappear.

20

Regardless, the homeward voyage began merrily.
When you have had your life given back to you, the
loss of a treasure trove seems no large matter.

"Besides, a report on *Sherrek* and her beamcast,
plus what we collected ourselves, should be worth a
substantial award by itself," Saxtorph observed. "And
then there's the other one, uh, *Swordbeak*." Dorcas
had read the name when they flitted across and
attached a radio beacon, so that the derelict would
be findable. "In a way, actually, more than the black
hole could've been. Your navy—or mine, or the two
conjointly —they'll be overjoyed at getting a complete modern kzinti warcraft to dissect."

"What that artifact, and the phenomenon within,
should have meant to science—" Peter Nordbo sighed.
"But you are right, complaining is ungrateful."

"No doubt the authorities will want this part of our
story hushed up," Saxtorph went on. "But we'll be
heroes to them, which is more useful than being it to
the public. I expect we'll slide real easy through the

bureaucratic rigmarole. And, as I said, get well paid for it."

"I thought you were a patriot, Robert."

"Oh, I s'pose I am. But the laborer is worthy of his hire. And I'm a poor man. Can't afford to work for free."

They sat in the Saxtorphs' cabin, the most spacious aboard, talking over a beer. They had done it before. The instant liking they took to one another had grown with acquaintance. The Wunderlander's English was rusty but improving.

He stroked his beard as he said slowly, "I have thought on that. Hear me, please. My family shall have its honor again, but I disbelieve our lands can be restored. The present owners bought in good faith and have their rights. You shall not pity me. From what I have heard since my rescue, society is changed and the name of Landholder bears small weight. But in simple justice we shall have money for what they stripped from us. After I pay off Tyra's debt she took for my sake, much will stay with me. What shall I then do? I have my science, yes, but as an amateur. I am too old to become a professional in it. Yet I am too young to . . . putter. Always my main work was with people. What now can I enjoy?" He smiled. "Well, your business has the chronic problem that it is undercapitalized. The awards will help, but I think not enough. How would you like a partner?"

Saxtorph goggled. "Huh? Why, uh, what do you mean?"

"I would not travel with you, unless once in a while as a passenger for pleasure. I am no spaceman. But it was always my dream, and being in an enterprise like yours, that should come close. Yes, I will go on trips myself, making arrangements for cargoes and charters, improvements and expansions. Being a Landholder taught me about business, and I did it pretty well. Ask my former tenants. Also, the money

I put in, that will make the difference to you. Together we can turn this very profitable for all of us.

"You cannot decide at once, nor can I. But today it seems me a fine idea. What do you think?"

"I think it's a goddamn supernova!" Saxtorph roared.

They talked, more and more excitedly, until the captain glanced at his watch and said, "Hell, I've got to go relieve Dorcas at the mass detector. I'll send her down here and the pair of you can thresh this out further, if you aren't too tired."

"Never for her," Nordbo replied. "She is a wonderful person. You are a lucky man."

Saxtorph's eagerness faded. After a moment he mumbled, "I'm sorry. I often bull ahead with you as though you hadn't . . . suffered your loss. You don't speak about it, and I forget. I'm sorry, Peter."

"Do not be," Nordbo answered gently. "A sorrow, yes, but during my time alone, assuming I would grow old and die there, I became resigned. To learn I missed my Hulda by less than a year, that is bitter, but I tell myself we had already lost our shared life; and God has left me our two children, both become splendid human beings."

The daughter, at least, for sure, Saxtorph thought.

Nordbo smiled again. "I still have my son Ib to look forward to meeting. In fact, since Tyra tells me he is in naval intelligence, we shall be close together—Robert, what is wrong?"

Saxtorph sat moveless until he shook himself, stood up, tossed off his drink, and rasped: "Something occurred to me. Don't worry. It may well turn out to be nothing. But, uh, look, we'd better not discuss this partnership notion with Dorcas or anybody right away. Let's keep it under our hats till our ideas are more definite, okay? Now I really must go spell her."

Nordbo seemed puzzled, a bit hurt, but replied, "As you wish," and left the cabin with him. They parted ways in the corridor and Saxtorph proceeded to the detector station.

Dorcas switched off the book she had been screening. "Hey, you look like a bad day in Hell," she said.

"Out of sorts," he mumbled. "I'll recover. Just leave me be."

"So you don't want to tell me why." She rose to face him. Sadness tinged her voice. "You haven't told me much lately, about anything that matters to you."

"Nonsense," he snapped. "We were side by side against the kzinti."

"That's not what I meant, and you know it. Well, I won't plague you. That would be unwise of me, wouldn't it?" She went out, head high but fingers twisting together.

He took the chair that was not warm after her, stuffed his pipe, and smoked furiously.

A light footfall raised him from his brooding. Tyra entered. As usual, her countenance brightened to see him. "Hi," she greeted, an Americanism acquired in their conversations. "Care you for some company?"—as if she had never before joined him here for hours on end, or he her when she had the duty. "Remember, you promised to tell me about your adventure on—" She halted. Her tone flattened. "Something is woeful."

"I hope not," he said. "I hope I'm mistaken."

She seated herself. "If I can help or console, Robert, only ask. Or if you wish not to share the trouble, tell me I should hold my mouth."

She knows how to be silent, he thought. We've passed happy times with not a word, listening to music or looking at some work of art or simply near each other.

"You're right," he said. "I can't talk about it till— till I must. With luck, I'll never have to."

The blue eyes searched him. "It concerns you and me, no?" How grave and quiet she had become.

Alarmed, he countered, "Did I say that?"

"I feel it. We are dear friends. At least, you are for me."

"And you—" He couldn't finish the sentence.

"I believe you are torn."

"Wait a minute."

She leaned forward and took his free hand between hers. "Because you are a good man, an honest man," she said. "You keep your promises." She paused. "But—"

"Let's change the subject, shall we?" he interrupted.

"Are you afraid? Yes, you are. Afraid of to give pain."

"Stop," he barked. "No more of this. You hear me?" He pulled his hand away.

An implacable calm was upon her. "As you wish, my dear. For the rest of the journey. You have right. Anything else is indecent, among all of us. But in some more days we are at Wunderland."

"Yes," he said, thickly and foolishly.

"You will be there a length of time."

"Busy."

"Not always. You know that. We will make decisions. It may take long, but at last we must. About the rest of our lives."

"Maybe."

"Quite certainly." She rose. "I think best I go now. You should be alone with your heart for this while."

He stared at the deck. "You're probably right."

Steadiness failed her a little. "Robert, whatever happens, whatsoever, you are dear to me." Her footfalls dwindled off into silence.

A squat black form stood at a distance down the passage, like a barricade. "Hallo," said Tyra dully.

Carita fell into step with her. "That was a short visit."

Tyra bridled. "You watched?"

"I noticed. Couldn't help it. Can't, day after day. A kdat would see. I want a word with you."

Tyra flushed. "Please to be polite."

"We're overdue for a talk," the Jinxian insisted. "This is a loose hour for both of us. Will you come along?" Although tone and gait were unthreatening, the hint lay beneath them that if necessary, she might pick the other woman up and carry her.

"Very well," Tyra clipped. They walked on mute to the pilot's cabin and inside.

Carita shut the door. Eyes met and held fast. "What do you want?" Tyra demanded.

"You know perfectly well what," Carita stated. "You and the skipper."

"We are friends! Nothing more!"

"No privacy aboard ship for anything else, if you're civilized. Sure, you've kept out of the sack. A few kisses, maybe, but reasonably chaste, like in a flirtation. Only that's not what it is any longer. You're waiting till we get to Wunderland."

Tyra lifted her arm as if to strike, then let it fall. "Do you call Robert a *Schleicher*—a, a sneak?" she blazed.

Carita's manner mildened. "Absolutely not. Nor you. This is simply a thing that's happened. Neither of you would've wanted it, and you didn't see it coming till too late. I believe you're as bewildered, half joyful and half miserable, as he is."

Tyra dropped her gaze. She clenched fists against breasts. "It is difficult," she whispered.

"True, you being an honorable person."

Tyra rallied. "It is our lives. His and mine."

"Dorcas saved your father's," Carita answered. "Later she saved all of us. Yes, Bob was there, but you know damn well he couldn't have done what he did without her. How do you propose to repay that? Money doesn't count, you know."

"*Ich kann nicht anders!*" Tyra cried. "He and I, we are caught."

"You are free adults," Carita said. "You're trapped in nothing but yourselves. Tyra, you're smart, gifted, beautiful, and soon you'll be rich. You've got every prospect bright ahead of you. What *we've* got is a good marriage and a happy ship. Bob will come back to her, if you let him go."

"Will he? How can I? Shall I leave him hurt forever?"

Carita smiled. She reached to lay an arm around the taller woman's shoulders. "I had a hunch that'd be what makes you feel so helpless. Sit down, honey. I'll pour us a drink and we'll talk."

21

The Jinxian relieved Saxtorph at the end of his watch. Lost in tumult, he barely noticed how she regarded him and forgot about it as he went out.

Oh, hell, he thought, I'm getting nowhere, only churning around in a maelstrom. Before it drags me under, I'd better—what? Have a bite to eat, I guess, take a sleeping pill, go to bed, hope I'll wake up clear-headed.

That he came to the place he did at the minute he did was coincidence. Nobody meant to stage anything. It made no difference, except that he would otherwise have found out less abruptly.

The door to Tyra's cabin stood half open, Kamehameha Ryan in it. His hair was rumpled, his clothes hastily thrown on, his expression slightly dazed. Saxtorph stopped short. A tidal wave surged through him.

The quartermaster said into the room: "—hard to believe. I never would have—I mean, Bob's more than my captain, he's my friend, and—"

Her laugh purred. "What, feel you guilty? No need. I enjoy his company, yes, and I had ideas, but he is too much married. Maybe when we are on Wunderland. Meanwhile, this has been a long dry voyage until now. Carita was right, she told me you are good."

He beamed. "Why, thank you, ma'am. And you are terrific. Tomorrow?"

"Every tomorrow, if we can, until journey's end. Now, if you excuse, I am ready for happy dreams."

"Me, too." Ryan blew a kiss, shut the door, and tottered off. He didn't see who stood at his back.

After a space Saxtorph began to think again. Well. So that is how it is. *Du kannst nicht treu sein*.

Not that I have any call to be mad at either of them. I've got no claim. Never did. On the contrary.

Even so—

Vaguely: That's the barbed wire I've been hung up on. Because the matter, the insight that hit me, touches Tyra, no, grabs her with kzin claws, I couldn't bring myself to consult Dorcas. I couldn't bring myself to see that she is the one living soul I must turn to. Between us we'll work out what our course ought to be.

Later. Later.

He walked on, found himself at Peter Nordbo's quarters, and knocked. The Wunderlander opened the door and gazed at him with surprise. "Hi," Saxtorph said. "Am I disturbing you?"

"No. I read a modern history book. Thirty years to learn about. What is your wish?"

"Sociability. Nothing special. Swap stories of our young days, argue about war and politics and other trivia, maybe sing bawdy songs, definitely get drunk. You game? I'll fetch any kind of bottle you like."

22

Both suns were down and Munchen gone starry with its own lights. Downtown traffic swarmed and throbbed around the old buildings, the smart modern shops. Matthiesonstrasse was residential, though, quiet at this hour. Apartment houses lined it like ramparts, more windows dark than aglow, so that when Saxtorph looked straight up he could make out a few real stars. A breeze flowed chilly, the first breath of oncoming fall.

He found the number he wanted and glanced aloft again, less high. Luminance on the fifth floor told him somebody was awake there. He hesitated. That might be a different location from the one he was after.

Squaring shoulders, setting jaws: Come on, boy, move along. Rouse him if need be. Get this goddamn thing over with.

In the foyer he passed by the *Fahrstuhl* and took the emergency stairs. They were steep. He felt glad of it. The climb worked out a little of the tension in him. Nonetheless, having reached the door numbered 52, he pushed the button violently.

After a minute the speaker gave him an uneven *"Ja, was wollen Sie von mir?"* He turned his face straight toward the scanner, and heard a gasp. *"Sie!"* Seconds later "Captain Saxtorph?" sounded like a prayer that it not be true.

"Let me in," the Earthman said.

"No. This is, is the middle of the night."

Correct, Saxtorph thought.

"You had not even the courtesy to call ahead. Go away."

"Better me than the patrol," Saxtorph answered.

He heard something akin to a strangled sob. The door opened. He stepped through. It shut behind him.

The apartment was ascetically furnished and had been neat, but disorder was creeping in. The air system failed to remove the entire haze and stench of cigarette smoke. Ib Nordbo stood in a civilian jumpsuit. His hair was unkempt, his eyelids darkly smudged. Yes, thought Saxtorph, he was awake, all right. I daresay he doesn't sleep much any more.

"W-welcome back," Nordbo mumbled.

"Your father and sister were disappointed that you weren't there to greet them personally," Saxtorph said.

"They got my message. My regrets. They did? I must go offplanet, unfortunately, at that exact time. A personal difficulty. I asked for compassionate leave."

"Except you holed up here. I figured you would. No point going anywhere else in this system. You'd be too easily found. No interstellar passenger ship is leaving before next week, and you'd need to fix up identity documents and such." Saxtorph gestured. "Sit down. I don't enjoy this either. Let's make it as short as possible."

Nordbo retreated, lowered himself to the edge of a

chair, clutched its arms. His entire body begged. Saxtorph followed but remained standing above him.

"How long have you been in kzinti pay?" Saxtorph asked.

Nordbo swallowed dryness. "I am not. I was not. Never."

"Listen, fellow. Listen good. I don't care to play games. Cooperate, or I'll walk right out and turn this business over to the authorities. I would have already, if it weren't for your sister and your father. You damn near got them killed, you know."

"Tyra— No, I did not know!" the other screamed. "She lied to me. If I knew she was going with you, I would have gotten your stupid expedition stopped. And my father, any reasonable person believed him long dead. I did not know! How could I?"

"Bad luck, yah, but richly deserved," Saxtorph said. "I might not have guessed, except that a clue fell my way. At that, the meaning didn't dawn on me till a couple days later."

He drew breath before driving his point home. "You'll have followed the news, as much of our story as has been released. Before then, being who you are and in the position you are, you'll have been apprised of what we told the Navy officer we requested come aboard as we approached. A kzinti warship caught us at the black hole, later than you expected it might, but still something you knew was quite likely."

"I—no, you misjudge me—"

"Pipe down till I give you leave to speak. The encounter *could* have been by chance. The kzinti might have happened on the beamcast from the earlier ship and dispatched this one at the precise wrong moment for us. Her captain knew who I was and what vessel I command. He *could* have heard that on the starvine or through his intelligence corps. *Rover*'s name wouldn't matter to that mentality and would scarcely have been in any briefing he got, but conceivably he'd heard it somehow, lately, and it was fresh in his mind. Yah. The improbable can happen. What blew the whistle, once I realized what it meant, was that he told me he'd hoped to find me. He believed it was entirely possible we'd be there, we of all humans, *Rover* of all ships.

"We'd never disclosed where we were bound for or why. Nobody else knew, besides you. Nobody but you could have sent word about us to Kzin.

"I imagine you informed them as soon as Tyra discovered your father's notes and showed you. The matter would be of interest to them, and might be important. When she got serious about mounting a search, you did everything you could to discourage her, short of telling your superiors. You dared not do that because then they might well order an official look-see, which could open a trail to you and your treason. They aren't as stodgy about such things as you claimed. The disclosure about Markham had cast suspicion your way, and you must be feeling sort of desperate. When we made clear that we'd embark in spite of your objections, you got on whatever hyperphone you have secret access to and alerted the kzinti. If they scragged us, you'd be safe.

"Okay, Nordbo. How long have you been in their pay?"

"Tyra," the seated man groaned. He slumped back. "I did not know, I swear I did not know she was with you."

"Just the same," Saxtorph said, "betraying us to probable death was not exactly a friendly act. For her sake and your father's, I just might be persuaded to . . . set it aside. No promises yet, understand, and whatever mercy you get, you've got to earn."

For their sakes, grieved a deep part of him. Yes, Peter has suffered, has lost, quite enough. He's so happy that Dorcas and I will take him on as a partner. Christ, how I'd hate to dash the cup from his lips.

He wouldn't be ruined. His vindication, the reparation to him, the family's restoration to the clan, those will stand, because *he* was and is the Landholder, not this creature sniveling at me tonight. I think he has the strength to outlive it if he and the world learn the truth about his son, his only son, and to get on with his work. But if I can spare him—if I can spare him!

Nordbo looked up. He was ghastly haggard. The words jerked forth: "I never did it for money. I got some, yes, but I did not want it, I always gave it to the Veterans' Home. Markham was like a, a father to me, the father I had worshipped before he— Well, what could I believe except that my real father turned collaborator and died in the kzinti service? I thought Tyra was a wishful thinker. I could not make myself say that openly to her, but I thought my duty was to restore the family fortune and honor by my efforts. Markham was faithful in those first years after the trial, when many scorned. He helped me, counseled me, was like a new father, he, the war hero, then the brilliant administrator. When at last he asked me to do something a, a little irregular for him, I was glad. It was nothing harmful. He explained that if the kzinti knew better how our intelligence operations work, they would see we are defensive, not aggressive, and there would be a better chance for lasting peace. What should I trust, his keen and experienced judgment or a stupid, handcuffing regulation? That first information I gave him to pass on to the kzinti, it was not classified. They could have collected it for themselves with some time and trouble. But then there was more, and then more, and it grew into real secrets—" Again he covered his eyes and huddled.

Saxtorph nodded. "You'd become subject to blackmail. Every step you took brought you further down a one-way road. Yah. That's how a lot of spies get recruited."

"I love my nation. I would never harm it." Nordbo dropped fists to knees and added in a voice less shrill, "Even though it did my father and my family a terrible injustice."

"You got around to agreeing with Tyra about that, eh? And what you were doing couldn't possibly cause any serious damage. Such-like notions are also usual among spies."

Nordbo raised his head. "Do not insult me. I have my human dignity."

"That's a matter of opinion. Now, I told you to listen and I told you I want to make this short so I can get the hell out of here and go have a hot shower and a change of clothes. Snap to it, and perhaps I'll see if I can do anything for you. Otherwise I report straight to your superiors. For openers, how many more are in your ring?"

"N-no one else."

"I'd slap you around if I had a pair of gloves I could burn afterward. As is, goodnight."

"No! Please!" Nordbo reeled to his feet. He held his arms out. "I tell you, nobody. Nobody I know of. One in my unit at headquarters, but she died two years ago. An accident. And Markham is dead. Nobody more!"

Saxtorph deemed he was telling the truth as far as possible. "You'll name her," he said. "That, and what else you tell, should give leads to any others." If they existed. Maybe they didn't. Markham had been a lone wolf type. Well, investigation was a job for professionals. "You will write down what you know. Every last bit. The whole story, all you did, all you delivered personally and all you heard about or suspected, the works. You savvy? I'll give you two-three days. Don't leave this apartment meanwhile."

Nordbo's hands fell to his sides. He straightened. A sudden, eerie calm was upon him. "What then?" he asked tonelessly.

"If I judge you've made an honest statement, my

wife and I will try to bargain with the authorities, privately, when we bring it to them. We can't dictate what they do with you. But we are their darlings, and the darlings of the public and the media more than ever. Our recommendations should carry weight. The Markham affair has shaken and embarrassed a lot of the brass pretty badly. They'd like some peace and quiet while they put their house in order. A sensation involving the son of hero-martyr Peter Nordbo is no way to get that. Maybe we can talk them into accepting your resignation and burying the truth in the top secret file. Maybe. We'll try. That's all I can promise. And it's conditional on your writing a full and accurate account."

"I see. You are kind."

"Because of your father and your sister. Nothing else." Saxtorph turned to go.

"Wait," said Nordbo.

"Why?" Saxtorph growled.

"My memory is not perfect. But I need not write for you. I kept a journal of my, my participation. Everything that happened, recorded immediately afterward. I thought I might want it someday, somehow, if Markham or the kzinti should— *Ach*, let me fetch it."

Saxtorph's heart banged. "Okay." He hadn't hoped for this much. He wasn't sure what he'd hoped for.

Nordbo went into an adjacent room. He strode resolutely and erect. Saxtorph tautened. "If you're going for a gun instead, don't," he called. "My wife knows where I am."

"Of course," the soft voice drifted back. "No, you have convinced me. I shall do my best to set things right."

He returned carrying a small security box, which he placed at the computer terminal. He laid his palm on the lid and it opened. Had anyone else tried to force it, the contents would have been destroyed. Saxtorph moved closer. He saw a number of minidiscs.

"Encoded," Nordbo said. "Please make a note of the decoding command. A wrong one will cause the program to wipe the data. You want to inspect a sample, no?"

He stooped, inserted a disc, and keyed the board. A date three years past sprang onto the screen, followed by words. They were Wunderlander, but Saxtorph's reading knowledge sufficed to show that the entry did indeed relate an act of espionage. Copies of photographs came after.

"You are satisfied?" Nordbo asked. "Want you more?"

"No," Saxtorph said. "This will do."

Nordbo returned the disc to the box, which he relocked and proffered. "I am afraid you must touch this," he said matter-of-factly.

Sudden pity welled forth. "That's okay." In several ways he resembled his sister: eyes, cheekbones, flaxen hair, something about the way he now stood and faced his visitor. "We'll do whatever we can for you, Ib."

"Thank you."

Saxtorph took the box and left. *"Gute Nacht,"* Nordbo said behind him.

The door closed. Saxtorph went the short distance along the hall to the stairwell and started down. *Whatever I can for you, Tyra,* he thought.

His mind went on, like himself speaking to her, explaining, though they were not things she would ever hear.

I'm not mad at you, dear. Nor at Kam, as far as that goes. You weren't deliberately playing games with me. You honestly believed you were serious—confusing horniness with love, which God knows is a common mistake—till the impulse itself overwhelmed you.

Or so he supposed. Nothing had been uttered, except in the silent language. They simply understood that everything was over. Apart from friendship. Already he hurt less than at first. He knew that before long he'd stop altogether and be able to meet her, be with her, in comradely fashion. Dorcas would see to it.

I do wish you'll find a man you can settle down with. I'd like you to have what we have. But if not, well, it's your life, and any style of living it that you choose will be brave.

Saxtorph had reached the third-floor landing when he heard the single pistol shot.

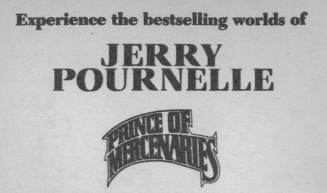